VALENTINE'S DAY

—✦•————————•✦—

By
Tony Buckingham

DEDICATION

I wrote three books after I sold my company Bonham, in 1997. The first, *The Grave Digger's Apprentice*, was an amusing account of how we started Benham. The next two, *The Stamp of Treachery* and *Valentine's Day*, were both murder mysteries and I had plans to develop them but despite a major publisher taking an option on *Valentine's Day* (they wanted changes) I started a new company that suddenly needed all my time.

I meant to continue later but alas I have Idiopathic Pulmonary Fibrosis so I would like to dedicate both books to the NHS. Starting with the Royal Brompton and Toby Maher for putting me on Pirfenidone which I think has given me an extra year of life, Adrian Morris my local consultant, Dr Farrow my GP, Gemma, my lung nurse, plus all the wonderful district nurses thanks for everything.

***

But the person to whom this book is really dedicated is Cath, my wife of fifty years, who didn't realize when she said, "In sickness and in health," she would be a carer for 24/7 for years. Without her I would never have completed these last two books. My thanks to her are more profound than I can express.

CONTENTS

PART I. THE MAIN PLAYERS 1

PREFACE 3

CHAPTER 1. The Perfect Accountant *9*

CHAPTER 2. The Perfect Bastard *34*

CHAPTER 3. The Perfect Wife *49*

INTERLUDE. How unlucky can one person be? *62*

PART II. THE STORY 69

CHAPTER 4 .... *71*

CHAPTER 5 .... *91*

CHAPTER 6 .... *102*

CHAPTER 7 .... *108*

CHAPTER 8 .... *113*

CHAPTER 9 .... *120*

CHAPTER 10 .... *129*

CHAPTER 11 .... *143*

CHAPTER 12 .... *150*

CHAPTER 13 .... *161*

CHAPTER 14 .... *169*

CHAPTER 15 .... *182*

CHAPTER 16 .... *188*

CHAPTER 17 .... *198*

CHAPTER 18 .... *226*

CHAPTER 19 .... *237*

CHAPTER 20 .... *251*

CHAPTER 21 .... *257*

CHAPTER 22 .... *262*

CHAPTER 23 .... *266*

CHAPTER 24 .... *273*

CHAPTER 25 ....*277*
CHAPTER 26 ....*282*
CHAPTER 27 ....*296*
CHAPTER 28 ....*299*
CHAPTER 29 ....*307*

POSTSCRIPT 313

PART I

THE MAIN PLAYERS

Preface

Why don't they stop that bloody dog howling?

Mike Burton was sitting at his computer trying desperately to work on a programme for satellite television. It was an extremely complex operation and needed intense concentration. Ever since he'd taken the step to become freelance he had been plagued with constant interruptions. Yesterday it had been a baby crying. The day before, dogs barking, and at the weekend the noise of children playing on the green outside his window was almost deafening. If that wasn't bad enough it was hot, stifling hot. God! He'd never known it quite so oppressive.

There seemed to be two clear alternatives. He could stop the noise by shutting the window, in which case he'd probably end up like the Sunday joint, or he could open the window and bear the noise. Either way, he wasn't going to get much work done.

Perhaps he had made the wrong decision. He had naively thought it was going to be easy working from home. He assumed there would be no more interruptions from stupid people wanting to pick his brain about this and that. He thought it would be an end to vile cups of darkish gunk purporting to be coffee, always brought to him just at the right moment to break his concentration and set him back hours. No more gossiping about who's going out with whom and what they were doing to each other. He imagined that he would be able to just focus and get the job done. Back in that overcrowded office it had seemed an ideal solution. However, here in his noisy, scorching oven of a flat he had begun to understand that it was not going to be that easy.

In reality Mike shouldn't even be doing the programming, after all, he was a senior systems designer. He should have had someone doing the donkey work for him, but he found that by the time he'd corrected some underling's work, it was easier to do it himself.

Oh bugger it, he thought, *I might as well go and make myself a cup of coffee. I'm certainly serving no useful purpose here.* He went out into the galley kitchen, got down his cafetière and opened the fridge to select a coffee for that particular morning.

Coffee was something that Mike really enjoyed. He took it seriously. What would it be this morning? Should he choose Kenya AA, Colombian, mountain blend, or his local delicatessen's special mix? In the end he chose the Colombian. Measuring the coffee carefully with the precision one would expect of a man used to being accurate in all his work, he let the water go slightly off the boil, warmed the pot with hot water, then poured the water away. He added the coffee and poured just the right amount of water into his cafetière to ensure the perfect cup. Despite the seductive aroma that dominated the room, he resisted the desire to rush his brew. He timed it exactly one minute before he pushed the plunger down and poured the resulting perfection into his Wedgwood bone china mug. He had splashed out on the mug especially to make the coffee taste even better. He was just about to drink it when he heard the horrific screams.

In the flat next door, Mavis Lucas was getting more and more concerned about the howling of the dog. *It's not right,* she thought, *that poor dog must be suffering. Something should be done about it.* The more it howled the more worried she got. She found that she couldn't settle to do her weekly washing. Eventually she dug out her battered phone book and looked up the number of the RSPCA. She kept looking but she couldn't find a local number. There was only a general number in Horsham and that, she knew, was a long way away. She was reluctant to phone it as she was sure it would probably be an expensive phone call and a waste of time. In the end the howling got to her so much, she thought it would be worth the money. She dialled the number and was immediately answered by a sensible young lady called Carol. She not only took all the details down and told her that she would report it to a local inspector, but also sensed that Mavis was worried about the cost of the call, so she reassured Mavis that she would only be charged at the local rate.

The inspector apparently would be there within half an hour. Mavis felt much better. At least she'd done something. She put the phone down and went back to her paper to read the disgusting details of some minor soap opera's sex life. She was happily being shocked when she too, heard the scream.

On the floor below, Emma and Thomas Pickup were recovering from measles and were still probably contagious and so weren't allowed back to school. However, the children were at that stage where they had far too much energy. They needed to get out and do something to calm them down. Their mother thought it would be an excellent idea if they were to go across onto the green and get rid of this surplus energy.

"Come on both of you," she called, "get your coats on, I'll take you over the green so you can do some playing."

They both excitedly ran round the flat getting their coats on, giggling and shouting as they did it. She took them carefully down and saw them across the road, even though it was quiet at this time of day. She always preferred to do so, dreading the thought of hearing the screeching of brakes, then looking out and seeing one of her treasures hurt or even worse. She unlocked the gate, which to a certain extent was an irrelevance. She knew children could squeeze through holes in the fence in many places, but she preferred to do it properly as it showed they had the right to go into the private gardens. She would have preferred to have lived in one of the houses on the south side of the square. They had the advantage that their gardens opened straight onto the communal ones. This would have meant no dangerous roads to cross. The problem was that not only were they rarely available, but also they cost at least twenty pounds more a week and the Pickups couldn't afford that. When they were in the garden, the first thing the children did was to take off their coats and throw them on the grass. The day was excessively hot but Joan felt somehow, because they'd been ill, they ought to wear a coat, even if it was the middle of summer. She watched them running round enjoying themselves for some time before she crossed the road and went back to get on with her housework.

"Let's play hide and seek," said Thomas. "I'll hide,

you come and find me."

He ran off first to the right and then skirted round the back of the bushes, tacking round until he was actually behind Emma. His idea was to make it more difficult for Emma to find him. The children were so noisy that they hadn't bothered with the howling that had certainly got quieter. Thomas noticed the small dog first; it was howling softly, lying close to one of the big houses. As he got nearer he saw the dog lying next to what appeared to be a large bundle of rags, just outside an open door. He went over to see what it was and to his horror he found it was an old white-haired man. It didn't need much intelligence to work out why he was lying so still. It was pretty apparent. A large carving knife was sticking out of the middle of his back with a black patch round the wound. As Thomas looked he realised, to his disgust, that the black patch was moving and to his total revulsion he realised it was ants, thousands upon thousands of ants, congregating round and inside the wound. Although he was scared and disgusted with this vile sight he found his legs had frozen and much as he would have liked to leave, he just couldn't.

At that point he heard Emma coming up from behind him.

"Found you, found you!" she shouted excitedly.

"Don't come here! No, go back!" he shouted at her.

However, it was far too late. She'd already seen the body and started to scream. It started slowly and then built up into the most horrific scream he'd ever heard. It was a sound that was to haunt him for the rest of his life.

Mrs Pickup heard the scream, dropped her favourite glass jug she'd been polishing at the time and rushed down the stairs across into the park, terrified as to what had happened to her children.

Mike tipped his carefully prepared coffee over his computer in his haste to get out. He almost knocked down Mavis, as she too hurried out of her flat.

All three of them arrived almost simultaneously and stared in horror at the body.

Mrs Pickup immediately dragged her two children away from such a terrible sight.

"I'll go and phone the police," she called as she rushed the three of them back to the flat, grateful to get away.

"Look," said Mavis, "it's old Mr Gregory. I was only talking to him yesterday, he was so excited about winning something and now he's dead. Why on earth would anyone want to kill him? He's never done anybody any harm, he only cares about dogs."

CHAPTER 1

The Perfect Accountant

In retrospect there was no doubt in Jason's mind that it was all Zoë's fault.

Jason Roberts had been the perfect child. Well, that's not entirely true. I suppose over the last fifty years he would rank in the top twenty perfect children born in England. As a baby he rarely cried; not only was he quickly weaned away from his night feeds but he was an enthusiastic potty-user from the beginning. He was also a beautiful baby. People would stop in the street and remark just how pretty he was. His mother, Rosemary, was exceptionally proud of him. He was a late addition to the family. Both Rosemary and James, her husband, had long since given up any hope of children, so when Jason came along it was true to say they were the happiest parents in the country. Jason's progress through school was one triumph after another.

He won swimming cups, starred in dramatic presentations, and sung in the choir. His departure to Rugby would have been a formality, but his father was made redundant after thirty years with the same company. This meant Jason had to take his place at the local free grammar school.

Again, he was always the perfect scholar. He starred in all the yearly dramatic presentations and was exceptionally fortunate in being taught by a drama teacher obsessed with detective stories. He thoroughly enjoyed acting in *Who Killed the Count?* and *Murder in the Nile*. It was here that Jason was to acquire a lifelong fascination with Wimsey, Alleyn, Marple, Campion, Poirot and co. He achieved the best examination results the school had ever had, which made it a formality for him to be admitted into Oxford.

He couldn't be bothered with a year off. He could see no point in voluntary services overseas. How was slumming it with a bunch of savages in some distant banana republic going to help his career? So he took his place at Oxford at the earliest opportunity. Being one of nature's natural workers and with a superb intellect, Jason found Oxford ideally suited to his talents. He enjoyed the dramatic opportunities and starring in many productions, as well as being active in the Oxford University Murder and Mystery Club.

His first was a foregone conclusion.

His biggest dilemma on leaving Oxford was whether to take up the lucrative offer from Coopers and Lybrand or the one from Price Waterhouse. Being practical, he chose Coopers simply because the offices at Charing Cross would be more convenient for him. He could easily commute up from Maidstone where he still lived with his doting parents.

Jason was perfect in every way but one. He had never, ever, had a regular girlfriend. He had gone out on dates, but mainly when he needed an escort for a particular function. He considered that girls were a distraction. There was plenty of time for that sort of thing later.

He settled down to work at the offices of Coopers and Lybrand. It didn't take him long to establish himself as a man to be watched. He passed each stage of his accountancy qualifications with flying colours. He was lucky enough to have the services of a pleasant secretary, Jane Taylor, whom he considered to be efficient and capable.

Jane Taylor was not beautiful. She was not even vaguely attractive. You couldn't call her ugly, but certainly she lived up to the name Plain Jane. She had had affairs, but none had lasted the distance and she was facing the prospect of being alone throughout her life. However, what she really wanted was children, a big house, and a presentable husband and she wasn't too worried how she achieved it. She was lucky that Jason Roberts was far more interested in getting the work done well, rather than having fun. He consequently preferred her to the short-skirted, long-haired girls that most of the other accountants chose. It didn't take her long to realise that here was a bargain just waiting to be snapped up. Jason was reasonably good looking, though he wasn't yet aware of it. He was fairly tall, clever, kind, considerate, in fact everything that would make an excellent husband. He also had the added bonus in the fact that his job carried a large salary, so that Jason Roberts' wife would always be comfortable. Jane liked the idea of being rich and comfortable. Jane set about making herself pleasant and indispensable to Jason. Gradually they began to go out for drinks after work, followed by the odd meal and finally to the theatre and shows.

One evening after enjoying The Phantom of the Opera at Her Majesty's, they went on to Café Fish. Here, at Jane's insistence, they drank far too much wine and they ended up back in her flat and into her bed.

Jane wasn't a virgin, so she found it easy to guide Jason through the beginner's stages and help him to lose his virginity in the best possible way. He had little talent for sex but she made him feel like one of the world's great lovers. It was not by chance that Jane got pregnant, she'd intended it from the start. She knew full well that Jason, being a gentleman, would not disappoint her. She didn't love Jason, but she thought that wasn't important, after all, he would be at work for most of the time.

They were married in the picturesque old parish church in Lenham. As Jane's elderly parents had died some years before, Jason's parents were delighted to organise the event, particularly as Lenham was such a romantic place for a wedding. The reception was held just up the A20 in Leeds Castle, the most beautiful castle in England. Well, that's what it said in the literature that came with the booking, so it had to be true.

Rosemary and James were very pleased with Jane. She was exactly what they had wanted for their son, a sensible decent girl who would quietly help him build his career. Jason and Jane bought a beautiful country cottage in a village called Mersham, south of Ashford, and Jane set about making it the perfect executive home. Jason's life was comfortable. He travelled first class from Ashford to Charing Cross every morning and returned home late most nights. He always phoned Jane to give her the exact time of his arrival and there was always a gourmet meal waiting for him on his return.

Their son William was followed quickly by a daughter, Sophie, and everything as far as Jane was concerned was pure heaven.

She had the perfect husband.

Coopers, naturally, were upset when out of the blue Richard Valentine, a successful entrepreneur, offered Jason a job as chief accountant with the Redwood Group plc. After all, he had been the perfect employee. The remuneration was excellent but as well he was also offered a golden hello amounting to a hundred thousand pounds of share options. It didn't take Jason long to make the decision to leave Coopers and start to build his commercial career.

At Redwood Jason drifted straight back into a routine. He was always at his desk early in the morning and was one of the last to leave in the evening. He was just another computer as far as most of the staff was concerned. Over the years he became indispensable to the company. One of the biggest fears of the board was that they would lose him to a larger organisation. His salary rose accordingly. His whole life would have been perfect if it hadn't have been for Zoë.

Round about coffee time one morning, after Jason had been in the company some ten years, the Chairman Roland Silverman, an old Thatcherite war-horse, came blustering into his office. He was always in a rush and never spoke in full sentences. It was as if his brain was working too fast for his tongue to keep up.

"Jason, you were complaining about not enough backup for your work. Well, I have good news. A very efficient young lady will be with you on Monday. Wants some experience. Thought of you immediately. Pay her a hundred pounds a week pocket money. Nice innocent girl, daughter of a friend of a neighbour, make sure you look after her. Must rush, got another board meeting."

Jason would have liked to refuse, but it's not easy when you're the Finance Director to refuse your Chairman, particularly with something apparently so trivial. Besides, if the girl was quiet and shy she shouldn't be too much of a problem. There was always plenty of ticking and checking work she could do and who knows, he could be right, perhaps she could be useful. Jason thought no more about it and settled back into his previous occupation, looking at the statistics and checking figures. By the time he got back to Jane that evening he'd forgotten all about it. He was quite surprised the following Monday morning, when an extremely glamorous young lady, who'd apparently forgotten to put on her skirt that morning, was shown into his office by Mrs Robinson, Jason's middle-aged and efficient personal assistant.

Jason may not have had much experience with women, but he certainly could tell a pretty girl when he saw one. Zoë Walker was a particularly gorgeous creature. Her outfit really wasn't suitable for an accountant's office, though at the same time extremely pleasing to the male eye. The skirt, or rather the lack of it, barely covered her thighs, her blouse was virginal see-through white, her nipples could be seen protruding from her transparent bra. Her hair was long and golden, her eyes blue and she seemed to laugh as she spoke.

"Good morning, Mr Roberts," she said, "I'm told I must report to you. What would you like me to do?"

Jason set her some filing and as she went out of the room he found himself looking at her white briefs, barely hidden below the pelmet of her skirt. *I suppose I ought to tell her to dress more appropriately for the office, but it's so embarrassing,* he thought. *Perhaps she'll notice and come dressed more suitably tomorrow.*

Over the next few weeks Jason found himself more and more preoccupied with Zoë. He found he could hardly take his eyes off her when she was in the office with him. She hadn't changed her way of dressing and he hadn't somehow got round to telling her that she should really wear slightly longer skirts. It was amazing how often she dropped things in the office, bending down to expose herself to him. She also had a habit of sitting on his desk while talking to him, her long legs apart, giving him a perfect view of her pubic hair through her thin, transparent briefs. It was getting so bad that he fantasised about making love to her while making love to Jane in one of their monthly sessions. He found more and more he couldn't get her face out of his mind. He realised he was becoming obsessed and it was beginning to affect his work.

It was inevitable that Jason would fall. Zoë was absolutely determined to have him. He was amazed to find that she actually found him attractive. She always preferred the older man. What her mother had conveniently left out when she asked Roland Silverman for a job for Zoë, was that she'd been expelled from her expensive private school for having an affair with her young history teacher. He suffered instant dismissal which in his case was justified but hardly fair. He just didn't stand a chance. What Zoë wants, Zoë gets.

Although she was not yet twenty her sexual exploits could easily create a best-selling bonkbuster novel. Unlike Jason, she was experienced in all aspects of lovemaking. Her preference was for older, richer men who could also provide her with things that she liked, designer clothes, expensive meals at restaurants, and generally treat her like she expected to be treated, like a lady. Poor old Jason, he got into such a state that he'd even taken up masturbating again, thinking of course of Zoë each time. His personal assistant, Mrs Roberts, was due for retirement soon and he decided that it would be nice for her to have two months' paid leave before she went. As Finance Director he had total power and so Zoë Phillips, not yet twenty, became his personal assistant with a salary rise of seven thousand pounds.

There were of course strings attached. She had to improve her typing, but the cost of the course would be paid by the company. The course would take place in company time to save her inconvenience. She would have to achieve the necessary standard. Of course there were a few eyebrows raised at her appointment at the Redwood Group headquarters but as Jason was so perfect, nobody seriously thought there could possibly be anything in it. After all, they were talking about goody-goody Roberts.

To celebrate Zoë's elevation Jason suggested tentatively that he took her out for a celebration dinner at Quaglino's. To his surprise she instantly agreed. He phoned Jane and told her that he had a boring evening meeting and afterwards he'd have to go to a business dinner and she shouldn't wait up for him. The evening went well. Zoë, as usual, looked scrumptious and Jason was extremely proud to be out with such a desirable girl. He ordered for Zoë, she acting the part of the little girl lost, even though she'd been there twice before, but she never let on. He kept the meal simple, a galia melon with port, followed by oven-baked sea bass, not the tasteless farmed variety, but the real thing, fresh from the sea, accompanied by new season's asparagus and Jersey royal potatoes. They washed it down with a Sancerre rosé. For pudding, he selected the apricot brulée and it was delicious. By the time they were drinking their cappuccino and eating their petits fours, they both were a little tipsy. Jason took Zoë back to her flat in a taxi and kissed her for the first time. She responded passionately and by the time the taxi drew up at the door Jason was more excited than at any other time in his life. If he'd had more confidence he might have at least tried to go in for a night-cap but his usual decent feelings rejected such thoughts and he contented himself with a final goodnight kiss.

Jane put Jason's unexpected passion that night down to far too much booze, but nevertheless enjoyed a rare burst of spontaneous sex. As they lay in the darkened room afterwards, Jane asked him about his evening.

"Was it a good meeting?"

"Yes, exceptionally good," replied Jason, "it all went better than I expected. The deal is going ahead so we're now in the middle of another acquisition and I'm going to be out late a lot for the next few weeks. I know it's a bore but that's the penalty of the job. Still, when it's all over I'll take us all away for a luxury holiday."

Even as he lied he felt the guilt swelling up in him, but he had no alternative, he just had to have Zoë.

The next evening he took Zoë out again, this time to the grill room at the Savoy. He realised it was a bit public but he'd worked out that he was better keeping it open, after all, why should he not treat his personal assistant to a meal after a boring meeting? This time Zoë asked him in for a night-cap. He readily agreed.

The flat was small, almost a bed-sitter, having just one main room with a galley kitchen and a bathroom off it. The bed rather dominated the room and Jason much hoped he'd end up in it that night.

"How do you like it?" asked Zoë suggestively. Then she spoilt it by adding, "Black, white, sugar or no sugar, cup or mug?"

"Black in a cup not a mug, with no sugar, please. Come here first, I want to kiss you some more."

She was a good kisser and Zoë set about teaching him what she liked. Jason, as always, was a brilliant pupil and had soon graduated up to a B plus standard. He gradually started using his hands and finding no resistance, was soon caressing her breasts. Again, he was poor and she had to instruct him about what he should be doing. By the time he was reasonably proficient and was expecting to bed Zoë, she surprised him by saying, "Well, it's been a super evening but I really must get some sleep. I'll see you tomorrow."

By the time he got home Jane was fast asleep so he had to provide self-help in the bathroom – that was not the way he'd intended the evening to end.

Zoë was somewhat distant during the next day and pleaded a prior engagement when he asked her out again. On the Friday she confided to him her problems.

"I was so ashamed of my flat the other night. It's so poky and squalid. I've really got to get myself something better. To do that I need more money. I don't suppose there's any chance of a rise, is there?" she asked hopefully in her best little girl voice.

Oh God, thought Jason, *so that's it. I give her what she wants and she'll give me what I want.* Even though it was blackmail he still was powerless to refuse her anything.

"I'll see if I can arrange something. Come out for dinner on Monday and I'll let you know if I've been successful."

The weekend was the longest he could remember. A dreadful dinner party on Saturday night followed by a boring trip to his parents' on Sunday. Before Zoë he would have thoroughly enjoyed the weekend but now all he could think about was Monday night.

This time he took her to a small Italian restaurant close by her flat. After all, he didn't want to waste time travelling, he had to get back to Mersham at a reasonable time.

"Well, did you manage to get me a rise?" asked

Zoë while devouring her Tournedos steak.

"I think it could be arranged, in fact I can get you up to twenty thousand pounds but it will be tricky. I'll have to exaggerate your qualifications, but it could be done." Even as he told her he felt disloyal to Redwood, after all, it was a form of theft and if it came out he would be in trouble.

"I'd be so grateful, I'd work much harder. I'd do anything."

He had no doubt he'd cracked it, in fact he was counting on it. They finished their meal and didn't bother with the coffee and rushed back to the flat. He quickly went through stage one and two which Zoë had taught him so enjoyably last time. He moved on to stage three. Their first lovemaking was not brilliant. He was in too much of a hurry and he knew he'd disappointed Zoë.

"Don't worry about it," she said, "I'll soon have you up and running again."

He'd read about oral sex but never imagined a nice girl actually doing it. He assumed it was something only prostitutes and tarts did, and then only for money. Zoë was quite right, she did get him up extremely quickly. The second time was a great improvement.

During the next few months Zoë taught him about sex. It seemed strange to him that a girl so young should teach a father of two about sex. But as far as Zoë was concerned he was like a little boy all over again. It amazed him just how much she knew and gradually as he became more adept, their lovemaking sessions lasted longer and longer. There was always one big snag. At the end of every evening he had to leave her bed and get back to Mersham. Both of them hated it; at last, Zoë snapped.

"I'm fed up with you always leaving. I want you to stay all night for once. I want to wake up with you beside me in the morning, make love slowly, have a shower together, make love again. I want to prepare breakfast for you. It's not much to ask, is it?"

He thought about it and he liked the idea of the morning sex.

"Perhaps we could go on holiday together. I could be called away on a business trip. Where would you like to go?"

"Hollywood! Los Angeles!" she squealed immediately. "I've always wanted to go there. Take me to Disneyland!"

*

"I'm afraid I'm going to have to go to the States for a week or so," Jason told Jane over breakfast on the Tuesday after Zoë's demand to go to Hollywood. "We're thinking of expanding out there by buying the Elite Card Group. I've got to go out and do the due diligence exercise. It's not a large outfit so should be back fairly quickly, say seven to ten days."

"Well, that's a shame," said Jane, "I know you hate travelling and it's rotten to be all by yourself. Do you want me to talk to your mum and see if she'll look after the kids, then I could come out there to keep you company?"

"NO," he said loudly. He was immediately aware that his 'no' had been too strong and far too quick, and so he repeated it again quietly. "No, it would be boring for you, I'd be working round the clock. It could also be rather dangerous because it's a rough area, which means I'd be worried about you. I'd love to have you with me, darling, but it won't work this time. It's only going to be a week so I'll be back before you've even noticed I've gone."

"I suppose you're right but you make sure you phone regularly and don't you be tempted by any of those gorgeous American girls," she joked.

"You've got absolutely no problems there," he answered a hundred percent truthfully. He could only just cope with Zoë's demands, let alone any others.

As Jason drove in to the office that morning he felt rather smug. It had gone much better than he'd hoped. Ten days alone with Zoë in Los Angeles. It would be absolutely fantastic. He started planning the trip in his head. They would stay in Beverly Hills, perhaps somewhere on Rodeo Drive. Zoë would love all the shops, after all, it was one of the most famous shopping streets in the world. Perhaps they would fly in via New York and stay a couple of nights at the Waldorf Astoria. While they were there they could take in a show on Broadway.

As it turned out there was only one hotel on Rodeo Drive, the Summit. Jason booked them the luxury penthouse suite. The flights to the Big Apple were fully booked and so he had to drop the New York idea. In the end they flew with British Airways in business class, on a direct flight to Los Angeles. Zoë was excited about the trip, as well she might be. Hollywood, Beverly Hills, Disneyland, Universal Studios and Santa Monica, all places she had only ever seen in films. Jason had to admit it was the thought of having Zoë to himself for ten days that excited him. It would make a change from the hurried sex in her poky flat, with him always having to think about time, hoping he didn't smell of her perfume or of sex when he got back to Jane and the children. He'd never even spent a full night with her. While she could explore Hollywood, he'd be happy exploring her body. It seemed amazing that it had taken him so long to find out how good sex could be.

He arranged for a limousine to pick him up from home and left a tearful family as he sped off down the drive. He did feel a little guilty, but that completely left him when he saw Zoë at Heathrow. She looked stunning in an expensive red Christian Dior suit. Her legs appeared to go on forever and the skirt was one of the briefest he'd ever seen. It seemed a shame that he would have to wait at least fourteen hours before he would have her alone in their luxury Beverly Hills king-size bed.

The journey was, as usual, delayed. Someone had become ill on the plane before they took off and they had to taxi back to the departure point while the old man was taken off and his luggage was located. By the time all was well they had lost over an hour. After that it was a reasonably pleasant trip. The food was surprisingly edible, the films reasonably interesting, the constant refills of champagne were free.

They arrived eventually thirty-five minutes late, and after queuing for about forty minutes to get through the customs and passport control they were in a taxi, stuck in a traffic jam in the blistering heat. Despite the fact there were six lanes, all were solid and moving slowly.

Being a non-smoker, Jason was delighted with some of the anti-smoking posters on the route. One he particularly liked showed a handsome man asking a pretty girl, "Do you mind if I smoke?"

Her reply was, "Do you mind if I die?"

There was also an elaborate electronic display board continually ticking over counting those who have died from smoking-related diseases. The digits moved continuously and the figures were large. If he'd been a smoker, it would certainly have made him think seriously about giving up.

Luckily they had to turn off the turnpike and away from the massive traffic jams. Shortly afterwards they pulled up outside the Summit. From the exterior it was not an impressive hotel but after travelling for over fifteen hours, lusting over Zoë's body, any bed would do. They were checked in by the friendly Mexican staff on reception and shown to their room. The suite was pleasant enough. The view from their rooftop terrace was boring, they just looked down onto a small roof garden and the courtyard restaurant below. On the other hand, the king-size bed looked to Jason exactly what he had been dreaming about all through the flight.

As soon as the Mexican porter had left he pulled Zoë to him and kissed her hungrily.

"Stop it, you'll ruin my suit," squealed Zoë, "just wait a minute, don't be so impatient!"

She carefully took off the jacket and removed the almost invisible skirt, carefully hanging them up. Standing there in her white blouse and white silk cami-knickers, she looked irresistible. He stood still, silently taking in her sheer beauty.

"What's wrong, changed your mind?" teased Zoë. "Getting too old?"

With that, Jason grabbed her and threw her onto the bed. He was so excited that he couldn't be bothered with foreplay or removing much of their clothing. They were so hot that they both exploded within seconds.

"Silly, isn't it?" he said, lying back, looking at the ceiling. "The first time we've got all the time in the world we try to break the world record."

"It's not silly, that was just the appetiser, darling. Now for the hors d'oeuvres, then we can have the main course and dessert to follow."

They didn't bother with dinner that evening.

They awoke early and after Jason had said good morning properly to Zoë they emerged to have a leisurely breakfast sitting in the window of the Cafe Rodeo. They had decided to take things easy for the first day and strolled out into the bright morning sunshine to look at the various shops along the drive.

Rodeo Drive certainly lived up to its reputation. If you wanted to spend real money, any of the various shops were delighted to oblige. Zoë was in seventh heaven. She bought three pairs of shoes at Bally, a beautiful dress and top from Chanel and a suit from Yves St Laurent. They then crossed the road and she booked herself a hair appointment for later that morning. The credit card bashing continued with Zoë adding a Gucci belt and a handbag and scarf from Hermes. By that time Zoë and Jason were exhausted;

they returned back to Cafe Rodeo for morning coffee. If Jason thought he'd overspent in the first session he was to be proved wrong.

If you haven't been to Rodeo Drive recently you probably would not have seen Rodeo Two. This is an old-fashioned looking European street newly developed incorporating cobbled streets and Victorian buildings, all completely authentic with original air-conditioning!

As they walked down this new road, there on the corner was the magic of Tiffany & Co. Zoë loved the Audrey Hepburn film and wanted to buy some trivial item just like Holly Golightly did. Jason didn't really consider a twenty thousand pound bracelet a trivial purchase but then what the hell, he thought, she was certainly worth it.

By the time they'd been in Cartier, Christian Dior, and bought an exquisite negligee in Valentino's, Jason was feeling extremely poor. He'd totted up the cost in his head of that morning's expenditure. He reckoned it worked out at around ninety thousand pounds and that was just for starters.

While Zoë was prettying herself up at the hair designers Jason studied the tourist brochures he'd picked up in the front of the hotel. Apparently they could visit the sister hotel at the Bel Air Summit where there was a large swimming pool. He booked them the hotel limousine and waited for Zoë's return. Of course, she needed a new swimming costume. Why it was called a swimming costume, he didn't really know. Nobody in their right mind would splash around in a four hundred pound outfit in that chlorinated water. Zoë simply sunbathed, showing off her magnificent body to all the other loungers, most of whom were men who envied Jason his gorgeous companion. He was self-satisfied. He was sure that most of them thought she was a film star and that he was probably a director or producer.

They had a pleasant meal at the hotel. What was unusual was that they had to catch the hotel limousine to get from the pool down to the main hotel even though it was only a few hundred yards. It was also up the hill. Apparently Americans don't walk anywhere if they can help it.

Being at the pool during the afternoons had one obvious advantage – Zoë couldn't shop. Jason realised he had to keep her away from Rodeo Drive as much as possible and so he started an intensive tourist programme.

That evening they ate at the Pretty Woman hotel, the Regent Beverly Wiltshire Hotel. It was a great disappointment to them both. The service was slow and the food boring. The only amusing part of the evening was that they observed a real Pretty Woman. A prostitute entertaining her sugar daddy. There was, however, a great difference between this couple and the Julia Roberts and Richard Gere version. For a start, this man looked more like someone who would need to pay for sex and she looked like the tart to avoid. Her behaviour was also rather embarrassing. They both wondered why they couldn't wait to start in the bedroom. Nobody else took any notice so they assumed this was normal behaviour.

Jason had often wondered why men would pay for sex, he would never do such a thing!

On their return to The Summit, Zoë ordered a bottle of Bollinger and they settled down to watch a naughty film on the pay TV. The next morning Jason felt tired. He was forcibly reminded of a joke he'd heard recently. What do you call a man over forty who has sex twice in a night? The answer – an ambulance.

Poor old Jason wasn't yet forty but the way things were going with Zoë he'd soon get there, though hopefully not in an ambulance.

Afterwards they took a taxi to Universal Studios and despite the fact the dinosaur experience was closed for maintenance, they certainly enjoyed the day. Jason thought the theatre tour was the highlight, whereas Zoë enjoyed the Wild West show.

By that evening, jetlag was catching up with them and they ended up in the Rodeo Cafe and retired early. After all, the best part of the trip as far as Jason was concerned was the bedroom.

The rest of their time was spent visiting Disneyland. Zoë was like a little girl rushing from one attraction to another, Jason found it endearing as well as a considerable sexual turn on. Each night they returned, had a meal, and settled back into their king-size bed. He thought all his increased activity might have an effect on his performance. If anything though, his stamina improved and with Zoë's help they became more and more adventurous.

On their last night in LA Jason had managed to book an outside table at Spargo, which was the most fashionable and probably the best restaurant in Beverly Hills. It was a fantastic experience. They sat in the courtyard with dozens of overhead heaters keeping them warm. Zoë was continually pointing out minor stars of stage and screen who were dining there. Jason's age certainly showed as he'd got no idea who any of these celebrities were, but he certainly noticed the girls. He'd never seen quite so many beautiful women in any restaurant in his life. In many ways Jason's next mistake was directly the fault of Spargo. Having eaten so well and drunk so much wine, he agreed to buy Zoë a flat in London on his return so they could enjoy many more similar evenings. Why he made the promise, he didn't know, but the one thing he did realise, whatever happened he had to keep Zoë at all costs.

All the way back to Heathrow, Jason was worried about how to buy Zoë a flat. She was so excited about it all that he really couldn't let her down. The problem was that he had no money. He was already considerably in debt. He was already only too aware that he had overspent on the trip. How was he going to keep it all from Jane? As he sat stranded in that aeroplane limbo, he began to work out how it could be done. He could see the solution immediately. He handled millions of pounds every week. It didn't take much ingenuity for him to divert a small amount to a worthy cause. The answer was to set up a few bogus suppliers and that way he could pay money from the company to himself.

He arrived back at Mersham bearing the usual guilty gifts – perfume, flowers, and chocolates and goodies for the kids.

He set up a number of off-the-shelf companies. His first creation he thought rather poetic. He named it the Flat Printing Company, a very appropriate name given the circumstances. After all, it was a company set up to buy a flat and it would literally print money for him! He organised it as a limited company and supplied himself regular invoices for services never received. He made sure all the printing services not supplied, were also non-vatable. The last thing he needed was some super-efficient VAT inspector looking for promotion picking it up from the accounts and causing trouble.

They went flat hunting together. Zoë particularly wanted a river view so they trawled the river from Kew to Canary Wharf. Jason found that river views sell quickly and as such, were expensive. Zoë's idea of a river view and some of the estate agents' seemed to be widely different. River peek would be more appropriate. In some cases he felt you needed a giraffe neck to cram out of the window to actually see the river. Eventually though, Zoë found her perfect flat. It was right on the Thames at a place called Jacob's Island. The views were spectacular and at three hundred and eighty-five thousand, it certainly looked a bargain. Jason had managed to embezzle over two hundred and fifty thousand by that time and with the aid of a short-term bank loan, he paid for the flat outright. Zoë was delighted and tried to thank him in all the ways she knew would please him, she even bought a gymslip.

To Jane's surprise Jason seemed to find more and more reasons not to return to Mersham. She suspected that he was having an affair but by then really couldn't be bothered. At least it meant he didn't try to paw her on his return. She had enjoyed their lovemaking at first but now was tired of it. She was prepared to put up with it as her part of the marriage bargain. Jane was now chairman of the local PTS, served on the parish council, and had many girl friends in the location. The way she saw it was that if she confronted him and they divorced, they would have to sell the house. She certainly didn't want that. Her life was far too comfortable.

Jason continued to plunder the company's resources and like most thieves, began to get complacent. He should have known that Richard Valentine would spot the fraud sooner or later. Jason, though, just didn't care. Zoë was so happy with her new apartment nothing else seemed to matter. Their sex life had never been better, there seemed no end to her inventiveness. Most of her ideas, she told him, ironically came from women's magazines. They had great fun furnishing the apartment, spending a fortune at the Conran Shop, Heals or Harrods. The result was the flat looked stunning. Jason had never been so happy, but then all good things come to an end.

When he arrived in his office one morning in early September there was a message from the chief executive. It was to see him at nine thirty on an urgent matter.

Jason was soon to learn the nature of the urgent matter. As he entered the room, Richard indicated that he should sit down. He didn't waste time with niceties.

"What the fucking hell do you think you're playing at?" started Valentine.

This shook Jason. He'd never heard Richard swear before.

"What do you mean?" said Jason.

"I mean Flat Printing Ltd, Cardboard Supplies Ltd, Office Supplies Ltd and all the others. You know what I'm talking about; the fictitious companies you've made up to milk the company. That's what I mean!" shouted Valentine.

"I don't know what you're talking about."

"I'm sure you don't, so let's put it this way. I'm going to call you into this office on the sixteenth of February, that's six months' time. Hopefully when we look at the books then, we'll find that no such companies exist. If we do find they still exist then it will be a matter for the police. I hope we understand each other. Incidentally, this meeting never took place. Do you understand me?"

Jason had started to feel faint. He should have realised Valentine would get wise to what he was doing. He was so thorough, looking at areas to save money. The only surprise was to be given the six months to sort it out. He didn't know if he could, but he certainly would try. The thought of prison, or losing Zoë, was too horrific even to think about. Over the next few days he gave it more and more thought and discussed how to make real money with some of his financial cronies at the local. He steered the conversation to how they would make easy money.

"Put it on a good horse," said one. "Even better, put it on three or four horses on an accumulator. If you're lucky you can make a pile." Jason didn't fancy horses though. He had no knowledge and to him it was far too risky.

"Play on the lottery," said another, "you've as much chance as anyone else. I try every week. Mind you, I haven't won anything."

Share options was another suggestion. Jason took this one more seriously. The trouble was, he couldn't really see himself making six hundred thousand pounds in six months on share options, but it was certainly worth considering.

The final suggestion, though, did appeal.

"Currency speculation," said one of the city currency dealers. "That's the way to make a real killing. Put your money on future currency purchases. The nice thing is you can gamble enormous sums and only play for a small margin. I regularly make thirty, forty, or fifty thousand pounds with almost no risk."

Now this sounded more like it, and as he could do it through the company, he wouldn't need any capital to start with. It could all be done on futures.

"If you were going to do a gamble at the moment, which currencies would you go for, the dollar, deutschmark, franc?" asked Jason.

"No, I'd go for the tiger economies. I'd go for Korea, Indonesia, Malaysia, possibly even Japan. That's where you'll really make some money."

Jason took the advice. He bought ahead three months' contracts, four million pounds worth of currency spread equally between the yen of Japan, the wong of Korea, the Malaysian dollar and the Indonesian rupee. With a bit of luck, before Christmas his problems would be over. He felt pleased with his gamble and chuckled to himself.

After all, what could go wong?

CHAPTER 2

The Perfect Bastard

Richard Valentine was a bastard. In most cases being a bastard was an accident of birth. In Richard Valentine's case he was a self-made man. There is a commonly used expression that you should be nice to people on the way up, as you might meet them on the way down. Richard Valentine had no interest in coming down, so he kicked all and sundry as he continued his rapid elevation into becoming seriously rich. He was born with no scruples, he was naturally amoral. He'd listened seriously to the words of Tom Lehrer's song, 'Plagiarism', and had adopted the words as his own. He had particularly liked the verse that went:

> *Never let anyone's work evade your eyes,*
> *Remember why the good Lord gave you eyes,*
> *Plagiarise, plagiarise, plagiarise,*
> *But please always call it research.*

He was an excellent plagiarist. He stole ideas from

anybody. He was never too proud to stoop to any level so long as he could see a good profit in it for him.

Richard had two main interests in life, sex and money. The bottom line was all he understood and cared about in business, and privately, his creature comforts and pleasures were a priority. He was of course, happy to mix both wherever possible. The Jesuits say give me a boy until he is seven and I will show you the man. Richard was a selfish, greedy, spoilt boy. He hated losing and was adept at cheating at an early age. By seven there was no better cheat at marbles and Monopoly than Richard Valentine. He was quick to spot an opportunity, particularly when it provided him a good profit.

His mother was persuaded by the vicar to donate a weekly fee to the local church. Being efficient, she put together fifty-two church appeal envelopes, each with a pound note in it, so she wouldn't have to think about it again. The vicar was delighted to receive on the offering plate ten shillings each week from her. Richard had painstakingly steamed open each envelope and replaced the pound note with a more acceptable ten shilling one; that is, more acceptable of course, to Richard. This annual income of twenty-six pounds continued for many years with neither the vicar nor his mother ever finding out the truth.

Being a keen stamp collector, he spotted many ways of adding to his wealth. Most of his contemporaries at school had no idea of the values of the stamps that they had in their collections. In many cases they had been given them by their grandparents or other elderly relations. Because of this, many of the albums contained valuable gems. With some of his capital he invested in brightly coloured triangular stamps from Monaco, San Marino, Hungary, and other such countries that specialised in making money from issuing stamps. He'd then swap these worthless pretty stamps for dull, valuable Victorian ones, which the stupid boys didn't want. His favourite swap was a large football diamond-shaped stamp from Monaco depicting Wembley Stadium for a British, orange five pound stamp issued in 1882.

One was worth one thousand six hundred pounds, the other about five pence. I'm sure you can guess which one was which.

By the time Richard was fifteen, he had a superb collection worth tens of thousands of pounds. In addition, he'd sold many unwanted stamps to a local dealer, netting himself thousands of pounds in the process.

Money makes money, he'd been told by his father, and he had taken his advice seriously. With his father's help he had started investing on the stock market before he was ten. He listened carefully to the grown-ups talking about investments and picked up many valuable tips. He usually bought blue chip shares such as Marks and Spencer's, ICI and Grand Metropolitan, but he wasn't averse to a gamble. He was lucky in purchasing Antofagasta shares, when they were out of fashion. He could hardly believe his luck when he saw his capital increase twentyfold.

Richard was an unpopular boy at school despite the fact that his work was excellent. His contempt for the teachers and the other boys, added to his persistent boasting about all of his money, meant he had no friends. That didn't bother him as he spent most of his time working out fresh schemes to make even more.

At sixteen he discovered there was more to life than money. He caught the train to Kings Cross, then the tube to Leicester Square. From there he walked through Soho, until he found what he was looking for, a discreet brothel. He walked in as confidently as he could manage and asked about prices. The madam, who was used to public school boys, realised that this was probably to be his first time. She kindly ensured he had a sympathetic instructor. He was an enthusiastic pupil with a natural aptitude for the subject. He learned quickly and after several visits decided that although pleasurable, it was a waste of money. He was sure that the same services could be obtained free, locally, thereby not only saving the prostitutes' fee but also the train fare. So began a phase in his life when he got to know the local girls of easy repute. After using them to enjoy further his newly found skills, he advanced to the nicer girls. He was pleased to find that under the surface they often enjoyed the game even more than the more common ones.

As soon as he was seventeen he quickly learned to drive and passed his first driving test with ease. He liked flashy cars and built up a part-time business buying them from auctions and selling locally using free ads in the newly published free house-to-house weekly newspapers. He had a magnificent collection of invented reasons why he had to sell each car. He was either an impoverished student, about to emigrate, or selling it for his mother who was dying in hospital. This proved to be so lucrative that he took a lease on a car lot and employed a retired car salesman to run it for him.

He sold his stamp collection through Phillips the auctioneers and was pleasantly surprised to receive, after commission, over fifty thousand pounds. He chuckled as he received the cheque, thinking of all those worthless stamps he had swapped to build up this useful capital. How stupid all those small boys were who had given him all this money.

With the help of this new capital, the garage went from strength to strength. It specialised in selling low mileage cars. Richard wouldn't touch anything else, particularly as he'd become quite an expert in 'clocking'. Within two years he had three other sites operating in the area and was in the process of acquiring a legitimate garage with a Rover franchise.

The garage business was making good money but it was not enough to satisfy his need to become very rich. He had noticed a growing market in greeting cards and felt this could be the area for him. The profit margins were incredible. All you needed was some good cheap designs, an adequate printer, a good sales force, and you'd created a cash cow.

*

He used young artists from the local art colleges for his new company. The nice thing about the students was that not only need you pay them virtually nothing, but they had no idea about business. He was astute in acquiring the copyright, so they were unable to get any more money regardless of how much Valentine made. Some of these youngsters' designs became classics, making enormous profits for him. The young designers of course, got nothing. His nose for money helped him quickly build up a sizeable card business. He'd opened his first three card shops by the time he celebrated his twenty-first birthday. By now he employed a manager for his garage business and had eight forecourts selling second hand cars, as well as his main garage. He'd also, as luck would have it, found a designer with considerable commercial experience to take over the day-to-day running of the greetings cards side. The man seemed to be under the impression that he would be allowed to purchase a good size stake in the company. He worked especially hard in building up the company to its first million-pound turnover.

Richard, meanwhile, turned his eye to property. He bought his first house at the age of eighteen and traded it three years later to make him a capital gain of over seventy thousand pounds, tax free. As easy money was to be made out of property, he bought an ailing estate agency and quickly turned it round, putting in a sharp young surveyor to run it. The two of them ran a particularly unpleasant scheme buying houses at well under the market price from old and trusting people and reselling them for an excellent profit. The agency did so well that they quickly opened up a second and then a third branch. They also started a property auction. Richard started to invest in property and used the auction and the agencies to acquire houses, always, of course, at advantageous prices well below market value.

The nice thing about property was the generous grants given to the poor and deserving people in order that they could repair their roofs, rewire, add a bathroom or kitchen, insulate and to do all sorts of necessary improvements. Richard couldn't imagine for a moment that there could be anybody more deserving than him. He got to know the right people on the grant panel. Not that anybody would ever guess, they never seemed to speak to each other in England. It was a different story in Greece or Florida where their families enjoyed Valentine's generous hospitality. This sideline was incredibly profitable. He bought cheaply from unsuspecting widows and old people prior to auction. As the houses were in such a mess he convinced the owners that he was being kind by taking them over. The taxpayer paid for renovations, he then rented them through the estate agency to the DHS.

He had learned early that money made money, and continued to play the stock market.

He had an excellent nose for financial matters; he made a killing with Body Shop and was pleased to have sold out of Polly Peck before the billion pound scandal and Azil Nadir's subsequent moonlight trip to Turkish Cyprus. In the summer of 1987 Richard's stock market wealth was well over two and a half million pounds.

Richard was becoming increasingly anxious about the high level of share prices. It seemed to him that the P/E levels were far too high both in the UK and in America. He had been discussing it with his old friend James Goldsmith and they both decided to get out of equities and sit with cash. Against all the other experts' advice, he sold out and put the money on deposit overnight at the bank. Nobody was more happy than Richard when the market collapsed in October, the day after Michael Fish had told the world that Britain never had hurricanes. He even made a profit out of the hurricane damage. All the unsaleable cars appeared to have been damaged by the freak conditions, so the car business made an excellent one-off profit. Richard was amused as it was recorded by the auditors in the official accounts as windfall profit!

A month after the crash, Richard re-entered the stock market, buying the same shares at a fraction of the price he sold them for. By this time his estate agencies had expanded to eight branches. The sharp surveyor was a natural and was always spotting excellent openings.

The Prudential approached Richard and offered to pay him the absurd sum of three and a half million pounds for his business. He couldn't believe such a large and successful company would be so stupid. Although Richard had promised his manager a future partnership, he had been careful to ensure nothing was on paper. He did wish him well in his new position with the Prudential and ensured he at least had a lucrative contract. After all, he owed him that much. After his kindness, Richard had no qualms about pocketing all of the money. Despite the temper tantrums he was forced to witness from the man, he still wished him no ill.

He was advised by his accountant to roll-over the tax by buying a further business and investing in his pension. This, he was told, would save him at least one and a half million pounds in tax. To make that sort of money tax-free and honestly was something that appealed to Richard. He was always keen on tax avoidance, which of course was completely legal. He often couldn't see the difference between what he did, and tax evasion which was illegal, it was a fine line after all. He invested the money, acquiring the shares of an extremely large greeting card manufacturer that had expanded too quickly in the boom years of the eighties and had suffered badly in the recession. Ironically, the same recession and the subsequent housing crash had made his old estate agency almost worthless. In the end it amused him when the great Prudential virtually gave their estate agencies away.

He left the choice of pension portfolios to his pension advisor, Mr Kon. He seemed to know what he was doing. The main thing, as he continually advised him, was to never put all your eggs in one basket. The more policies the better, he insisted. Richard took his advice and had dozens.

The greeting card side of his empire was now growing at an enormous rate and employed over five hundred people. They exported to all over the world and they were even selling cards in Harrods. The garage side was hardly less successful and by now had acquired franchises for Jaguar and Ford to add to the original Rover one. At the same time the auction had grown into a national name. The combined profits for both were now well over three million pounds.

In 1995 Richard put them into a group and floated on the stock market. The new company predicted profits of not less than four and a half million for its first year and the shares were oversubscribed by three times. At the time of the sale Richard sold twenty-five percent of his own shares. After the float, Richard's shares were worth on paper nearly a hundred million pounds. In addition, he had a further twenty-five million pounds in cash, less whatever tax his artful accountant would agree with the Inland Revenue.

Prior to the public offer of the shares Richard had persuaded Roland Silverman to become Redwood's chairman. Roland was a well-respected city figure, a company doctor with many successes behind him. He was also chairman of many listed companies. He was more importantly a tough old bird and gave the company some respectability. He had worked with Jason Roberts while he was at Coopers and it was at his suggestion that Jason was recruited as financial director.

He had succeeded in seducing an endless list of local beauties, many of whom thought, as it turned out incorrectly, that they were engaged to him. With his large and flashy cars, access to the best London restaurants and night clubs, his luxury country house, a London flat, and a house on Longboat in Sarasota, Florida, Richard found every opportunity to enjoy his second favourite pastime – women.

Richard was an almost perfect bastard.

Eventually he decided he would like to have a son and heir to take over his ever-expanding empire. He set about it, in his usual efficient and profitable way, to find a suitable wife. When he was introduced to Nicola Provest at a dinner party he realised that she was ideal. She was blonde, attractive, clever, the only daughter of an elderly shipping magnate who had already lost his wife. From all accounts Ernest Provest was worth something over twenty million pounds and all of that would eventually go to Nicola. It was that, that clinched it for him.

It was a marriage made in the boardroom. Luckily she was good in bed, which to Richard, was an acceptable bonus. Nicola was an excellent hostess and their dinner parties were always full of useful people. The only drawback for Richard was that no children appeared on the horizon.

Richard couldn't have a better home base and most men would have been ecstatic with Nicola. They had bought a delightful terraced house close by the Thames on Oakley Gardens. Nicola had scoured all of the auction houses for miles around and had furnished it in period style for a fraction of what it would have cost from the London antique shops. Although very wealthy, her parents had brought her up to respect money and to look after it. The house looked just as if they had employed an expensive interior designer.

Nicola had put all of her energy into being a proper wife, however, while she was being good the same couldn't be said for Richard. His sexual appetite had become accustomed to more variety, so he continued to take mistresses, the first being within a month of his marriage. The score increased rapidly. It was as if he had a bet with Peter Stringfellow. However, until he met Rebecca, none was ever serious.

Rebecca Fielding was one of those amazingly attractive girls. If you were to ask why she was so attractive it would be hard to put your finger on it. She oozed personality and was full of life. Her voice was deep and husky and incredibly sexy. She was always immaculate in her appearance but somehow always managed to flaunt her legs or breasts. Never apparently on purpose but always in an extremely erotic way. She also never seemed to be overawed in any situation, she was one of life's natural posers.

Rebecca had money in her own right. She'd been left a small legacy by a childless aunt who had always been a favourite as a child.

When she met Richard Valentine at an advertising meeting for his new card range, she was immediately attracted. The feeling was mutual. Rebecca did not at that point in time know that for Richard, this was his usual routine. She was swept off her feet and they began a passionate romance that she thought would eventually lead to something a little bit more permanent.

Richard confided to her that his marriage was a total sham. He had only married Nicola because she had told him she was pregnant, which as it turned out was a lie. As of course was the whole of his well-used story. He told her he only stayed with Nicola for appearance's sake, they didn't even sleep in the same bed, and he was lonely. He gave her the impression that he would leave his wife for the right woman. He made it clear to her that she was that right woman.

Despite Rebecca's obvious charms and beauty, she had not been particularly successful with lovers. In many ways her appearance, wealth, and confidence put most of them off. The ones that were attracted were often the fortune-hunters who clearly only wanted her for her money. She had been disappointed so many times but with Richard she was sure, at last she had found her partner for life.

Richard clearly felt the same as he gave up all his other mistresses for her. They spent all of their spare time together and for a change, Richard even missed the odd meeting. They spent an idyllic holiday in Jamaica at the Sandals resort. It was the happiest she had ever had. Richard often took her to his house on Long Boat Key near Sarasota in Florida and they constantly spent time on the French Riviera.

Richard usually kept his extramarital affairs fairly low key, but with Rebecca he just didn't seem to care.

Nicola knew he was regularly unfaithful, otherwise why would he have to be away from home so often? She had come to terms with it. She was not prepared for this public show of their problems. So many of her 'friends' showed their 'concern' for her by telling her all about his latest sightings. It was humiliating for her, but Richard just didn't seem to care.

Eventually she plucked up courage and confronted him.

"Richard, I want a divorce. I'm sick of your screwing around. At least in the past you were decent enough to try to hide your affairs from everyone, but now you just don't care. I can't take it anymore. I feel completely worthless so I'm going to talk to a solicitor and get things moving."

Richard was shaken. He couldn't care less if she left him, but there were more important considerations. A divorce would mean a financial settlement. Nicola would then have a sizeable stake in the company. More to the point, it would mean he could lose control of the company. That was the one thing that Richard could not contemplate, it was his baby, he had built it up and no city bastard was going to take it away from him. Much as he loved Rebecca, he realised he would have to give her up. It was a shame, but business always came first.

"Look Nicola, I know I've been stupid but I can change. I'll stop seeing her and I'll try to be a good husband. Look, you don't have to believe me now, give me three months. I know I can do it."

Nicola was extremely doubtful about the whole thing but reluctantly agreed, provided he got rid of all his lovers and started behaving himself.

In the back of Richard's mind he thought he could possibly get Rebecca back when things had quietened down. In the meantime he'd have to dump her. At least he could do it in a civilised fashion. He'd take her to Paris for a few days and break the news to her gently.

That's how Rebecca found herself in an extremely expensive night-dress lying on a bed in one of the Meurice's finest suites. It had been a glorious three days; the weather had been hot, the food delicious and the sex unbelievable. Richard had been the perfect companion. Rebecca was convinced he was going to ask her to marry him at any moment. You can imagine her feelings, as she lay on the bed, relaxing after a very satisfactory lovemaking session, when he told her that he'd have to stop seeing her. It didn't take her long to realise that he'd brought her to the Meurice to tell her but had decided to enjoy her for a few last days before getting rid of her.

God, he's an unfeeling bastard, she thought. She couldn't even bring herself to travel back with him in the car. So she got the hotel limousine to the Gare du Nord, caught the Eurostar back to Waterloo and a taxi back to her home.

On her return to the flat she broke down and sobbed uncontrollably for what seemed like days. How could he treat her like he had? She'd thought he loved her, how could she be so wrong? She didn't think she had ever been so unhappy in her life.

CHAPTER 3

The Perfect Wife

John Carrington had been all Nicola Provest had ever wanted. When as a dreamy teenager she'd lay snuggled up under the duvet with her favourite cuddly toys and dream of her perfect man, John filled all her criteria. For a start, he was incredibly good looking; well, Nicola certainly thought so, even if some of his features were not quite even. They say that beauty is in the eye of the beholder and Nicola was completely and utterly hooked.

John was a Cambridge graduate working as a solicitor in an old and well-established partnership in the ancient county town of Henchester. He was doing exceptionally well and it was just a matter of time before he was offered a full partnership.

From the time they'd met at a recital when she was only twenty, at the local church and then again at a party at the vicarage, they had been inseparable. Like Nicola, he loved classical music, they regularly attended concerts at the South Bank complex, the Barbican, and Albert Hall. They both loved the countryside and although John didn't ride, Nicola was always trying to persuade him to start. They certainly enjoyed their long walks at the weekend, ending with real ale and bread and cheese in remote country pubs.

John was a fantastic yachtsman. He'd already had represented Great Britain in the Olympics at Atlanta and had his heart set on an Olympic medal in Sydney. Nicola had never enjoyed sailing, due to persistent seasickness. This was the one area of their lives that they remained independent of each other. John would go down to Hamble where he and his friends continually practised working on moves that they hoped would bring them glory. Nicola used the time to keep up with her old friends and dream of wedding bells.

One grey damp November evening, after attending a superb concert of the London Mozart Players at the South Bank, John took her to the Ivy, one of the most famous restaurants in London. Certainly the Ivy was a place to be seen, the trouble was though, the waiters and waitresses seemed to be prefer the celebrities in as far as their service was concerned. John and Nicola were shown to a table in the far corner and shown scant service for the rest of the evening. Even the food was disappointing, but in the great scheme of things it meant little to Nicola, for when John asked her to marry him suddenly the restaurant was again the best in the world, and the food was exquisite. It took her all of a second to answer him yes, and the rest of the evening and the journey back was spent discussing dates, possible honeymoon destinations, and where they'd like to live after the wedding.

Nicola's wedding dress was enchanting. She'd gone

for a traditional full-length one with a long train. While wearing it, she looked truly beautiful. The banns had all been read, the White Swan booked, and the cake baked. Nicola had never been so excited in her life. It certainly topped her previous high, waiting to see what Father Christmas brought her on the night of the twenty-fourth of December. She couldn't imagine there was a more lucky girl in the whole world.

The phone call telling her of John's death came out of the blue. She'd just been luxuriating in a hot, deeply filled, oil-infused bath when she'd been summoned to the phone. It was the police in Southampton. There had been an accident, they said, they'd found her name and address in the car. Did she know a Mr John Carrington of Crosswinds, Mill Lane, Henchester? When she confirmed she did, they asked if she was a relative. After she told them she was his fiancée, and was due to be married next week, there had been a long pause. It couldn't have been easy for the young policeman to break the news. Death is never easy, but under those circumstances a horrendous undertaking.

On the surface Nicola took the news calmly. Thanking them politely for letting her know, she went back to her room, finished off her make-up, got dressed, and was about to go downstairs for dinner when she broke down. She had of course hoped it was a nightmare and she would wake up from it, but as realisation hit her she cracked open at the seams.

People handle grief in different ways. Nicola turned to her music for comfort. She sat for hours on end staring into vacant space listening to her CD collection. She continued with her job, as personal assistant to a structural engineer. He liked her and was a great help, putting no pressure on her. She did her job well and conscientiously but rarely went out, other than to work. She refused all invitations to social functions, stopped going out to concerts and became a recluse for the next three to four months.

But as the old cliché says, time is a great healer; life must go on and eventually Nicola started again, slowly rebuilding her life.

At first it was the odd evening with a friend at the house. A visit to the pictures, a quiet restaurant meal. Slowly but surely she learned to hide her dreadful sadness. Her friends started trying to get her to meet eligible bachelors. She was invited to dinner parties where she would be sitting next to some unattached male, but she couldn't even start to think in those terms. However, on one of these matchmaking evenings she found herself sitting next to a tall, fairly handsome and sophisticated businessman. Apparently, he was a self-made multi-millionaire and was the chief executive of a plc. Nicola had to admit he was amusing company and enjoyed the evening far more than she ever would have believed possible.

At first everything was wonderful. Richard appeared to be the perfect gentleman. He made no demands on Nicola, their evenings were spent at musicals, shows or restaurants. Afterwards they would go on to visit Stringfellows or one of the other many night-clubs that Richard was a member of. Step by step she relaxed and found that life was after all worth living. Richard was clever, amusing and devilishly handsome. He also could dance and Nicola enjoyed gliding round the dancefloor with him. It certainly made a change from the wriggling or smooching which was the height of ambition of most of her other men friends. With Richard they felt as one as they glided around the floor. Eventually, after he'd given her enough time over a number of months to adjust to the new circumstances, he used one of his more effective romantic weekend on her.

"Nicola, I've got to go to Paris for a few days, I thought you might like to come. Paris is beautiful this time of the year." Richard could see some doubt written across Nicola's face and so he played his little boy hurt card.

"No, no, I'm not asking you to come on a dirty weekend, we'll have separate rooms, surely you know me better than even to think that."

Nicola was embarrassed; she had thought he was moving in for the kill and he seemed so upset.

"I'd love to come; I know I can trust you, when do we go?" she asked enthusiastically, warming to the idea; she hadn't been to Paris for years.

"Next weekend."

The new International Station at Waterloo was very impressive, it was more like an airport than a station. The Eurostar purred into the platform and they were shown to their extremely comfortable first class seats. It was all extremely civilised.

They ate an excellent breakfast of scrambled eggs and smoked salmon washed down with champagne. The train was slow moving through the Kent countryside. Nicola found she could read the station signs easily. Tonbridge, West Malling, Ashford and then, just before the tunnel, the romantic-sounding

Sandling Junction. Shortly afterwards they suddenly plunged into the darkness of the Channel Tunnel. For about twenty minutes their journey was underground as lights flashed by outside at regular intervals. Just as abruptly they rushed out into the sheeting French rain. The speed of the train changed and they flashed through the wet, flat northern plains. Nicola's thoughts went back to the fact that her grandfather and uncle died on these plains, their deaths separated by thirty-five years and two world wars. They were the graveyards of so many young men. A testimony to the futility of war, they were still the same as they were before the conflict and would be the same for thousands of years to come. No trenches, tanks, nor man's stupidity would ever change that.

She shook herself out of such morbid thoughts, and enjoyed her mid-morning coffee as they rapidly approached the Gare du Nord. The rain had disappeared by the time they arrived. They were met by a limousine from Richard's chosen hotel. They drove through the congested streets, noisy with continual hooters blaring. This being the way the Parisians register their distaste for bad driving, or for anyone to have the audacity to suggest that they were also guilty of such a crime.

The car drove the down past the Galeries Lafayette; Nicola was determined to shop at that most famous of stores. She recognised the Opera and knew when they stopped at last at the hotel, they were close to the Champs-Élysées and the Seine.

The hotel was sheer five-star luxury. Richard had booked a two bedroomed suite; Nicola was delighted with the fantastically large bathroom and the luxuriously appointed room. It was like staying in a chateau rather than a hotel. As soon as they had unpacked, they set out to walk round the local sights. Nicola was tempted by the chic boutiques, their attractive windows full of gorgeously expensive clothes. The air was full of enticing smells emulating from the plethora of pavement cafés. They walked through the park and then Richard grabbed a taxi and took them to the Cathedral of Notre-Dame. It was magnificent. Nicola had been before as a schoolgirl, but that visit had been spoiled as they rushed round shouting, "The bells, the bells." She remembered the big disappointment of not seeing a deformed hunchback. She assumed it would be like the beefeaters at the Tower of London, there would be hunchbacks on tap.

The rest of the afternoon was spent idling round the island. They ate in the Meurice that evening, Richard seemed to be well known and they had one of the best tables overlooking the Tuileries. After a truly memorable meal accompanied with a superb wine for each course, they went for a late evening stroll down to the Seine. Nicola felt incredibly happy, she seemed to be able to float and realised she must have drunk rather more than she had intended. They kissed passionately in the gardens as they looked at the crescent moon reflected on the still water. It was as Richard had intended it to be, very romantic.

On their return to their suite, Richard opened a special bottle of champagne that was already chilling in a silver bucket. It was his usual seduction clincher. He was indeed well known at the hotel. Well known and envied, as he returned regularly with different women, always gorgeous and never repeated. The staff were surprised to find he had booked two bedrooms, but you would have found few of them that believed he and the latest flame would not end up in one.

Nicola was no match for Richard's experience. In fact she was still a virgin; she and John had all but made love properly, but he was old fashioned, something that she loved him for. He wanted it to be special on the first night of their honeymoon. If it were possible to go back, she would certainly have changed that part of their courtship. How sad that she didn't experience sex for the first time with her one and only love.

She couldn't in all honesty remember how it all started on that evening. They started kissing and it seemed natural for him to caress her breasts. He must have somehow opened her bra, and unbuttoned her blouse because his hands were hot on her naked flesh. The sensations she was getting from her nipples were almost as if she was receiving electric shocks through them. Her eyes were closed and as she opened them she saw him playing with them gently with his teeth. The waves of pleasure went on and on; she had never felt anything like that ever before. When he removed her skirt she couldn't say, all she knew was that his fingers were working the same magic between her legs. She should have asked him to stop, but the pleasure was so intense she just couldn't. At last he carried her to his bed, removed his clothes quickly and before she had a chance to think about it, she was no longer a virgin. Richard made love to her many times that weekend and each time seemed better than the last.

On the Sunday while drinking coffee on the Champs-Élysées, Richard at last proposed. Nicola was surprised how quickly she said yes. She didn't at that time really know anything about the real Richard. If she had, she would certainly have refused.

The wedding was a grand affair. Her father organised a marquee on the lawn at their beautiful Georgian house. The guest list was a veritable who's who of Hampshire society. Nicola thought something was wrong with Richard at the reception. He seemed suddenly more distant and certainly gave more attention to the bridesmaids than was strictly necessary. At the time she put it down to wedding nerves. It didn't take her long to realise that Richard was not, as the songs say, a one-girl guy. In fact, quite the contrary. Even on their honeymoon he was eyeing up the talent blatantly in front of her. On their return to London he started on his extra-marital affairs. He tried to cover up his sordid activities but she could always tell. He would smell of a strange perfume and even worse, sex. He also had so many unexplained last minute business trips. The only consolation was that there was no-one special, unless they changed their perfume regularly. He at least kept these affairs fairly discreet, which at least was something.

Nicola didn't really know what to do, she started thinking of herself as worthless. She had little confidence and she assumed that there had to be something wrong with her. If there wasn't, why would he be unfaithful so quickly? She didn't want to admit that her marriage was already a failure. When she thought about it she hadn't really got firm proof, only her suspicions. They were still making love, so in the end she took the course many women had taken before her, and turned a blind eye.

She started joining things: the local Conservative Party, where she became the chairperson of the women's lunch club. Charity work took a great deal of her time and she organised regular dinner parties for Richard's business colleagues. Ironically, it was a combination of these that proved to be her own undoing.

Piers Lamont was the Director General of her favourite charity. As the local chairman, she met him on many occasions. They gradually became more and more friendly. It was obvious to all of the staff at the charity headquarters, that they didn't need quite as many lunches together to keep the work of the charity going smoothly.

At first it was all very innocent, they just enjoyed each other's company. They seemed to have so many things in common. They were both born in Hampshire and they had many mutual acquaintances. Unlike Richard, Piers liked all sorts of music, not just musicals and pop. He took her to the Royal Opera House in Covent Garden for a charity gala night. This was followed by several charity concerts and even a star-spangled Royal Premier in Leicester Square.

Eventually she invited him to one of her dinner parties. From the onset Richard took against Piers. As a state school boy, Richard had a definite chip on his shoulder. In general he disliked all the public school types he met in business. Most of them were deviants who learnt their disgusting ways in the dormitories. As for the rest, they were a mixture of wimps, wets, and professional con artists. He made no effort with

Piers, in fact he ignored him, putting all of his effort into flirting outrageously with the attractive young second wife of a Cabinet Minister. Over the next month or so Piers attended a number of Nicola's dinners. He was always useful if Nicola had an odd female for dinner, which as luck would have it was a fairly regular occurrence. In the end, as so often happens, fate lent a hand. It was almost inevitable that they would become lovers, it was just a matter of when. On one hot, steamy summer evening, Nicola had two unexpected cancellations; the lawyer friend, who was due to be Piers' particular partner, cried off at the last minute and then Richard suddenly felt the need to fly to America on business. Piers stayed behind to help her with the clearing up, one thing led to another and before Nicola had time to think about it, she was an adulteress. She supposed she ought to feel a little guilty but what with Richard's disgraceful behaviour she found she had no guilty feelings whatsoever. Quite the contrary, as it turned out she enjoyed their coupling and it was obvious from Piers' excitement and his subsequent repeat performances throughout the night that he did too. Nicola found it reassuring that a man liked making love to her. After Richard, her only other lover, she had been worried that she was no good at sex.

Piers was an attentive lover, yet strangely detached at the same time. He was very skilled, ensuring she enjoyed everything to the full. Nicola had never really enjoyed sex before Piers. True, Richard was good at the mechanics and at first the sex seemed good, but it didn't take long for her to realise that for Richard it was just an acquired skill, there seemed no love there at all. With Piers she felt tenderness and a genuine desire that she should enjoy everything just as much as he did. Richard phoned to say he was detained in the States, and wouldn't be back for at least a week. It was during this period that Nicola fell in love with Piers. Normally she would have done nothing about it. Piers certainly wouldn't want to be involved in a messy divorce case. It would affect his position as Director of the charity and Piers was always aware of his social position. However, Richard had seemed to have changed character. Not only was he now content with one lover, the perfume never changed, but somehow he didn't seem to care. He was no longer covering up this affair, in fact quite the contrary. He seemed to take delight in flaunting it in every way possible way. Her so-called friends took great delight in reporting seeing them together and Nicola's self-esteem had fallen to a new all-time low. Eventually she had asked him for a divorce, assuming that he would be delighted as he could then marry this Rebecca creature he was seeing. This would leave her free so she could marry Piers. When he refused, she was amazed. Perhaps he did care for her after all; if so, he had a funny way of showing it.

Despite Richard's assurances that he would be faithful and change his ways, Nicola didn't have much faith that he would keep his promises. She certainly didn't feel any inclination to stop seeing Piers. Luckily Richard couldn't imagine any man wanting her and what's more, he had no time for Piers. He thought Piers as the kind of gutless wonder that ran charities, the sort who couldn't get a decent job in the real world, so they used their social connections to secure amazingly well-paid charity jobs. Most of the charitable income was spent paying the staff and holding lavish parties. He had no time for it all. Piers could spend as much time as he liked with Nicola. All the time, though, Nicola and Piers were getting closer and closer to forcing the issue.

INTERLUDE

How unlucky can one person be?

1997 had been a year of pure hell for Henry Hill. At Christmas 1996 he had still thought of himself as a reasonably successful businessman. His electrical contracting company had been expanding slowly throughout the decade. He was not rich by most people's standards, but he could certainly be described as comfortable. He had a lovely home. Admittedly he shared ownership with the bank, but then, who didn't?

Alissa, his wife, didn't work. She stayed at home looking after their two children and ensured that they had a good social life. They had the usual little luxuries, a heated swimming pool, and all-weather tennis court. He drove a BMW and she a Toyota MR2. As Henry tucked in to the Christmas turkey, there was no doubt in his mind: life was sweet.

Life is full of 'if onlys'. For Henry, everything would have been fine if only he hadn't met Tim Smeeth. At first, Henry thought how lucky he had been. The contract that he had won from Tim was the biggest he'd ever had. Perhaps he should have wondered why he, as a small local contractor, should have beaten all of the large London players. However, like so many other small businessmen before him he just thought he'd been lucky. Of course, if he's been a better businessman, he would have submitted his bills in earlier. He might have even asked for an advance, but for Henry, book-keeping was a pain that had never been his priority.

When Tim's first cheque for £125,000 bounced, Henry assumed it had been a mistake. At that point, he wasted valuable time writing to Tim about the problem. After ten days, his letter came back marked 'not known at this address'. Henry knew it had to be a mistake, as he had visited Tim in his office. He immediately dropped everything and drove over to visit him personally. He parked the car and took the lift up to the sixth floor, where he knew Tim's office was. To his horror, the door was now marked 'James Export Services'. He rang the bell and a small, white-haired old man opened the door.

"How can I help you?" he asked.

"I am looking for Tim Smeeth of Smeeth enterprises. I thought his office was on this floor, but I've obviously got it wrong."

The old man looked agitated.

"Does he owe you money?" he asked.

"I don't see that's any of your business!" snapped Henry.

"I'm sorry, but all of the others have been after money."

"The others! How many others?"

"About twenty or so. We've had the CID round. It would appear that Mr Smeeth is a crook. I do hope he didn't owe you much."

Henry just stood in silence. A crook? He just couldn't believe it. Tim owed him over £400,000! Still, the work was being done for a major bank so it couldn't be that bad, could it?

"Are you all right? Would you like to come in and sit down? You look very pale."

"No, I'll be fine. I've got to get to the bank as quickly as possible. Henry went straight round to the regional offices of the bank and waited patiently to see the director. After about forty minutes, he was shown into a very impressive office.

"I'm glad you've come in. There were one or two small problems we'd like sorted out, but overall we are very pleased with your work. You've done an excellent job."

"Thank you. We always do our best. But it's not about the work that I'm here, it's about the payment." Henry picked up a pencil off the desk and fiddled with it anxiously.

"Don't worry about money. We've already paid Smeeth Enterprises in full."

The pencil snapped in Henry's hand.

"They said they wanted to pay all their small suppliers as quickly as possible so we advanced them the money early. You will probably get a cheque in the post in the next few days."

"You paid them in full? Oh my god! What am I going to do?"

He put his head in his hands and just sat there.

"Are you all right? Is there anything I can do to help?"

At that, Henry sat up.

"I don't think there's anything anyone can do to help me," he said coldly. "I have just learnt that Tim Smeeth is a crook who has just disappeared with all the money. I don't suppose the bank would pay for the work twice." Seeing the reaction from the director, he continued, "I thought not."

As Henry left the bank, he knew he was finished. From there, things went fairly quickly. He could not pay his bills, so he was cut off from his supplies. He couldn't pay his men, so his company collapsed into bankruptcy. Some years earlier, his bank had got him to sign a piece of paper which gave him unlimited liability. This meant they took everything – his house, his furniture, his cars were leased and had to be returned. Alissa left, taking the children with her. He even had to sell his endowment policy just to raise cash to live. He'd gone from riches to rags in one nightmare of a year.

He would never have thought that he could have got so excited about some silly advertising stunt. It just went to show how sad his life had become. According to a personal letter he had received, he had won a major prize in a national competition. Its value was not less than ten thousand pounds and it was being delivered at eight o'clock that very evening. To celebrate this change in his fortune, Henry had bought himself a bottle of cheap white wine. He had already drunk half of it when the knock on the door came.

A shortish man, carrying a smart brown leather briefcase and a small parcel tied up with string, was waiting on the doorstep.

"Have I the pleasure of addressing Mr Henry Hill?"

"I'm Henry Hill. I suppose you're here about my win?"

"Yes. I'm here to change your life for good. Have you the card to prove that you are definitely Mr Hill?"

Henry produced his winning voucher. The man checked it carefully, looking slightly worried.

"Is anything wrong?" asked Henry, terrified that he might miss out yet again.

"You haven't still got the letter have you?"

Henry rushed off. He knew exactly where it was. In the bin in the original envelope. He grabbed it and returned to the man, who by now had limped his way into the kitchen. He gave him the letter and the man was immediately pleased.

"Good. I can see it's all correct now. Have you, by any chance, a pair of scissors so I can open up the prize?"

As Henry turned, the man opened his briefcase. Henry was still searching the drawer for his scissors when he sensed the man behind him. He half turned, and to his horror he saw that the man had a long, thin knife in his hand. It was the last thing he saw as the man plunged the knife into his side. The pain was excruciating. The knife plunged again and again, but he didn't feel anything anymore. Henry Hill's *annus horribilis* had finally ended.

The man wiped the knife clean on a drying up cloth. He carefully removed his outer coat, which was spattered with blood. He folded it up carefully and wrapped it into the brown paper parcel along with the knife and the gloves. He left Henry's last resting place, ensuring that nobody saw him. He walked round to the next road, got into his dark BMW and drove slowly away, stopping at a building site where he had already observed a blazing fire. He changed his shoes and threw all the incriminating evidence into the furnace-like blaze.

Pleased with his evening's work, he drove off again. He switched on the car radio and listened to his favourite country and western CD as he sped off down the motorway.

PART II

THE STORY

CHAPTER 4

The letter that had annoyed Richard Valentine on the morning of February 14th was from the Ombudsman for the pension industry. Richard had lodged a complaint against his previous pension adviser. In common with most businessmen, Richard had left his pension matters to the experts. Fair enough, he accepted he had to pay for their services. In fact he was so naive about how much he paid that he thought his agent was an incredibly hard worker. After all, he always drove the latest Porsche and spent a great deal of time on holiday, regularly in the Caribbean.

It wasn't until the changes brought about by Margaret Thatcher's government that he learnt the painful truth. He'd just decided to invest a further hundred thousand pounds into his pension and had, as usual, taken advice. The difference this time was when the paperwork came back, he was notified just how much commission the agent earned. He doubted if commission was the right word. Legalised theft is how he would describe it. At first Richard had thought it was an error, it had to be. Four thousand three hundred and eight pounds paid for the little help he'd received seemed a little steep, but he could have lived with that. The form, however, said forty-three thousand eight hundred pounds. It had to be a mistake, so Richard phoned the insurance company. When they confirmed that it was not a mistake and forty-three thousand eight hundred pounds was the correct commission, he almost hit the roof. Apparently every time you opened up a pension fund, your agent struck gold. He did wonder why he had so many pensions but then Harry Kon had convinced him that it was prudent.

"Don't put all your eggs in one basket," he constantly told Richard. No, as it turned out most of them went into Kon's pocket. He used to chuckle at Kon's name and now to his horror he found the joke was on him. He had been conned. Richard was used to getting his own way, and was appalled to find there was almost nothing he could do about this bare-faced robbery.

He stopped the hundred thousand payment which at least deprived Kon of his forty-three thousand eight hundred, but as for the hundreds of thousands he'd already given to Kon, it was, as they say, water under the bridge. The only other way he could stop Kon getting any more of his money was to cancel his one endowment policy. It was redundant, it had been started many years ago, as part of a purchase of a house; there was no reason to continue it. He phoned up the Scottish Equitable about how much he could get for it. He thought the forty-two thousand pounds was better in his pocket than sitting with them. He mentioned this to Jason the next day in the office. Jason told him not to surrender it.

"Get in touch with Policy Portfolio, or one of the other outfits that regularly advertise in The Times."

Apparently, according to Jason, he'd get considerably more for the policy by auctioning it. Taking his financial director's advice he phoned, and was immediately told he should get somewhere around fifty-five thousand pounds for it. Well, thirteen thousand pounds tax-free was not to be sneezed at, so Richard sent the company all the necessary papers duly signed and sealed. A few weeks later he was pleased to receive a cheque for fifty-seven thousand two hundred pounds.

He had, however, put in a complaint against Kon over a year ago and according to the letter he had received that morning, after deliberation, it was ruled that Kon had not acted improperly. As far as Richard was concerned the whole pension industry was a pack of rogues. After all, the only time you found out if you'd been robbed was normally when you were old and weak. By then, there was nothing you could do about it.

Richard angrily threw the letter in the waste paper basket and opened the other envelope. To his amazement he found he had won a major prize in a financial competition. *What is it, a chance to buy a pension?* he thought cynically. He put in on his desk with the rest of his papers. He was just about to leave for work when he heard the doorbell ring. Nicola, he knew, was in the kitchen which was at the far end of the house, so he opened the door himself. To his astonishment he found a rather worried-looking Roland Silverman waiting there.

"What do you want, Roland?

"I can't stay long, I've got a meeting at ten."

"Well you'd better come in, we can't talk on the doorstep."

He took him through into his study and firmly closed the door behind him. Before Silverman had a chance to speak, Richard started.

"If this is about your insider trading, it's a waste of time. I've told you, you only have two options. Resign as Chairman, or face a stock market enquiry. Personally I think I'm being too kind. We both know it should be both, for if the fraud squad got hold of it, you would go to prison. When you were selling the shares you knew that Roberts was up to no good and the price would drop if the information became public. If that wasn't enough you also knew that we were negotiating with Intercards. Insider trading, is, as you very well know, illegal in this country; you could easily go to prison!"

"It's all right for you," snapped Silverman, "you've got plenty of money. This Lloyds thing's bloody crippling me. I've had to sell the shares, I had no alternative, you know that as well as I do. For God's sake man, help me. We've been a good team, the company's done well, why can't you help me through this?"

"Do you honestly expect sympathy? You're pathetic! All of you Lloyds people are the same. You got the money for doing nothing in the good years. You knew the risks, how else did you expect to get double paid on the same money? Anyway, it's got nothing to do with me. You sold shares, knowing they would drop after the Jason Roberts scandal broke. No, it's get out of the company, or jail. It's entirely your decision."

Richard smiled coldly at him, after all, he'd never really liked Silverman. Fair enough, he had been useful in the early days, but he was an embarrassment now. This was the perfect way to get rid of him.

Silverman was so angry, he looked as if he would explode.

"You cold-hearted bastard. I could kill you for this!"

"Yes, but you won't. We both know you're gutless. Now get out."

Silverman stared at Richard aggressively, and for a moment indeed looked like he might do Richard physical harm. Then he turned quickly, looked back and shouted, "I'll get you Valentine! I don't know how, but I'm going to get even with you!" He then left, violently slamming the front door, as if he wanted to take it off its hinges.

Richard left shortly afterwards. He had told Silverman the truth, he did have a meeting at ten. It was one he wasn't particularly looking forward to, but it had to be done.

Alec Nash arrived on the dot. He was immediately shown into Richard's palatial office, as per his instructions. The last thing Richard wanted, or needed for that matter, was a public scene.

The reason for Valentine's concern was that he believed there may have been a misunderstanding when Redwood bought Nash's greetings card company. There hadn't been any such problem as far as he was concerned; he always knew what he was going to do with it. He hoped Nash would be sensible about it, after all it was too late to change anything.

Nash was a well-preserved man of about seventy, with white hair and strong, piercing blue eyes. He was dressed in a smart, grey, worsted three-piece suit and wearing old, but really well shined shoes. He was a man who wasn't going to let age stand in the way of his appearance.

"How nice to see you again Alec, what's it like to be the idle rich? Would you like coffee or perhaps tea, or even something stronger?"

"Don't give me any of that pseudo politeness crap," said Nash loudly, in a deep-throated voice. "You know very well why I'm here. What the bloody hell's going on with my company?"

Richard smiled at him, in the way you might to a mental defective that just told you he wanted to be a brain surgeon.

"I think you'll find it's our company, Alec. We did pay you a lot of money for it, or has that slipped your mind for a moment?" said Richard slowly, as he began to enjoy himself.

"Don't patronise me, Valentine, you lying bastard. I was doing business while you were crawling around in your dirty nappies. You know well what I'm on about, so don't play games with me. You promised me, from the beginning, that there would be no job losses and that the company wouldn't move out of its present area. I now find out that you're sacking all but a handful of my staff and moving the whole bloody operation, and selling the premises. It's not bloody good enough. You know I'd have never sold to Redwood, if I knew that was what you were going to do."

Having finished his speech, Nash glared at Valentine.

"What do you want me to do then, Alec, give you back the company?" sneered Richard. He grinned unpleasantly.

"What I want, is you to keep your word. That's all I want. It's not that much to ask, is it damn it?"

As he spoke, Nash went redder and redder in the face and sweat started running down his forehead. He was in one hell of a temper.

"Did I promise to keep all the staff on and that we wouldn't relocate? I don't remember agreeing to it. If you're right, of course, Alec, I'll obviously keep my side of our bargain." Richard smiled reassuringly at Alec as he pressed a buzzer on his desk.

With that, his personal assistant entered the room.

"Ah, Miss Hastings, will you ask Roger to come in, and bring the Nash contract with him? We seem to have a small problem."

Roger Devon, Redwood's in-house lawyer, cut an impressive figure – young, sharply dressed and intelligent-looking.

Nash looked at him as he came in and thought to himself, *That's all I need, another smart-arsed yuppie.*

"Roger, we seem to have a small misunderstanding with the Nash contract. Can you remember what was in the contract re jobs and location? Alec here says we promised no job losses and we would never move the operations. I wonder if you can find it for me in the contract." Richard leant back in his chair and looked straight across to Nash.

"Oh I'm sure there's nothing in the contract about either. In fact, I know there isn't. If there was I would be able to put my finger on it straight away but I'm sure there isn't," said the clever lawyer. "Besides, we would have never agreed to that, the intention was always to close it down. We only wanted the contracts."

"Thank you Roger, that will be all. I was worried that perhaps I was going senile, luckily for the company that's not the case. Shut the door on your way out." Richard smiled at Nash. "So there you are Alec, no such promises. Sorry."

Alec was getting angrier and angrier.

"But you bloody well promised me! I know you did, you bloody promised," he shouted almost hysterically.

"Alec, Alec you've been in business for a long time. In fact, as you reminded me only a few minutes ago, you were doing business even when I was still crawling in my dirty nappies. You and I know very well, that if it's not in the contract it doesn't count. That's why we have a contract, so both parties know exactly where they are."

Richard was enjoying himself. He knew it was game, set and match to him, but he was quite happy to continue and rub Nash's nose further in the dirt.

"If I were you I'd have a word with my solicitor, Alec, they seem to have let you down rather badly. Let me see who were they, ah yes, Fletcher and Co., wasn't it? From Buntingford. Perhaps in retrospect you should have had a London firm to represent you. Of course they would have been be more expensive, but as they say, you get what you pay for!"

He sat looking expectantly at Alec Nash, wondering what his next move would be. He wasn't at all prepared for what actually happened.

Nash was a rather large man; he got up quickly, reached over and grabbed Richard by the throat and pulled him violently across the desk.

"You lying bastard! I ought to kill you! You've made me the villain out of all this with your clever tricks!"

All the time he was shouting he was shaking Richard, who was gradually turning an interesting pinkish colour.

Valentine's PA and the young lawyer rushed into the room and pulled Nash away from Valentine. He then seemed to come back to his senses. He let go of Richard, and pushed past the other two on the way out of the room. As he got to the door he stopped, turned back and said menacingly, "You haven't heard the last of all this. You're a miserable lying shit, Valentine. Someone's going to give you what you deserve one of these days."

With that, he left, much to the relief of Richard and his immediate staff.

Brushing aside their concerns, he got them both to leave and then sat quietly, rubbing his throat. He reflected that he'd been threatened twice with death, and it wasn't yet coffee time.

If Richard was thinking that things would improve that day he was going to be disappointed.

He'd just got back to his favourite work, thinking

how he could force another one percent profit out of his operation, when his personal phone rang. He picked it up and was surprised to find it was Rebecca.

"Richard, I've got to see you. It's important. Meet me for lunch at the American Bar at the Savoy. I'll be there at one p.m. Don't let me down, will you?"

Before he could reply, she rang off. He tried to phone her back to tell her he couldn't make it but there was no reply from her number.

Damn, he thought. *I'd better go and see what it's all about.* He certainly didn't need any more trouble.

Richard found he couldn't concentrate on the endless stream of statistics in front of him. Normally he'd be in seventh heaven. He loved trying to work out from the information where margins could be improved but somehow today they had no interest for him.

Richard sat pondering on the morning events. He had no doubt that Silverman would go. He was a stubborn old fool, but he knew he was licked. Richard had a replacement in mind, someone that would do as he was told. He always thought Silverman gave himself too much credit for the success of the company. Richard was the company, and Silverman was nothing, and never had been. When he had first floated the company he had needed someone to become Chairman who was respected by the city. At the beginning, he only wanted him for his name. Nobody had heard of Valentine and it was important to hire Silverman. He had been warned Silverman had an ego the size of the American debt (currently standing at one point five trillion dollars). He had been told to butter him up. Unfortunately, he had been too lavish with his praise and Silverman had the ridiculous idea in his head that he was indispensable. It would be good to get rid of him. As for Alec Nash, he rather enjoyed the confrontation. Not the attempted throttling, that was painful and slightly frightening, but the rest went beautifully. He particularly liked the dirty nappy crack. Alec Nash would bitterly regret using that particular argument, as it had so badly backfired on him. It always struck Richard as amusing that even the most discerning businessmen often never fully understood that everything had to be either disclosed, or in the contract. Poor old Nash, what a fool he had made of himself. The thing that Richard really couldn't understand was why he still worried about his old company. Why should he concern himself with a lot of pathetic losers who used to work for him? They had, after all, served their purpose. He'd got the money, so why did he bother?

He was disturbed from his thoughts by the phone ringing. He noticed it was an internal call and it was from Jason Roberts.

"Yes, Jason, what do you want?" he snapped.

"I need to see you, this afternoon, it is important," said Jason.

"Can't it wait? I've had a very busy day and I've got to finish a contract, Monday would suit me better."

"I really do need to see you now. Monday is the sixteenth, after all. Please, can you spare even a few minutes!"

"All right, come at four o'clock sharp, I can spare

you ten minutes, that's all." With that, he put the phone down.

Could Jason have raised the money to sort out his problems? Well, he'd have to wait to find out that afternoon. But he doubted it; judging from his voice he was in a bit of a state. It would be a pity though, as Roberts had been a good accountant. That was before he started to get itchy balls. That brought him back to think about Rebecca. He was certainly missing her and not only for the sex, which was always good, but also for her amusing stories. The fact that he didn't seem to have to put on an act with her, it was all so easy, he could just be himself.

He got a taxi to the Savoy and made his way through the foyer, up the steps to the famous American Bar. Rebecca was already there sitting at a corner table drinking a cocktail. A non-alcoholic one, as it turned out. Richard ordered a scotch and water and joined her.

"What's so important to drag me here during business hours?" he asked.

"I'm pregnant," she said, "and before you ask, yes, it is yours. I only found out for certain this morning."

"I see," said Richard in a matter-of-fact tone. "So what are you going to do about it? Have an abortion, bear it and get it adopted, or are you thinking of keeping it?"

"As always you are the realist, aren't you? Covering every possible angle. You ask me what I'm going to do. It's not just me is it? I'd like to have our baby and be married to the father. It's not a lot to ask, is it?"

It wasn't much to ask and, if Richard was

completely honest with himself, he'd have liked the scenario himself. He would like to have a son and heir. He was disappointed that Nicola had so far failed to deliver on her part of the contract.

"Nicola won't give me a divorce, you know that," lied Richard. "I have asked her but she's strict about these things. It's to do with her religion."

"We could still live together. It's no big deal these days, it won't hurt your position in the city. Why, one Chief Executive even boasted about his sexual adventures recently. If we did move in together perhaps your wife would see how silly she was being and give in."

This, of course, put Richard in a difficult position. The idea appealed, but he had promised Nicola and he couldn't risk a divorce. If he lost control it wouldn't be long before some toffee-nosed pouf would oust him from his job. He knew he had many enemies who were itching to get rid of him.

"I'll arrange that you are both well provided for," he said coldly. "A thousand pounds a week should cover everything. I'm sorry Rebecca, but anything else isn't possible just at the moment."

"You really are a miserable bastard! You deserve to be put down. I don't know why someone hasn't killed you before now. I really could kill you myself!"

Here we go again, he thought, *three times in one day.* Luckily all three were incapable of actually doing anything about it.

"I'm sorry Rebecca, I really am, but it's the best I can do. I wish things could be different. If only we'd met first."

With that, he got up, put a twenty pound note on the table, and left. If he'd looked back he'd have noticed Rebecca trying to hide the fact that she was crying.

Despite the fact that Richard had acted so coldly, he was upset. As he walked down The Strand he found himself questioning almost everything he believed in. He even began to wonder if control of the company was that important. What did it really matter? He had no doubt that he did love Rebecca and they could make a go of it. His wealth exceeded one hundred and fifty million pounds. He could invest it and even if he could only get six and a half percent tax-free it added up to around a million pounds income. Perhaps he might like a change of direction; he could always start another business, after all, he sold the estate agency and never looked back. Even if he didn't leave, he wanted a son to carry on his name and perhaps take over the company one day. He might even work it so he'd get a divorce and keep control. Nicola was naive about money. She had always been wealthy so money wasn't that important to her. He almost went straight back to Rebecca at the Savoy but decided he better give it more thought, so he popped into another Strand watering hole for a sandwich and one more scotch.

When he came out into the sunshine he found himself outside the Stanley Gibbons Strand shop. Although the shop was different, it brought back memories. All those stupid small boys who helped to give him his start. He had even considered buying Gibbons a few years ago. They had gone through some rough times after being taken over by Letraset.

He remembered talking to a merchant banker acquaintance that had stupidly got some trust involved in lending it a lot of money. Luckily he didn't take up the offer as Stanley Gibbons was a disaster area for many years. Even the world-famous entrepreneur Sir Ron Brierley had got out, and he was a stamp collector. As he walked round he wondered if there was any truth in the rumour that a bunch of flower sellers from Jersey were buying it. Well, if they did, good luck to them. It was, in his opinion, a difficult business to run. He went in and bought a catalogue for old times' sake. Who knows, perhaps he might start collecting again. After all, he could afford to pay the market price for his stamps now.

On his return to the office he found Jason waiting for him. If he had any doubt concerning Jason's ability to pay back the money, they were dispelled in the first few seconds of seeing him. Jason looked distinctly ill, in fact he looked like a man who'd been on the red-eye to New York and back a number of times in quick succession, without any sleep at all. His eyes were a ghastly red, and if anything slightly wild-looking. His shaving had been less successful than usual and it certainly wasn't the old goody-goody Roberts that everyone was used to seeing in the office.

He sat down and drummed his fingers regularly on the desk. It was an annoying habit. He only did it when he was worried. Judging by the incessant drumming he was worried almost out of his mind now.

"Well, Jason," started Richard, "I hope you've managed to solve your little financial problem."

"That's what I wanted to see you about," said Jason.

Richard watched the tapping finger. He hardly needed him to tell him that he'd failed.

"I just need a little bit more time, Richard. If you could give me, say, another two to three weeks I'm sure I could sort it out. I've almost got the package put together."

"Jason, I told you clearly I'd give you six months. Today is the fourteenth – your time runs out on the sixteenth. I really shouldn't have even given you the six months, as it turns out it's been an embarrassment to me. You do know that Roland also knows about your problem, for all I know along with half the company. I cannot leave it any longer. I promised you I wouldn't do anything until the sixteenth and I'll keep my word but on the sixteenth then it becomes public knowledge. I realise that it will involve the police and you will undoubtedly go to prison. I'm sorry but that's the best I can do."

Jason looked as if he was going to burst into tears.

"Look, Richard. How about my share options? Could you not bring them forward for me? If I could cash the options it would solve all my problems. I know they're two years off, but you could make a special resolution and get them through the board quickly."

"Oh yes, that would solve everything wouldn't it? I could become a party to insider trading. How would it look if it ever came out? I'm not going to prison for you Roberts, or anyone else. As far as I'm concerned, it's your problem. I'm not the one who has been stealing hundreds of thousands of pounds so I can fuck some young tart so young she could be my own daughter! You got into the mess you're in, so you get out of it."

"Could you, could you not lend me the money?" stammered Jason. "I-I'd pay it back and give you a good rate of interest. I just need a little bit of time. Please for God's sake, Richard, give me a chance. Please, help me."

"You have already helped yourself Jason, that's the problem. You must face the consequences of your own stupidity. Nobody can help you but yourself. Now if you don't mind, I've really got to get on. I've got a contract to read and it's got to be done today."

"That's it, is it?" said Jason, changing from pathetic to aggressive. "So all the years I've given the company counts for nothing. All my loyalty, my hard work, all those nights I've stayed working late to make you a fortune and then at the end of the day it's just 'your problem, Jason'. You make me sick. I know some of the tricks you've pulled since I've been here and yet you sit there sanctimoniously telling me what to do. I ought to kill you, you bastard."

Christ, thought Richard, *four times in one day.* They were all so predictable.

"Don't be so stupid, Jason, you know you don't mean it. Just get out and leave me to get on with my contract work."

Jason changed character yet again.

"Oh God, Richard, I didn't mean it, I don't even know what I'm saying. Please, please help me. I'll do anything. I'll work for nothing, just help me, please," he begged.

"No, Jason. I've told you it's your problem. Just get out, will you? I've got a contract to sort out."

Jason got up and slowly left the room. As he was just about to close the door he looked back,

"I just hope one day you get your just desserts, so you know what it's like."

With that, he left the room. Richard buzzed out to his assistant.

"No visitors, no calls, I really must get some work done." With that, he settled down, looking at the contract that had been given to him by his lawyers Nabarro Nason (for the purchase of yet another small company to fit into his empire). There were a number of points raised by the lawyers that he had to consider and to ensure that there were no loopholes. It was work he thoroughly enjoyed. He worked late and at about nine thirty decided that there was no more he could usefully do to the contract. He packed it up so it could be sent back to be reviewed by the lawyers the next day. Before he left he made an important phone call. Afterwards, feeling better, he left, driving the short distance back to his Chelsea house.

He parked the car in the garage and was surprised to find the front door double locked. He wondered why Nicola had used the Chubb lock. She never normally used it, but he thought no more about it. He closed the door and looked for Nicola inside the house as he wanted to get the divorce issue settled as soon as possible. He was hoping she would have cooked him a meal so they could talk while eating. He found instead a note informing him that she'd gone to the theatre and would be late in, and he shouldn't wait up. It was a pity because he really wanted to talk to her about the divorce and financial matters. Instead he made himself some cheese sandwiches, opened a decent bottle of wine and went into his study to work out a strategy to try to appease Nicola and keep Rebecca. After a while he went back to the kitchen and opened a second bottle of wine. He sat in the study trying to work out what to for the best.

He phoned Rebecca again but he only got her answerphone; he left her a message telling her that he loved her and he hoped to have good news soon. He would come and see her in the morning and tell her what happened with Nicola. Eventually, after drinking the two bottles of wine he became rather tired and drifted off into a drunken sleep. In one of his many dreams he found himself on a fast and frightening roundabout. Every time it went round he bashed his head on an iron girder. The amazing thing was, the pain seemed real. He was rudely awakened to find he was being beaten across the face with his own gavel. He sat up, trying to fend off the blows but collapsed again into a deeper, more permanent sleep. He died exactly at one minute past twelve, for as Richard had already predicted, tomorrow was the first day of his new life, in all probability in hell!

His assailant dropped the hammer that had been conveniently placed on the desk, thus saving his knife for another day. He picked up a paper from the desk, checked to ensure it was the right one, and then carefully put it into his pocket. He then let himself out of the unlocked front door, removing the surgical gloves afterwards so he didn't leave any fingerprints behind. The murderer walked slowly around the corner back to the car that had been parked well away from the house, so as to attract little attention. The gloves were dumped in a convenient waste paper bin many miles away from the scene of the crime. The paper was torn up carefully; the pieces scattered as they blew out of the car window. On his return home he removed all of his bloodstained clothes and burned them; the ashes, he dug into his vegetable plot. The next day he thoroughly cleaned his car, drove it through the muddiest lanes he could find, and then booked a professional valet. Once all was well he made a mental note to stick to his plan in future. Satisfying as the hammer had been, it was far too messy.

CHAPTER 5

Ex-Chief Inspector Sandy Neil, late of the Serious Fraud Squad, was sitting round the debris of his breakfast in his small kitchen reading the Daily Mail. The meal didn't look particularly appetising. The toast was burnt and he had allowed the tea to stew far too long, making it rather rank and unpleasant. The kitchen also had that unmistakably masculine look, in other words unkempt, messy, and distinctly unhygienic. Sandy had however, done the washing up, the evidence proving it was stacked high on the draining board.

Although in most ways he was glad to see the back of his wife, he did miss her cooking. At least her breakfast was good. Sandy hadn't just lost a wife, for at the same time she had totally destroyed his career. He was honest enough to admit that he wasn't the perfect husband, he hadn't always been there for her when she needed him. In fact he had hardly been at home with her at all. That was the trouble with the job, it took you over, body and soul. To him it was exhilarating, he became alive while engaged in a case; he was so absorbed that he lost all sense of time. Sandy had neglected June, he knew he had. He never meant to. His career had always come first – as a young copper he was always the one that volunteered for overtime. As he climbed the ranks, he went on course after course, finally taking an external degree in criminal psychology. This of course meant even when he was at home he was always preoccupied with his studies.

June just couldn't cope with it. She liked company and was naturally lonely. It was inevitable that she would turn to other men for comfort. Perhaps if they had had children it would have helped but June had gynaecological problems and they were never fortunate in that way. Like so many other marriages of his generation, their union was based on pure lust. The early sex was good, but as the urgent hunger fades marriage needs more than sweaty couplings. Sandy gradually realised that they had nothing in common and slowly they drifted apart. Sandy didn't object to June finding another man, that would have been fine, but to work through half of Southwark, that was another matter. He hated being a joke with some of his colleagues but that was preferable than the sympathy he got from the rest. The final straw was when she started an affair with his boss. That, he found he just couldn't take. It had been a mistake to hit him, but when Sandy came home unexpectedly and found them in his bed, he just lost complete control. Still, it was no use crying over spilt milk. June was long gone and he had eventually returned the favour by ruining the Deputy Commander's career before he too, retired.

Sandy was a tall man but his body language indicated all was not well as he slumped over the table reading the paper. There was a story which interested him about a murder in Newbury, which was baffling the local police. There appeared to be absolutely no motive whatsoever for the crime. A man called Gregory had been found knifed by two young children in his own garden. Nothing apparently had been stolen. He had no money, no-one benefited from his death other than the Battersea Dogs Home, even then by only a few thousand pounds. There was no logical explanation of why anyone should want to murder Gregory.

One thing he was sure of, he was glad he wasn't the investigative officer. Where on earth would you start? No, he was glad to be out of the force. A chance to take things easy, do all those things he'd always wanted to do. Who was he kidding? He would love to have a good murder to investigate; come to think about it, he'd love to have anything to investigate. He realised he needed to do something, he needed to get a job, but what sort of a job? It would be easy to get something in the security world, working for one of the big companies. He knew though, that after a few months it would be as boring as hell. What he enjoyed doing was solving crimes. Sorting out the details, working out the problem. It was like doing a crossword puzzle to him. No, he'd have to do something and it had to be in that sort of area. He wondered if Peter Pike meant it when he talked about setting up a detective agency. At least that would give some sort of variety. *Oh hell,* he thought, *I'll go and see him, it can't do any harm.* With the idea firmly placed in his head, Sandy started to search for the telephone directory; it proved more difficult to find than he anticipated as he was using it for a door stop in his bedroom.

Ironically, on the other side of the Thames a similar scene was being acted out.

Peter Pike was depressed. He had been a staff sergeant for fifteen years in British Intelligence, but people with skills like him were redundant in the new post-Cold War era. It wasn't as if his skills were in short supply, today the KGV offered a full menu of services including spying, elimination (this was expensive but still probably highly competitive when compared to your local amateur hitman), or simply straightforward industrial espionage. With so much highly trained and remarkably cheap talent available, it was not surprising that Peter was depressed.

It was a bit of an anti-climax to wake up with nothing more stimulating to do than to walk down to the local shops to buy the morning paper. He tried to add a little spice by not deciding what paper to buy until the last moment. He had already had some professional work. Gupta, the owner of his local newsagent, asked his advice about thefts he had been experiencing in the shop. Peter was able to solve his problem very quickly. He pointed out that putting his takings in a biscuit tin close to the counter somehow asked for trouble. Needless to say, as soon as he put the cash out of reach of his more light-fingered and long-armed customers, all was well. Gupta was extremely impressed and gave him a large supply of his favourite pipe tobacco. In all fairness it didn't really compare to the bandit country of Armagh, or undercover work in the old Democratic Germany.

He was also rather lonely. Now he'd left the service his 'wife' was reallocated elsewhere. It was as Mark and Beth had guessed, a political marriage.

There was also the small problem of how to dispose of her. A tragic accident in Bavaria? A rare blood disease, striking with no warning? Or a messy love affair and a quickie divorce? That was always the problem with cover stories, they could always come back to haunt you later.

Come to think of it he rather fancied being the sad and lonely widower. Perhaps some beauty would feel sorry for him. He certainly felt sorry for himself sitting drinking a disgusting cup of black instant coffee. He didn't like the look or smell of the milk, perhaps he should buy it more than once every fortnight. He was reading all about yet another disaster in Zimbabwe for our cricket team. It amused him that an MP had actually stood up in the House of Commons and demanded that Parliament order the team back before they go to New Zealand rather than to risk fresh disasters. How could people take things so seriously? It was, after all, only a game, even though his cricket-mad friend Mark Cheshire would not agree with him. He was about to try his own daily personal humiliation, in the form of the crossword puzzle, when the phone rang. He was instantly cheered up, hearing Sandy Neil's voice. After all, here was one man who would totally understand him.

"Morning Peter," said Sandy, starting brightly. "How's retirement suiting you?"

"Don't even ask," replied Peter slowly. "The most enticing thing I've got planned at the moment is the washing up."

"Well, sounds good to me, I've done mine. Look, how serious were you when you talked about that detective agency?"

"Very serious. If you're interested I think we should get together fairly quickly, that is, before I sign up as a milkman, I'm that desperate. How about a beer? Where shall we meet?"

"How about the George Inn in Southwark? You know, the National Trust place, it's a great pub. We can have lunch there, it's bound to be fairly quiet at this time of the year."

"I've been there but not for a while. If I remember it's on Borough High Street, just over the bridge. Am I thinking of the right place?"

"Yes, you've got it. See you there, say twelve thirty?"

Peter's whole mood changed after the call. He got out his favourite pipe, lovingly cleaned it, filled it with golden flake, lit up and pulled an unhealthy drag down. He rarely smoked these days, what with the regular teasing in the office and the healthy brigade it had lost its joy, but occasionally in the privacy of his own home he savoured the taste and the feel of the bowl in his hand. He liked Sandy, and with their combined experience they should be able to build a good business. Perhaps life wasn't quite so bad after all. It was funny how they both met. Mark and Beth Cheshire had an unpleasant thief in their company. Mark turned to his two expert friends to help and they had found they got on like long-lost brothers. It was also in the back of his mind that they might just persuade Mark to join in. He had been a canny businessman and would be invaluable as part of the team.

"You're bored," said Beth Cheshire, as she bought in the tray of tea and crispy ginger thin biscuits.

"You're going to have to do something about it eventually. It's no good just sitting there moping. It's just not like you."

She was right, of course. When they sold their collectable company they were committed to working for four years at least. The problem was, they cared about people. The company that they had sold out to were only interested in the share price as it affected their share options and the profits, which of course determined their final annual bonuses. The only other interest, it seemed to Mark, was scoring points off the other directors. This didn't leave much time to worry about loyal members of their work force. It had been obvious from the first three months that neither Mark nor Beth were going to fit in. They both understood fully the need to make good profits, but not at the expense of their staff. They found it revolting to openly discuss hiring young people on the basis they would work themselves almost to death in order to succeed, then after a few years they could be replaced with fresh blood. As far as the company was concerned, forty was over the hill and anybody over thirty better look out. They were both elated when they got the chance to leave the company early and get on with living their lives. They were in that enviable situation, that everyone thinks they want, never having to work again.

At first it was bliss, laying in the morning, drinking endless cups of coffee, reading the newspapers from cover to cover. They had no stress, no responsibility, just endless free time. They bought a luxury London flat. In the evenings they went regularly to the theatre, concerts and shows.

Mark had an idea when he gave up Cheshire's that he could perhaps become a writer. It sounded the ideal solution. He soon realised that to be a successful writer you needed good contacts, a lot of luck and even more important, talent. He might have been able to find the contacts. He could have perhaps manipulated the luck, but talent? Well, two out of three wasn't bad, was it? He received a pleasant letter from a top agent based in Chelsea Harbour. What the agent said was, "Don't give up your day job." It was unfortunate in his case, as he already had sold out, so end all dreams.

He was the chairman of a local appeal, a fund raiser to a museum, but these were small activities. Beth knew as well as he did that he needed something meaty to get his teeth into. He might have started another collectable business but for the fact his contract wouldn't allow it for three years.

"Oh, by the way, I forgot to tell you, Sandy and Peter are coming to supper tonight. They particularly want to see you."

"Peter and Sandy together?" He wondered what they wanted.

Since they met while helping him with a particularly nasty problem they'd become good friends. Sandy was a brilliant ex-policeman. He was tall – about six foot four – with ginger-blonde hair and with the most piercing green eyes Mark had ever seen. He should have reached the top of the greasy pole but was stopped when his wife had an affair with his Commander. He'd recently retired from the force where he'd been working as a Chief Inspector in the Serious Fraud Squad, the elite force based at Elm House.

Peter was an old friend. He was short in comparison with both Mark and Sandy yet he always seemed taller. It was his breadth that gave this illusion. With his short haircut he looked exactly what he had been – an ex-soldier. However, despite the fact had Mark known him for over twenty years he never quite knew what Peter used to do for British Intelligence. He'd always been a bit of a man of mystery. Like Sandy, he'd recently retired. Unfortunately, with the end of the Cold War, spies were not so important as in the past.

Mark brightened up at the thought of the two of them amusing them that evening. They were both full of exciting stories from their previous careers. With both of them together it could prove to be an extremely interesting evening.

"What about Inga, is she coming?" he asked. Inga was Peter's wife and was even more of a mystery than he was. She always seemed to be in another country.

"Just Sandy and Peter, I'm afraid. No partners, no-one for you to flirt with," shouted Beth as she went back to the kitchen, where she was busy preparing the meal.

They both arrived together and seemed unduly anxious. Beth had done them proud. Seared scallops in a superb creamy sauce was the starter. This was followed by baked swordfish, she served it with fresh asparagus and new potatoes. The dessert of raspberries and cream was Mark's particular favourite. In his opinion, a meal fit for a king. While in New Zealand they'd got fond of Villa Maria Sauvignon Blanc, and it proved to the perfect accompaniment. By the time the meal was over, they had emptied three bottles.

After dinner they sat with their coffee in the main room, stretching their bellies and trying to work out why the Conservative Party should be doing so well with the economy, yet doing so badly with their public relations. New Labour were certain to win the next general election, which they all agreed was poetic judgement. Poor John Major should never have won the election in 1992 but paradoxically shouldn't really lose this one.

Eventually Sandy took the bull by the horns and brought up the subject that they had come to see Mark about.

"Now look, Mark, it's no good going round the bush. We need you."

"That's nice, it's good to be needed, but to do what?" Mark asked.

"We're going to start a detective agency. We're both good at what we do but we've got no business sense, and to be even more honest, very little money."

"What he's trying to say," added Peter, "we want you to come in with us, be our chairman or managing director whichever you prefer. We'll form a company. Sandy and I will do all the professional work but we need you to organise the business itself and to invest in it."

Both looked hopefully at Mark. It didn't take him long to think about it.

"I'll do it on one condition, that is that it's a part-time job and I might go away for the winters. If you still want me under those conditions, then I'm your man."

It was obvious they were both relieved. Sandy smiled as he answered my question.

"Well that's settled, so let's get down to brass tacks. Where are we going to operate from?"

They discussed it for the rest of the evening. Eventually they decided to open a prestige office in the city. Beth decided to join in and organise the design and publicity. She produced a superb leaflet and circulated it to all the leading city institutions, telling them about their services. Within weeks, work was piling in. Luckily both Peter and Sandy had an endless supply of extra extremely well-qualified helpers. The expansion of Neil and Pike was impressive.

It was soon obvious to Mark that his investment was going to prove lucrative, which is what so often happens when you don't expect it.

CHAPTER 6

There's often a catalyst or special event that brings about a crisis. It's like lancing a particularly nasty boil. In Nicola's case the crucial date was the fourteenth of February. Piers had arranged to take her out on her special day. After all, as he said, Mrs Valentine should be wooed on Valentine's Day.

The evening was a great success. He had managed to get hold of three tickets to see *Naked*, at the Almeida Theatre in Islington.

"Why have you bought three tickets?" Nicola asked him, puzzled. "Who else is coming? You haven't invited your mother again, have you?"

Piers was close to his mother, it was one of the things that worried Nicola. They regularly had to go and visit the old girl and this Nicola didn't mind. She did however, draw the line on letting her come out with them on dates. It had happened twice before and Nicola was dreading he was going to do it to her again.

"No, of course not, I told you at the time it was a one off," he assured her. "I bought three tickets as the seats in the theatre are absolutely dreadful. By having that an extra one it makes things bearable. It's an interesting theatre which produces superb plays but the seats, well, they're just beyond a joke."

Nicola was pleased, she really couldn't have put up with his mother again. It was great that he had arranged such a treat, particularly as she admired Juliette Binoche. It would be interesting to see how a French film star performed live on the English stage. The day itself was strange. Richard was in an odd mood. He seemed even more distant than usual over breakfast and one of his letters put him into a frightful rage.

Roland Silverman arrived to see him before he left for the office. They moved themselves into his study and although Nicola was at the far end of the house she could still hear raised voices. Silverman left suddenly, and Nicola reflected that it was good that the front door had reinforced glass as he almost slammed it off its hinges. Richard left shortly afterwards.

Nicola had arranged to visit a relation who was in hospital at nearby St Thomas's, and then on to the Brassiere at the Oxo Tower for lunch with a group of her old school friends. The day was a gem, crisp and dry with that beautiful, pale light blue skies that so often come along with a touch of frost. Nicola loved these perfect winter days. That evening she didn't see Richard and rushed off to meet Piers for her evening treat. As she left the house she found that Silverman had broken the Yale lock. It looked as if it worked as you locked it, but in reality nothing engaged. She locked the door on the Chubb deadlock and made a mental note to get in a locksmith the next day.

The play itself was a disappointment. It turned out to be more of a melodrama, but the acting was brilliant. Juliette Binoche was amazing. It was hard to believe that she was French, and that she was speaking in her second language.

After the performance they crossed the road to the White Onion, a French restaurant that served exquisite food and wine. It was here, over an excellent meal of turbot and spinach and a pleasant chardonnay, that Piers became far more serious.

"It's about time," he started, "that we considered getting married. You really have no interest in your husband and judging by the rumours going around he certainly doesn't love you. It's not helping my reputation to be involved in an adulterous affair. Mother is very worried about it all which makes things difficult at home. Couldn't you just get a divorce so we can spend all our time together?"

"I did ask him a while ago," said Nicola, "but I admit I didn't force it. I do want to marry you, I do love you. When I get home tonight I'll try again, I promise." It seemed to Nicola that this should be one of the happiest days of her life, but why did she seem so apprehensive? She assumed it was because of all her other bitter experiences. No, she was pleased, at last she had found another man that she wanted to spend the rest of her life with.

After that they discussed the play and the next production, *The Judas Kiss*, which starred the American mega film star Liam Neeson, and they both agreed they'd like to see it. Nicola said she'd get tickets, which were likely to be sought after as not only was Liam Neeson a big star but the subject, Oscar Wilde, was a fashionable one. She also joked that as it was at the Playhouse by Charring Cross Station, he would only need two tickets.

Piers drove her back home after the meal in his new Jaguar XK8, as she prepared herself for the confrontation with Richard about the divorce. Once out of the car and after Piers' goodnight kiss, she decided to go for a walk to clear her mind. It was important now that she got this divorce. She walked for what seemed hours. Eventually she realised how cold she was and so she headed back home.

She was shocked to find the door unlocked and then remembered Silversmith's temper. She opened the door and then relocked it on the Chubb. She was puzzled to find that the house was in complete darkness. She tried to put a light on but nothing happened. *That's great,* she thought, *the fuse has blown again and Richard just hasn't bothered. How typical of him!* She groped her way through the hall and as she passed the study door the moonlight shining through the study window gave her more light. She noticed that Richard's commemorative Toastmaster's gavel was lying on the floor. Whatever she thought of Richard, she knew that he was proud of having been a British President of Toastmasters International and that that gavel was one of his most treasured possessions. He would never want it on the floor. She picked it up and was surprised how sticky it was. Almost as if he'd been stirring jam with it. She crossed the room and put the gavel carefully back onto his desk. It was then as she turned she noticed him, lying motionless on the floor behind the desk, the light striking him at an odd angle. He looked strangely peaceful. *Drunk again,* she thought. *One of these days, Richard, your drinking will be the death of you. Why did you have to do it tonight? It's taken me ages to get up the courage to ask for a divorce and now I'll have to do it all again.* She had every reason to assume he was drunk, as there were two empty bottles of wine on his desk, yet only one glass. Nicola assumed he had passed out, the effects of the booze catching up with him. It was always his particular weakness; some men get aggressive when drunk, some romantic, others turn silly. Richard however, just went to sleep, and when he woke up he never had any after-effects.

As soon as Nicola turned him over she knew he had already suffered his after-effects this time. Even in the poor light of the study, she could see he was dead. His face, which had been so handsome, was grotesquely misshapen. She realised now that her hands were wet with his blood and for a moment she could do nothing but stare at the ghastly sight of his now lifeless corpse. She fell back into his chair in a form of paralysed shock and she found herself going over their life together; whatever she thought of him, he certainly didn't deserve this.

Eventually, after what seemed hours she came to her senses and she phoned 999.

"What service do you require?" came a distant voice.

"What service do you require?"

"What service do you require?"

Nicola pulled herself together. "I'm sorry, police please."

"Police emergency, can I help you?"

"Yes, it's my husband. He's dead. There's blood everywhere. I can't believe it, it just doesn't seem real. It's like a nightmare only I know I'm awake. Please come quickly."

"Your name and address please," came a calm voice.

Nicola gave the address.

As soon as she'd finished the phone call she realised that she had to get out of that death-filled study. There was an appalling stench in it, for one thing, that repelled her. She couldn't put her finger on what it was at first. When she at last placed it, it made her feel sick. It was the putrefaction that she associated with cheap butchers' shops.

CHAPTER 7

Sodding, bloody dog, thought Alistair, as it once again produced an alarmingly large string of turds. *Why on earth does anybody keep a dog? It's beyond me.* Once again he got out his pooper-scooper, knelt down and removed the vile-smelling obscenity, putting it into the Marks and Spencer's bag he brought with him. It was not a job that he would ever volunteer for.

In reality he would have liked to have refused his parents when they asked him to look after Jakey. The lurcher was the pride and joy of his elderly parents, they had spoiled him rotten as he was in some ways an Alistair substitute. He was an only child and since he had left home, he knew his parents had been lonely. In reality, really, he never had any choice, he knew he couldn't let them down.

It would never have happened but for fact that they won the competition. Who would have believed that they would go abroad for the first time at their ages? Jakey could hardly have gone to Madeira and stayed with them in the hotel as well. Hence, Alistair's problem. He didn't really mind looking after Jakey, the dog was fine, other than his constant bowel problem. It was only for seven days and most of that would be spent at his parents' country home. The problem was, for two nights he had to have him in London. His flat was not suitable for dogs and the lease strictly forbade pets of any sort. Lurchers are not the sort of pet one doesn't notice, in fact quite the contrary. On the first night Jakey had been fairly quiet. Alistair had got away with a short walk and an early night. The second night was a different story altogether. Alistair had hoped to spend Valentine's evening with a beautiful girl, wining and dining her back to his bed. Instead, he had a noisy and energetic lurcher to calm down. It was bloody cold, the last thing Alistair wanted to do was go out. However, a long walk seemed to be the most sensible course to take. Luckily on the fifteenth he could pack up and leave London, taking Jakey back to the country. He put on as many sweaters as he could and thick socks over his normal ones. God, he must be mad going out in this weather, for at the least he'd catch double pneumonia. After walking for what seemed hours, he hit the Thames Embankment. He walked along looking suspiciously at the water, expecting it would be frozen over. It wasn't and as they walked along he wondered just how cold it must have been when they regularly had frost fairs on the river.

Most sensible people, he reflected, were safely tucked up in their warm beds and he decided that was where he wanted to be. As he turned to go back home he was surprised to see her. She looked gorgeous but at the same time worried. He thought how cruel life was. You always saw women you could fall for at the wrong time. Long flowing blonde hair, light camel hair coat; she looked just like Grace Kelly, his ideal date. Almost as quickly as he saw her she disappeared down one of the side turnings. Perhaps she hadn't liked the look of him and the dog. *Oh sod it*, he thought, and strode back purposely to the flat, a cup of cocoa, and his warm, inviting bed. Just round the corner in Oakley Gardens a young lady was anxiously gazing out of the window.

Bella was fed up with furtive sex. Her landlady, an elderly lady who still had Victorian attitudes to these sort of things, had refused her permission to have male visitors in her room at any time or for any reason. Bella should have really found alternative digs, but Mrs Hamilton's establishment was so convenient for her college that she had never got round to it. Besides, she had always put off things that might be unpleasant. It would have been fine if Charles had his own flat, however, he shared it with four other guys. His room was small. In fact the smallness didn't matter as much as the smell. The whole flat had a revolting stench. The trouble with these all-guy places was that nobody ever cleaned up. The kitchen was always full of dirty washing and bits of food lay around in various stages of decay. She was always worried what she would catch just by being there. Bella's real name was Donna, but she'd been called Bella for some time due to her minor drug habit. Bella wanted somewhere romantic to make love. She didn't want just to do it, she wanted it to be special. She was sure she was in love with Charles and the flat made it seem sordid rather than special. She was repelled by the smell of Charles' room, it inhibited her so much that she hated going there. To her horror one day she found all his dirty washing, going back months, stuffed under his bed. Call her an old fashioned romantic, but such conditions didn't really help her relax. Nor did it help to hear the knowing sniggers of his flatmates every time they went into his room. They'd tried it in the back of Charles' Ford but that was even worse. Bella, however, had a short-term answer to her problems. Her parents were off to Klosters skiing for two weeks, and that gave Bella the perfect quiet and romantic place.

They had literally screwed their way through early February, but unfortunately all good things had to come to an end. That was why she had been cleaning up the house frantically as her parents would be back on February the fifteenth. Everything was looking as it normally was and she was glad that she had no need to call the Yellow Pages for French polishing services. She had only just started to relax; she had opened a bottle of Riesling and was drinking a glass while watching for him. Charles was coming round late that evening for one last orgy of sex. Then they would clear out of the house just in case her parents arrived back in the early hours of the morning.

There was no getting away from it, Charles was late. Bella kept looking out of the window hoping to catch a glimpse of him. It was extremely cold, few people were out on the street that night so there was little to keep her amused. She had been intrigued earlier by an odd-looking fat man hanging about. The man obviously had something wrong with one of his legs as he moved in an unusual way. At first she thought he might be a burglar but as he entered the house across the road she assumed he was a neighbour, who had been out getting some cold fresh air. She quickly put it out of her mind, instead starting to curse Charles for losing them precious time. It was particularly galling to her as it would probably be the last time they would be together for some time. She was off to Paris on February sixteenth, for a three-month intensive French study course.

While she was looking for some sighting of her missing lover she noticed a flashy new Jaguar XK8 coupé arrive. An attractive woman with long blonde hair got out followed by a man, tall and distinguished. He gave her a quick peck of a kiss and then drove off. Surprisingly, bearing in mind how cold it was, she didn't go into any house but just stood looking up at the sky for a minute or so. She then suddenly came to life and started walking and disappeared from sight. Before Bella could reflect on her movements, Charles arrived. She led him straight to the chosen bedroom. Bella had equipped it with ice-cold Riesling and her favourite egg mayonnaise sandwiches. Afterwards they straightened up the room and left at around two fifteen, wishing they had somewhere like that to live regularly. Charles had also proposed and Bella had told him she needed time to think about it. She knew in her heart really she would accept, though she thought it was better to wait until she returned from Paris before she gave him his answer.

CHAPTER 8

After Nicola had called the police, she decided to get completely away from the study and the lifeless corpse that used to be her husband. She walked cautiously through to the kitchen and poured herself a stiff brandy. She was shuddering with delayed shock; the brandy steadied her. She put on the kettle, made a pot of jasmine tea and sat drinking it, waiting for the imminent arrival of the police. Inspector Morse had provided her with an insight as to what to expect, so when the mass of people came and occupied the house she was not unprepared.

The officer in charge looked the sort of man her father would call a wide boy. He was not very tall and wore a double-breasted fashion suit. Nicola cruelly assumed it had been bought in a charity shop, it was more an out-of-fashion suit nowadays. He had sharp, piercing black eyes which went well with his black stubble, which for the record was not the designer sort, just the result of working incredibly long hours. His female colleague was not a good recruitment advertisement for attracting girls to join the police force. She wasn't the sort that had much bother at dances, not that Maggie Cook ever went to dances anymore for she was always too busy, and besides, she didn't like watching all the other girls dance.

"Good morning, Mrs Valentine. I'm Inspector Griggs, I am the officer in charge of this investigation. This is Detective Sergeant Cook. I realise this must have been an awful shock to you, but I'm afraid we will have to occupy your house for some time. I'll also need a room for our use and I'm afraid I do need to ask some questions. Are you up to it or would you rather wait till later in the day?"

Nicola couldn't see any point in waiting. After all, it was like going to the dentist, even if you put it off, it somehow was worse later.

"I'm fine, Inspector, let's get on with it. The only problem is, I don't think I know anything that might help you."

"Don't worry about it, just tell me everything that happened here tonight, from your point of view. D.I. Cook will take note so as to ensure we don't forget anything."

"I had been out for most of the day and got back at around five o'clock. I made myself a sandwich and went through to the study to get a piece of writing paper. At least I can tell you Richard wasn't in there then. I did a few jobs then I got dressed and went off to meet a friend at about six thirty. We were going to the theatre over in Islington and we had a meal in a French restaurant afterwards."

"Who did you go with to the theatre, Mrs Valentine?" asked Cook.

"I'd been there with Piers Lamont. He's the director of *Help*, a charity for the elderly."

"Can we have his address please, for our records? We'll need to talk to him too," said Griggs.

"After he had left me at about eleven thirty I went for a walk in order to clear my head. When I came back I found the lights had fused, so the house was in darkness."

"You think the murderer did this?" asked Griggs.

"Probably not, the house needs complete rewiring and it happens regularly. The fuse box is in a cupboard at the back of the study so I went in there to flick the switch. I was moaning to myself that Richard could have fixed it, when I noticed his Toastmasters Gavel lying on the floor. He was very proud of it as he was given it personally by the World President Len Jury, for services to promote the organisation. I picked it up to put it on his desk and found it was sticky as if covered with jam. On the desk were two empty claret bottles, but only one glass. That's why when I saw him lying on the floor. I assumed he was dead drunk, and not just dead as it turned out."

"How did you know he was dead?"

"Inspector, I may not be medically qualified, but anybody would have known he was dead. I have seen bodies before."

"Did you call the police immediately?" asked Griggs.

"No, I was so shocked that I fell back into the chair. My husband and I had been going through a bad patch, in fact I was going to ask him again for a divorce. He wouldn't give me one last time. I was going to insist tonight. He had a regular mistress,

Rebecca Fielding, and I thought he might be glad to be rid of me. Funny thing though, seeing his lovely face all smashed up like that. All I could think about was all of the good times we had. It was a bit like what they say dying is like when your life flashes through your mind. I knew he was dead, so perhaps I just wanted time with him. I know it must sound silly, but that's what I did."

"It must have been awful. How long did you sit there, Mrs Valentine?" asked Griggs kindly.

"About twenty minutes I think."

"And the walk, where did you go, and how long were you out for?"

"I'm not sure, probably for about an hour, I walked along by the Thames."

"Did you see anybody while you were out by any chance?"

"No, I don't think so."

"So to summarise, you were dropped outside the house at about eleven thirty. You didn't go into the house, instead you decided to go for a long walk even though it was late and freezing cold. You arrived back at about twelve twenty, found the body, then waited twenty minutes to call us. You picked up the gavel which you think was covered in blood and you moved the body to check if he was drunk. Nobody saw you from eleven thirty till the police arrived. Is that what you have been telling me?"

"Yes Inspector, that is what happened."

"Well thank you, I think that's quite enough for the moment but I will need to talk to you again."

After Nicola had left Griggs' interview room, or the room that used to be her dining room, Griggs started making a lot of notes. Cook had kept a good record of the interview but he liked to note down his initial observations as well. In murder cases the obvious suspect was either the person who found the body, the husband or wife, particularly if there were signs of problems, or failing that, the person who would benefit financially. Thinking about it, he should have told Mrs Valentine to get a lawyer, and a good one at that.

After all, she had his blood all over her, her prints were on the murder weapon. There was an hour and a half where she had no alibi, which was almost certainly around the time he was killed. Probably when he checked, she would stand to inherit a fortune. If that wasn't enough, she admitted that the marriage was rocky and she wanted a divorce. He knew he would be seeing a lot of Mrs Valentine. He turned to his assistant.

"Have you checked the phone, Cook?"

"Yes Guv, the last call was a London number, 0171 365 5456, at ten o'clock to a Miss Rebecca Fielding, I've got the address. I've also got the phone people to provide a list of all calls for the last week." Sergeant Cook wasn't the most glamorous woman in the world, but she was a good worker. Cook would never make inspector, but would nevertheless be an excellent backup. Griggs was delighted to be working with her.

"Is the Doc about? I'd like a word."

"He's been and gone, Guv. Would you believe he

had yet another killing to go to, apparently the department is short-handed."

"Did he give us anything?"

"Yep, death between ten o'clock clock and two this morning. He was killed by savage blows to the head, that's all he say till the p.m." Cook read this confidently from her notebook.

"We needed a doctor to tell us that! He was probably on the phone at ten o'clock and I was here at two. As for the death, it was a little obvious."

"Oh, I don't know, sir, he could have been poisoned first."

"He was, Cook, in a manner of speaking, but his was self-inflicted, two bottles of claret would knock out a mule."

Griggs looked round the house, talked to the scene of the crime mob, then gave them permission to remove the body. He watched the body bag being carried slowly out into the ambulance. He always hated death, it seemed a constant reminder that your number was due sometime. With that cheerful thought in his head he thought he'd go home for an hour. Before he went he came back to see Mrs Valentine.

"We're off then, I'm leaving an officer here and you won't be able to use the study for a while. I'm afraid you are going to have to identify the body officially. I'll send a car in the morning at about ten if that's all right with you."

"Tomorrow at ten then," replied Nicola, dreading the experience.

Griggs drove back home thinking it a shame that he was almost certainly going to have to arrest that pleasant lady. He wondered what the mistress Rebecca Fielding was like, after all, she had tempted Valentine away. Well, he'd find out soon enough, he would see her tomorrow.

CHAPTER 9

To say it was cold would be the understatement of the year. The apartment was more like an Arctic igloo. It was so cold that Rebecca wondered if she'd be warmer outside in the communal gardens. The problem was, as always, the antiquated central heating system which was meant to serve the whole building. There were never problems when it was warm, in fact quite the contrary. The stupid pipes then were often red hot, which was not ideal in the middle of the hottest spell of the summer. No, the problems with the heating system only arose when it was cold. At that time everybody turned up their thermostats with the inevitable result that the boiler broke down.

It happened every year, without fail, but when the residents were asked to cough up the money to repair the whole system, the meeting was always held on a warm day. The vote was always decided on meanness, the residents thinking more of their summer holidays, rather than the next winter's snows. Besides, some of them reckoned they would have moved by the winter so why waste the money? Most people have little imaginations, they cannot imagine the opposite of anything. This meant that the residents had to suffer on the few really cold days of winter. There was no doubt that February the fifteenth qualified. According to the papers it was the coldest February, since the previous coldest February. It may or may not have been colder than the one before. Rebecca, like most people, was becoming cynical about these continual breaking of records. Every month broke some sort of record – cold, wet, hot, dry, windy. You name it and some month's weather would break it.

Despite the cold, Rebecca felt great. Mind you, she was wearing trousers, a skirt, three sweaters and her dressing gown. She was sitting in front of an electric fire with a blanket over her, reading a slushy Mills and Boon. This was in total contrast to her mood of the previous evening. When Richard had phoned her back later yesterday afternoon, then she was sunk in lethargy, comfort-eating her way through an enormous box of Cadbury's Milk Tray.

When Richard walked out of the American Bar, she thought she'd seen the last of him. The phone call in the afternoon was an incredibly pleasant surprise. She could remember the phone call almost word for word.

"Rebecca? It's Richard."

"Oh, what do you want? Have you thought about your offer? Do you now want to reduce it, realising you were far too generous? Perhaps five hundred pounds was what you meant, or was it one thousand pounds a month!"

"I don't blame you for being cynical."

"No, you were quite right to be cautious. Are you sure you don't want me to have a blood test? After all, for all you know I could have been sleeping with all of the massed brigade of the Scots Guards. You can't be too careful about money, as you're always telling me."

"Go on, enjoy yourself, I deserve it. I panicked when you told me your news. I regret it dreadfully now."

"So that's it, is it? You just wanted to feel better?" she added sarcastically.

"No, it's not that," he snapped. "Just shut up, and listen. I've thought about it and I now know I want you more than anything else, even the company. I do love you Rebecca, and I want us to bring up our child. You must believe me, I love you."

"Ah, so we're going to live together are we?"

"Better than that, I'm going to make Nicola give me a divorce. I'll see her tonight. She won't stand in our way, I won't let her, I promise."

"You really mean it, don't you? What's brought about this conversion at the gates of Damascus?"

"I've been thinking about a lot of things lately and I realise I've been wrong. Money and power aren't everything. Life's too short. It's taken me a lifetime to understand it, but I'm going to change. Tomorrow's going to be the start of my new life."

Richard wasn't to know at that point in time just how accurate his prediction was to be.

"I'm just calling to let you know how I feel, I've got to go though, I've got a meeting to chair. Look, I'll see you tomorrow. I'll phone you. I love you."

He hadn't yet phoned, although he had left a nice message on her answering machine, telling her that he loved her. Why didn't he phone? She was dying to know how he'd got on with Nicola. Had she agreed to the settlement? Would they be able to be married before the birth of her baby? She sat looking at the phone, willing it to ring. But as they say, a watched phone never rings. Why didn't he phone and tell her?

She sat drinking her hot chocolate, listening to the latest Spice Girls offering, 'Spice up the World', when the nine o'clock news came on the radio.

She didn't know why she bothered to listen to the news as it was always the same. She listened to it half-heartedly as it droned on in the background. More ethnic cleansing in Kosovo, more empty threats to Serbia, further financial troubles in the Far East, speculation of whether Gascoigne would play for England in the World Cup, the death of a prominent businessman. The chairman of Redwood Group plc, Richard Valentine, was brutally murdered at his Chelsea house last night. Police are appealing for anyone who was in the immediate vicinity of Oakley Street between ten p.m. and two a.m. to come forward. New flood warnings concerning people living in low-lying West Country areas. The two runaway pigs were still at large. The news droned on. Rebecca sat silently, looking at her cup of chocolate.

At first she couldn't take it in. Did she hear what she thought she'd heard? No! She couldn't have, she must have dozed off and imagined it in some form of daymare, but it sounded so real. There was only one way to find out. She phoned the local police station.

"Duty officer. How can I help?" came a flat voice.

"Richard Valentine, I heard on the news he'd been murdered last night."

She desperately wanted him to answer, "Who? Oh, I don't think so," but she was to be bitterly disappointed.

"Yes, madam, do you know anything about the murder?"

The full implication of what she had heard on the news started slowly to hit her, and she found herself speaking in a voice she hardly recognised.

"Not the murder, as such, but I was with him yesterday lunchtime and he phoned me in the afternoon. I knew him rather well."

"Can I have your name madam, and telephone number and address? I'm sure the Inspector would want to talk to you."

She gave him all the details and then went slowly back to the bedroom. She lay down and with that, her resistance finally cracked. With a horrifying cry, the floodgates opened. She sobbed uncontrollably for what seemed like years.

By the time Inspector Griggs arrived, Rebecca had got over the worst of her shock. She had had a hot bath, made herself get dressed and put on some of Richard's favourite perfume. She opened the door and recognised Griggs and Cook for what they were immediately, even before Griggs flashed his warrant card. She wondered why the police were so easily recognisable. The man was wearing an extraordinary suit, it would have looked good ten years earlier but today it didn't do him any favours. He was not very tall, with short, dark hair and with a thin, intelligent face. Despite the pantomime suit this was clearly a man to be reckoned with. The woman was dumpy, and frumpy, she was the sort you rarely noticed. The only thing that Rebecca thought was that she really should go to a hairdressers', a beautician, and a decent clothes shop – she would be amazed at the difference.

"Good afternoon, Miss Fielding. It is Miss, isn't it? I'm Inspector Griggs and this is Detective Sergeant Cook. I know it's an intrusion but I do need to ask you a few questions."

"Come in, Inspector, I've been expecting you."

Griggs' first thoughts about Rebecca Fielding were of a sexy lady. Not tarty or cheap, but oozing sex just the same.

"I understand you know Richard Valentine," started Griggs.

"In all ways," said Rebecca, "let's not play coy. I was his mistress, his lover, and I'm carrying his child. That should save you a few questions."

Griggs was a prude and he was quite taken aback by her directness.

"How long have you been his mistress?"

"Over two years, but it was more than that. I loved him and he loved me."

"I understand he was already married?" said Griggs.

"She," Rebecca emphasised the word with a hiss, "wouldn't give him his freedom, she was religious or something and didn't believe in divorce."

Interesting, exactly the opposite of what Mrs Valentine had told him. Mind you, to be fair, he'd known a lot of men use that argument so as not to have to do anything. Valentine, from all he had been told, was somewhat of an expert in these matters, so he couldn't read too much into it.

"You saw him yesterday, I understand?"

"We had a drink at the Savoy. I told him about our baby."

"What was his reaction?"

"Not good at first. Said he'd make us a weekly allowance."

"But you said he was going to ask for a divorce," probed Griggs.

"That came later. He phoned me from the office. He told me he'd make his wife give him his freedom. He was determined about it."

Should have been an interesting meeting, thought Griggs, *both apparently wanting the same thing. Or did they?*

"He phoned here last night at around ten, what did he say?" asked Griggs.

"You can hear for yourself, it's on the answerphone." She walked over and switched the machine on.

"Hi darling, I suppose you've taken one of your pills, I'll speak to you in the morning. Nicola's not here so I've got no news. I love you."

It was obviously very distressing to her as her eyes were filled with tears.

"How did he die?" asked Rebecca. "Did he suffer?"

The last words were spoken as if she was trying not to cry.

"No, we don't think he suffered. Death must have been fairly instantaneous. But I can't talk about how at the moment, we're still in the early stages of the investigation. Now, if you think of anything else that might help, please contact me. We'll want a statement just for the record. Where were you last night between ten p.m. and two a.m.?"

"You can't think I could have anything to do with Richard's murder, can you?" said Rebecca loudly. "Surely it's obvious who did it!"

"Who would that be?" Said Griggs, anticipating the answer in advance.

"She did it. Nicola, of course she did it, who else!"

Who indeed? thought Griggs. "I'm afraid we do have to investigate. I still need to know your movements, I'm sorry but that's the rules in a murder enquiry," said Griggs firmly. "As I said, it's just for the record. We have to quickly eliminate all the people that knew him. As I'm sure you hear often on the television, it's just routine."

"I was here all evening, not terribly exciting I'm afraid. I went to bed early. I took a pill as I haven't been sleeping too well lately. I haven't got any witnesses, I'm afraid. But I can assure you I wouldn't murder the father of my child."

"Well, thank you, Miss. That'll be all. I'll see myself out, thank you."

Griggs couldn't imagine a more different pair of women. Nicola Valentine was tall, with long blonde hair – the virginal attractive type. She looked like butter wouldn't melt in her mouth, the mere thought of sex would be a shock to her. Blue eyes, blonde hair, little make-up, no glimpses of forbidden flesh.

Rebecca Fielding on the other hand, was short and incredibly sexy. She had black hair cut in a bob, wore plenty of make-up. Her blouse was open just enough so that as she moved you could see her breasts through her almost transparent bra. Her skirt was split, revealing tantalising glimpses of thigh. *Yes,* thought Griggs, *Miss Fielding knew she was sexy and made no attempt to hide it, in fact she enjoyed men looking at her.* From what he gathered about Richard Valentine he would have thought that Rebecca Fielding was far more his type. Nevertheless, she could be lying about the phone call, she hadn't got an alibi and a woman dumped with child could easily turn to murder. Mind you, the answerphone message would indicate all was well. That is of course, if it was last night's message and not an earlier one re-recorded. He reminded himself that he had to keep an open mind. Even though the circumstantial evidence against Mrs Valentine was very compelling.

CHAPTER 10

Griggs' next call was to the offices of the Redwood Group PLC in the city. His first appointment was with the chairman, Roland Silverman. He was shown into a big, flashy office. Silverman believed in large desks. Griggs didn't think he'd seen a bigger one. He wickedly wondered if desks were like cars and reflected lack of size in other areas.

"Good afternoon, Inspector. Dreadful business, absolutely dreadful. It's hard to take it all in. I was only at his house yesterday morning. I just can't believe he's dead. Poor old Nicola, it must have been a dreadful shock. I must go round and see her and offer our support."

Griggs looked at Silverman and thought to himself, if he was casting a play with the chairman of a company, he'd go for Silverman. He seemed exactly what everyone thought a modern chairman should be like. Small and round like a football. His hair, or lack of it, was a greasy brown, and his beady eyes looked immense through his thick glasses.

"I understand, sir, that while you were at his house yesterday morning you had an argument."

"Not an argument exactly, officer, it was more a

disagreement about policy. It happens all the time at board level. Nothing serious, I can assure you," said Silverman pompously.

"How did you get on with him?"

"No problems, we were friends. After all we've taken Redwood onto the market and made fortunes for all of our shareholders. We were a great team."

"Had Valentine any enemies that you can think about? Anyone that would benefit from his death?"

"Nobody I can think of. He did have a row with Nash yesterday, but I can't imagine that Alec Nash would kill him."

"Nash? Where would I find him, sir?"

Silverman flicked through a card index file, pulled out a card and passed it across the desk. Griggs looked at and passed it to Cook, who noted the address in her book. He looked straight at Silverman, weighing the honesty of his replies.

"I think you'll be wasting your time though."

"You're probably right, sir, but it's best to be sure when you're dealing with a murder inquiry. Now, I'd like to go and see Mr Roberts, your financial director. Oh, I forgot to ask you, just for the record, sir, what were your movements last night between ten p.m. and two a.m.? You understand that I have to eliminate all of the people that knew Valentine from our enquiries."

"Yes, I quite understand. I haven't got a strong alibi, though, if that's what you call it. I got a phone call from an old friend, Colonel Palmer, who'd lost a lot of money by being a name at Lloyds. He wanted some advice about what he could do, so we arranged to meet in the St Ermine's hotel."

"This Colonel Palmer, he'll confirm your meeting, will he?" said Griggs.

"No, I'm afraid not, the poor old fool committed suicide last night. Apparently he just couldn't face the shame of going bankrupt, and that Archer woman was no help at all. Mind you, how could she understand financial hardship when their income is in the millions? I waited there for the old fool for about an hour but of course he never showed up. I was bloody angry at the time, in the end I came home."

"Did you see anyone you knew there?" asked Griggs, thinking he'd check the suicide as soon as left the building.

"Nobody, I'm afraid. It was, as I'm sure you are aware, rather chilly last night, there were few people about. Someone may remember me at the hotel but I sat in a corner to keep warm. It was out of sight of the bar."

How convenient, thought Griggs. He noticed Cook's face and knew she was thinking the same way; that would be her afternoon's work, checking on Silverman.

"Well, thank you, sir. We'll need a statement, I'll get D.S. Cook to organise it now. I'd better see Mr Roberts, I understand he's the Financial Director."

Silverman buzzed his secretary, who took Griggs down to Roberts' office. Jason looked flushed but Griggs supposed that was only to be expected. After all, it wasn't every day your chief executive was murdered.

Roberts' office was smaller and less luxurious than Silverman's and looked over-cluttered with paperwork. Roberts himself was around forty, good looking but haggard. He looked like he needed a holiday urgently. *His Paul Smith suit must have cost a pretty penny,* thought Griggs, and the tie didn't come from a boot sale like his.

"I'm sorry to have to bother you, sir, but I have to ask a few questions."

"Of course, I'll do anything I can to help," said Roberts.

"How did you get on with your boss?"

"Great. He was like a father to me. This was my first commercial job and I've been here over twelve years. If I hadn't liked Richard I'd have been off. I've had lots of other lucrative offers."

"How's the company doing? Any financial problems?"

"On the contrary, the company has never been stronger. We've just taken over Intercards plc. We're a successful company that the city thinks highly of. Mind you, saying that, the shares dived today on the news of Valentine's murder. It's a big blow to us, Richard Valentine was a brilliant business man."

"Can you think of anyone who might want him dead?"

"No, I can't help you. I can only think it must have been a burglary, although..." Roberts stopped as if thinking better of what he was about to say.

"Although what, sir? It's all right, we are just trying to get a picture. Every little thing helps."

"Well I do know he had had some trouble with a woman!"

"Trouble, sir? And who would this woman be?"

"Rebecca Fielding. Richard had just dumped her and according to office gossip she even went as far as threatening his life. But then Richard was always in trouble with the ladies, love them and leave them was his motto. Believe me, he has done this to a lot of ladies in his time. I expect it's not much use to you though, as you would call it hearsay."

"Thank you, sir. We like to hear everything, we can always sort out what's important and all of that is extremely interesting." Griggs looked as if he was about to go, then turned back.

"Right, one last thing, just for routine, I'm afraid, sir. Where were you between ten p.m. and two a.m. last night?"

Griggs wondered why Roberts looked so worried by the question.

"I couldn't sleep and I went out for a drive. I had a personal problem that was bothering me."

"Where did you drive to, sir?"

"Oh, here and there. I recall parking alongside the Thames at some time. I remember looking at that cold grey water. You know how it is, Inspector, when you get uptight you just need time to think. Sorry, I know it's not a good one, but if I was going to commit a murder I'd be clever enough to make sure I had a good alibi, I can assure you. I read enough Elizabeth George detective stories to understand that."

Griggs had to agree with him. If it was a premeditated murder, the murderer would certainly have a better alibi.

He left the offices more and more convinced that he was dealing with a simple domestic murder. It seemed a pity as he had liked Mrs Valentine, and from what he had already learned about her husband he was sure he would not have liked him. His instinct was to arrest her straight away, however, he had to see Piers Lamont and Alec Nash first.

The Georgian building in which Piers' charity was housed was a gem. It had recently been steam-cleaned at great expense by the charity and it made it look attractive. The gleaming white paint set off the original Georgian windows; a strong mauve clematis grew up part of the building, giving a rural feel to it.

A blue plaque outside the door proudly proclaimed that Lord Skincross, the Victorian author of such religious treaties as 'God knows you're there', and, 'Know your own God', had lived there from 1861 to 1874. Unfortunately Skincross' works had not stood the test of time, nevertheless he had been successful in his own period.

The impressive double front door opened to reveal a wide hallway with incredible ornate coving. The pale blue walls made it look even bigger than it was. A magnificent mirror added to the effect. There was a small removable sign indicating that the reception was in the room to the right.

Griggs knocked and entered. Once again, he marvelled at the opulence of his surroundings. No expense had been spared. The attractive secretary sitting at an antique desk was talking on the phone. Fresh lilies infused their powerful perfume throughout the room. The thick carpet felt good under Griggs' tired feet. The attractive secretary indicated that he should sit. Again, the chair was expensive. Griggs looked round the room and had no doubts that the paintings were original, as was the rest of the furniture. God knows what on earth it was worth. Eventually, the girl put the phone down and turned to smile at Griggs.

"How can I help you?" she said in a silky, sweet, Sloane Ranger voice.

Griggs flashed his warrant card.

"I'm Inspector Griggs, I'd like to have a word with your Director, a Mr Piers Lamont."

"He's exceptionally busy at the moment, have you an appointment?" she asked doubtfully.

"No, but I think he'll see me, this is official business. It'll only take a few minutes if you don't mind."

With that, she phoned up to Piers' office. She looked up at Griggs and smiled.

"He says to show you straight up."

If anything, the upstairs of the building was even more luxurious than the ground floor. Prints and paintings filled the walls of the stairs and corridors. Piers' room was more like an antique showroom than a charity office. Griggs wondered what percentage of the annual funds raised by the charity went on maintaining these offices. He suspected it would be a high figure. He wondered if the fund raisers at their bring-and-buy sales had any idea – he doubted it.

Piers Lamont was a tall, distinguished man, greying at the temples. He was wearing an expensive grey suit. *Savile Row, if I'm not mistaken*, thought Griggs. The young lady introduced him and then left.

"Please sit down, Inspector," said Piers, in his unmistakably public school voice. "Now how can I help you, Inspector?"

"I need to ask you a few questions about your movements last night. It's very much routine, sir."

"How extraordinary! One hears it all the time on films and the television, but I never thought I'd be asked that question myself. Let me see, now, I picked up a friend at about six thirty and we drove to Islington. The traffic was awful at that time of night, I had a dreadful fuss trying to park the car. You know what it's like these days, you can never find a space. Anyway, we managed to park close to the theatre. We walked round and got there about twenty past seven. We saw 'Naked', it wasn't that good really. It was at the Almeida Theatre, that's in Almeida Street. After the play we walked across the road and had a meal in the White Onion. Quite a reasonable meal as it turns out, despite the fact it was in Islington. Then I drove the lady back to her house. I didn't stay. Afterwards I drove home and went to bed. I haven't got anyone to collaborate that part of the story, I'm afraid. Now what's all this about?"

"Was your friend a Mrs Valentine?" asked Griggs.

"Yes, but..."

"And what time did you leave her?"

"It was well after eleven p.m. I got home about eleven forty-five, so I should imagine somewhere around eleven thirty."

"Did you see Mrs Valentine go into her house, sir?" continued Griggs.

"Yes. No. Come to think of it I didn't. No, she was still in the road as I drove away. I assume she went straight in, it was rather cold last night."

"Thank you, sir. I'd ask you to pop into the station to make a full statement and that'll be all."

"It's not all, officer. Not by a long shot. Why are you asking me these questions?"

"Mr Valentine was murdered last night."

"Oh my god! At what sort of time?"

"We're not sure yet, but it was late last night."

Piers looked horrified. He realised immediately why all the questions.

Nicola might be involved. After all, she was going to ask Richard for a divorce. She wouldn't have killed him, would she? The most important thing though, was not to get involved, thought Piers.

"Have you anything else you want to tell me?" asked Griggs, sensing there was more to come.

"I feel a bit disloyal saying this, but, I suppose you should be aware that the Valentines' marriage was not a happy one. He was an absolute swine, treated her like dirt and went out with all sorts of other women all through their marriage. In fact, Nicola, that is Mrs Valentine, was going to ask him for a divorce last night. I'd asked her to marry me. She was going to confront him about it, once she left me."

Piers felt extremely guilty about telling the inspector all these personal details, but he felt it was better that he told him than he found out from elsewhere.

"Let me get this straight. You say Mrs Valentine went back to confront her husband and get him to give her a divorce. Had she asked him for a divorce before?"

"Yes, he'd always refused but she felt he might grant her one this time, because he seemed to have some sort of strong relationship with another woman."

"So you proposed last night? And Mrs Valentine accepted?"

"Yes, that is providing she could get a divorce."

"Thank you Mr Lamont, you've been very helpful."

After Griggs had left, Piers sat thinking. *Nicola couldn't have murdered Richard, could she? No, it's impossible.* The more he thought about it the more likely he thought it was. He tried to picture the scene. Richard drunk, violent and offensive. Nicola reasonable, but persistent. An angry row developing followed by Richard becoming more and more violent. He could see him hitting Nicola, Nicola picking up the scissors and plunging them deep in his heart. He could see it all, the kitchen covered in blood. Poor old Nicola. Even worse, poor old Piers, it'd be dreadful for the charity, let alone his mother. God, his mother. What would she say? She had not been keen on the idea of a divorcee. He'd have to get rid of Nicola as quickly as possible, but he'd do it as nicely as possible.

"Well, what did you make of him?" he asked Cook as they drove on through endless dreary suburbs on their way to the stockbroker belt.

"Not a lot," said Cook, "he certainly has a high opinion of himself. He's frightened of bad publicity and is worried that the mud will stick. For what it's worth, as far as he's concerned she's guilty as charged. Not that we've charged her yet."

"So you reckon she did it, no doubts?"

"Not really, sir. I reckon they had a row, he was drunk and went over the top, she picked up the hammer and killed him. Could well have been self-defence. She should plead guilty to manslaughter; she could be out in a few years. It's obvious that it wasn't premeditated. I feel sorry for her, by all accounts he was the perfect bastard, what do you think, Guv?"

"You're certainly right about him being a bastard, and yes, she probably did it. If she had been a nasty piece of work I'd have no doubts, it's just, I don't know what, but I'm not completely happy with it all."

"What about this walk, do you believe her?" asked Cook.

"Well, if she did it could easily be after she killed him. In which case she would have put her coat on, check all of the coats in the house for blood stains on the inside."

By now they were driving through sun-dappled leafy lanes, catching glimpses of thirties-style Tudor mansions hidden up the end of rhododendron-lined drives. Most of the houses here costs millions and if the owners had their way all the roads would be gated so as to keep out the riff-raff (locals). Cook spotted Nash's house and Griggs reversed the car back to the neatly raked gravel drive. As he pulled in he was embarrassed as he had ruined the neatly manicured effect, putting deep ruts across the drive.

As one would expect, Golf House was in the middle of a golf course. Griggs would have liked to play golf, but to play golf you needed free time, and since when did coppers have any free time?

Cook rang the bell and after a lengthy wait the door was opened by an elderly foreign-looking woman.

"We're not interested in joining the church, nor do we want any more copies of watchtower, thank you very much." With that, she shut the door firmly in their faces.

Cook rang the bell again. The woman opened it again; before she could speak, Griggs started.

"We are not Jehovah's Witnesses, madam, we are police officers. This is my warrant card." He flashed his card at the now slightly less confident woman. "We need to see Mr Nash, is he at home?"

"Mr Nash!" shouted the woman down the corridor. "Police at the front door. They wanta see you."

A tall, powerfully built old man came out of a side door.

"Thank you Mrs D'Avinia, but there's no need to shout."

Mrs D'Avinia retired, muttering. How was she supposed to know they were the police? They had never been before.

"Now, how can I help you? But first let's get out of the hall." He led them into a large room filled with what looked like junk to Griggs. Wasn't what he would expect in a house like this, rings on the tables, carpet worn and books, newspapers, and magazines everywhere. Jill, his long-suffering wife, would never leave a room like this.

"Mr Nash, I believe you sold a company to Richard Valentine."

"No, I sold it to Redwood, but yes I do know, or to be more correct, did know Valentine."

"Were you happy with your dealings with Valentine?"

"At first yes, but then the chiselling bastard went back on his word. He promised to safeguard the jobs but sacked them all. He lied to me and was proud of it. I was so angry I went up to see him on the day he died. That is why you are here, you have been told about the row. Well it's true, I did attack him. It was silly but he was so smug. I didn't kill him though, don't even know where he lives."

"What were your movements on the evening of February the fourteenth?" asked Cook.

"Here alone watching television, or to be more honest sleeping in front of it. So no alibi, I'm afraid, but I didn't murder the bastard. Good luck to whoever did, they did the world a favour." Griggs didn't see much point prolonging the interview, and so they got on their way back to London; he would get Cook to tie up the ends.

He thought that Nash proved to be extremely honest. He had admitted freely that he'd attacked Valentine and they had had quite a row. Despite that, he couldn't really see Nash murdering Valentine after he'd given him twenty million pounds for his company. Admittedly his alibi was almost non-existent, but Griggs couldn't see him as a plausible suspect.

It was strange really, thought Griggs. All five possible suspects all having dodgy alibis. Griggs, however, was convinced that he already had enough evidence to arrest Mrs Valentine. He decided he'd he would waste no more time and go and talk to the Crown Prosecution lawyers. The lawyers agreed with his logic, that there was enough evidence to charge Nicola Valentine with the murder of her husband.

CHAPTER 11

Nicola knew the exact day her nightmare began. Her childhood had been idyllic. She had wonderful parents. On the surface, her father was strict and rather frightening, but she knew that underneath, he was a loveable old teddy bear. Her best friend was her mother. She told her everything and valued her advice on all subjects. Her mother never told her what to do, but helped her by talking her through any problem she might have. Whatever happened, her mother was always there, a rock to lean on. She managed to help Nicola through the pain of her pony dying and her constant broken-heart problems as a teenager. She was the one constant thing in Nicola's life. Everything could be put right whilst her mother was there.

It was hard for Nicola to come to terms with her sudden death. Cancer is so indiscriminate and it strikes so quickly. One minute all was well, the next there was more pain than she had ever thought possible. She learnt afterwards that her mother had known for the last few months. It was typical of her mother's inner strength that she had kept it to herself, giving no clues to her impending death. It was for Nicola, the end of a chapter in her life. She had hardly recovered from the trauma when John had died in that awful car crash. During the months that followed, Nicola had been close to a total breakdown. All that saved her was her inner strength, inherited from her mother, and a particularly clever psychiatrist.

Now it was all starting again. Richard being murdered was bad enough, but for anyone to think that she could have done it, was horrendous. She had plunged back into total despair.

Just when she thought things couldn't get any worse, she was phoned up by Piers' overbearing mother, who explained in her sickly sweet voice that Piers had to think of his position. She was sure that Nicola would understand. In retrospect, Nicola thought she really should have been grateful. Imagine being married to a man of thirty-five who gets his mother to jilt his fiancée.

When the police first arrested her, Nicola thought it was a dreadful mistake which would soon be put right, but after she had appeared in the magistrates' court and was formally charged with murder, she realised that it was horribly serious. Her father stood bail of a hundred thousand pounds and she was released on the provision that she visited the police station every week. The Rear Admiral took her out to lunch afterwards and warned her how worrying her position was; he suggested that she should go to a private detective agency so they could investigate Richard's death. He recommended a new organisation called Pike and Neil, which is why Nicola found herself talking to Sandy Neil in her sitting room one dark evening in late March.

As Mrs Valentine opened the front door, Sandy was immediately moved. Pain was etched across her face. She looked so small, so sad and so vulnerable. Despite this, Mrs Valentine was incredibly pretty. She had long blonde hair which, although she had pulled up into a scruffy ponytail, still looked beautiful. Her face was pale and she wore no make-up. Sandy was very taken with her.

He followed her into the sitting room and they sat on either side of the open fireplace.

"Mrs Valentine, I have been through the file and I understand your present position. In all fairness I have to warn you that the prosecution case is a good one. Our job is to undermine it. It will involve a lot of work and, I'm afraid, expense, but it is necessary. I will have to ask you questions which may be embarrassing to you, but always remember that I am on your side and I will be ten times nicer than the prosecuting council."

She nodded.

"All right," said the detective, "if you didn't kill your husband, the sixty-four thousand dollar question is, who did? Had he got any enemies?"

Nicola laughed. As she did her face lit up, making her look completely different. Sandy liked the look of new Mrs Valentine better than the old sad one.

"How long have we got? The list is endless, I'm afraid. He was a ruthless businessman. He steered close to the wind at all times. There must be hundreds out there who'd be delighted to see him dead, but I doubt if any of them would actually do anything about it."

"Let's start with his present close associates. What's his chairman, Roland Silverman, like?"

"Roland? Well he's a bit of a rough diamond. He likes people to think he's old school, tie, old money and all that. In reality he's just dragged himself up by his boot straps. He's got himself drunk a few times at our parties. When he's drunk he starts feeling sorry for himself and likes a sympathetic audience, which usually turns out to be me. He's carrying a fantastic chip on his shoulder. You wouldn't believe that he's the youngest of a family of eleven. They were brought up in a small house in Woolwich. His father ran off when he was only three. Things were tough and it left its mark on him. He managed to get himself articled to an accountant and worked his way through night school. He got himself fully qualified but apparently he was not the right sort. Not that many people know that, he keeps it quiet."

"Can you think of any reason he might want your husband out of the way?"

"Not really. They never got on with each other but then few people liked Richard anyway."

"What about money? Silverman is rich, isn't he?"

"Yes and no. On the surface he's rich but he told me a while ago again under the influence that he'd got parasites crawling all over him, incessantly demanding enormous sums from him."

"Blackmail?" asked Sandy excitedly.

"No, I think he meant Lloyds." Nicola grinned as she said the last words, pleased with her wit.

Sandy couldn't remember being with a prettier woman in years. Talking to her, he was fairly sure that this decent woman was innocent. He was going to do his best to prove it.

"Ah yes, of course, the rich man's burden. Was he in for much?"

"Well it's difficult to know. Drink makes people say all sorts of things but he did say that each time he got a demand he always hoped they'd put a couple of noughts on by mistake."

Sandy found himself looking more and more into her blue eyes, which he thought were the most beautiful he'd ever seen. He had to push himself to keep asking the questions.

"So it was serious. Do you think he could have been dipping into the company accounts? If he was and your husband found out, that could be a strong motive for murder. I'll certainly look into that possibility. Were there any others with money problems?"

Sandy was trying desperately to concentrate on his work. He found Nicola disturbing and had a sneaking feeling he was falling for her. He had never felt this way before and he found her very exciting. It was ridiculous, he thought, as he had only just met her and besides, it would not be professional.

Nicola got up and walked over to the sideboard. She poured them both a sherry and handed one to Sandy.

"Sorry, I should have asked. I hope you like sherry."

Sandy nodded his approval and she continued.

"I suppose Jason Roberts is a long shot. He was Mr Goody-goody until about a year or so ago, then it all changed."

"In what way?"

"He found a new love, or to be more precise he found sex. He's been running round with a girl young enough to be his daughter."

"That's always interesting, it's amazing what men will do under those circumstances," said Sandy. "I'll certainly have to have a chat with Mr Roberts. What about women in Richard's life? Any jealous husbands? I'm sorry to ask you this but I gather he was a womaniser."

"Well he'd just dumped his present lover. I think her name was Rebecca Fielding. You'll probably be able to find out through the office what her real name was, but then she'd hardly murder him for that. If that was a motive then he'd be dead years ago."

"Probably not," said Sandy, "but on the other hand it's worth a look, after all, a woman scorned and all that. Anyone else?"

"Well he did have a row with someone in the office the other day. I can't remember the name but Richard had just bought his company. He apparently threatened to kill Richard. Come to think of it, Roland Silverman was at the house on the morning he died. There was a row and it certainly sounded to me as if Silverman threatened him. He certainly was extremely angry, he smashed the front door so badly it broke the Yale lock. I had to use the Chubb before I went out otherwise we'd have been open to burglars."

"Did you tell the police this?" asked Sandy.

"No, I've only just remembered it."

"I think you should. I think when we've finished we'll make a further statement and give it in to them. Right, business over for tonight. Are you hungry?"

"As it happens, yes, I've hardly eaten all day."

"Can I take you to dinner?" asked Sandy hopefully.

"You don't have to," said Nicola, "I could easily get something out of the freezer."

"No, I know I don't have to but I'd like to. Who knows, you might remember something while we are eating. Come out, I think it would do you good. Do you like Chinese?"

"I adore Chinese. I've hardly had any for ages. Richard didn't like 'foreign muck' as he called it and Piers preferred gourmet restaurants, preferably with two stars to their name."

"Right then, Chinatown it is."

Over the meal Sandy found himself slipping further and further down the slippery slope. Nicola was almost perfect. She reminded him of Beth Cheshire. Why was he thinking that way? She was rich and beautiful. He, on the other hand, was just an employee. Still, a cat can look at a king.

As he drove home after taking Nicola back he started working out his plan of attack for the morning. He had a contact who would be able to tell him all about Silverman's Lloyds problems. He'd also get Peter onto the financial records of both Silverman and Roberts. It was amazing what Pike could dig up. He never really wanted to know the methods Pike used as he was sure they were illegal, but then the end justified the means if it meant proving Nicola innocent.

CHAPTER 12

At first Jason's speculation in the tiger economies looked like saving him. The pound, despite rising against the deutschmark and the dollar, was still falling against the eastern currencies and he soon had a paper profit of approximately a hundred thousand pounds. For the first time in months, Jason could see he might get himself out of the debt situation. He was so grateful for the excellent advice given to him by Jim, his brilliant currency dealer friend, that he took him out for a superb lunch at the Brasserie at the Oxo Tower. As they sat looking across St Pauls and the city, he began to realise how lucky he was and how all his problems were going to sort themselves out.

If he'd been on the ball he might just have listened a little more carefully to what Jim was telling him over lunch. The trouble was, he was far too greedy with the wine; too busy boasting to Jim how fantastic Zoë was in bed and how lucky he was that such a beauty like her should want him. Because of his vanity, he didn't take much notice of what the serious city trader was saying. Anyway, what did student unrest in Indonesia have to do with him? It was hardly world-shattering news. The army in those places knew how to deal with that type of trouble. President Suharto had the army behind him and things would soon be back to normal again. Jason was far more interested in choosing the decent dessert wine to have with his crème brûlée to take much notice of Jim's worries over the Japanese economy. He thought he was rather overreacting about a solitary bankruptcy in Japan, after all, companies in Britain and America were always going bankrupt. If he'd have thought about it a little more he might just possibly either have pulled out from the market or hedged his bets, but he was far too busy thinking about Zoë and what he was going to do to her that night. Jim tried to tell him again as he was leaving that things were changing fast in the East, but it was to no avail.

Jason had told Jane that he'd be away for a couple of days. He was looking forward to a two-day orgy of fun. He rarely went to the pictures but was intrigued with the reviews and publicity for the new British film The Full Monty. They went to see it in Greenwich, which was only three miles from Zoë's new apartment. After they had laughed their way through it they had a rather pleasant Chinese meal in the nearby The Treasure of China, a rather sumptuous establishment in the town centre. They ate lobster stew and thoroughly enjoyed themselves, being bestial, eating with their fingers as they looked at each other suggestively. Afterwards, washing in the finger bowls and cleaning with the warm airline-style cloths provided by the thoughtful staff. They drank their coffee slowly, then drove back to Zoë's Thames-side flat at Jacob's Island.

Jason was pleased with the Berkeley Homes built-in wardrobes in the main bedrooms, as they created a wall of mirrors. He opened a bottle of iced Laurent-

Perrier Rosé Brut champagne and brought it through into the bedroom. This was the first chance Jason had to sleep with Zoë all night at the new flat. He had been anticipating what he was going to do to her for a long time. Like most men, Jason was a voyeur, he loved watching himself in the large mirror as he plunged into Zoë. He arranged their position so Zoë could watch as well. He enjoyed the sight of her watching them making love, it seem to inflame him all the more. What with the pictures, her enthusiasm, and his relief that all was going to be all right, he was insatiable. He took Zoë in every position imaginable that night. Where he got the stamina from he just didn't know. Eventually when even Zoë's powers of resurrection had failed and he was feeling extremely sore, he dropped off into a deep sleep. What with the effects of the champagne and a night of fantastic sex, Jason awoke late the following morning. He crawled out of bed, put the kettle on for coffee and then glanced at The Times headlines.

"Christ," he shouted aloud, "that's all I bloody well need!"

The headlines indicated that all was not well in the East. Trouble had started in Thailand and had spread into Indonesia. The Indonesian rupee had fallen heavily due to their internal problems. The knock-on effect was that all the other currencies fell sharply, almost wiping out Jason's profit.

Jason felt sick. Just when he thought things were going to change everything started looking black again. However, over the coffee and toast that he had taken in to Zoë in the bedroom, he started to relax. After all, the markets had probably overreacted and within a few days they would correct and go back up again. After the third cup of coffee he was sure it was just a blip.

Zoë had been keen to go to the controversial Sensations exhibition of modern art at the Royal Academy. It seemed the ideal thing to take his mind off his problems. They lunched at Quaglino's which was close to the Royal Academy, then went across and queued for forty minutes before they got into the exhibition. Neither of them could understand why anyone would want to buy most of the exhibits. The rotten meat with the bloated blueflies was probably the worst. Mind you, the chopped up cow, or the sculpture of a man's head carved out of eight pints of his frozen blood ran it pretty close. One exhibit they thought was just plain filthy, and set them both sniggering. As Zoë said, what else could you do with two melons and a bucket with the suggestive cucumber in the middle? After that they watched some strange film which went on for ages and did virtually nothing. The whole exhibition seemed to be a total waste of time.

"Modern fart would seem to be a more appropriate name for this exhibition. It seems more like the emperor's new clothes to me," said Jason as they walked back out through the courtyard.

They giggled their way over to Fortnum and Mason's for tea, Jason always enjoyed his visits there. It always reminded him of when he was a small boy and his parents took him up to London for a treat. He never imagined then that he'd return with one of the most beautiful women in London. Looking across the table, he completely forgot about Asia.

That night they dined locally at La Lanterna in Mill Street, an Italian restaurant. They were lucky enough to get a table in the courtyard. They ate fresh pasta along with a robust Chianti Classico. When they returned to the flat they watched their favourite cable programme called Live, enjoying yet another blue film in the Erotica, Erotica series. They both found these films helped them to enjoy their bedroom sessions, Jason was somehow less energetic that night, much to Zoë's disappointment.

Again, the wine didn't help Jason to wake up early in the morning. He got up, organised breakfast and didn't even look at the paper until he returned to bed.

The blip had proved to be short-lived but not in the way he had hoped. All of his speculated currencies had plunged heavily, he was now down fifty thousand pounds. He couldn't believe it. A hundred and fifty thousand pounds had disappeared in forty-eight hours.

As the days and weeks went on he began to understand the real seriousness of the Asian crisis. Some of the stories he read in the papers he could hardly believe. Peregrine Securities, a Hong Kong high-flying company, went bankrupt. Apparently they'd lent nearly eighty percent of their total assets to an Indonesian taxi company with the unlikely name of Steady Safe. *Christ,* he thought, *what kind of cretins lend that sort of money to a taxi company?* It had to be some sort of racket.

Bankruptcy followed bankruptcy and then the Japanese joined in with gusto, trust them to do everything better than the rest. Mega-bankruptcy after mega-bankruptcy, debts and losses mounted by the hour. The Japanese banks had bad debts of around the three hundred and fifty billion pounds, which in some ways made Jason's problems look small. However, these things are relative, of course.

When he first started he needed six hundred thousand pounds to sort himself out. As the events in the East unfolded he found himself in a position that he needed one million six hundred thousand pounds to get himself out of trouble. His position, though, was getting more and more serious day by day.

The Mersham house was mortgaged up to the hilt and beyond, there was no way he could persuade anybody to lend him any more, he'd already tried. All of his credit cards were overstretched and it was difficult even to pay the minimum charge. He began to curse the name of Jim, that bloody useless bastard who had put him in the position he was now. He should never have listened to the idiot in the first place. He knew he was a no-hope loser.

He kept hoping that somehow the tide would turn, but it seemed nothing could stop the panic throughout South East Asia. He was also aware that the company share price was dependent on the annual profit. They were, at the moment, trading at a multiple of thirty-two times this annual profit. That means his one point six million loss times the multiple of thirty-two, which gives the shares a false value of fifty-one million two hundred thousand pounds. If his mistakes became public knowledge it would have a serious effect on the share price. In fact, if the full implications were known the share price could fall easily by that fifty million pounds and that would certainly be disastrous for Valentine's latest take-over.

Jason realised then only too well why Valentine hadn't pulled the plug on him. He couldn't afford the scandal in the middle of a key take-over. Ironically, as it turned out he'd have been far better taking the pain earlier rather than later. The way things were going Jason could easily find himself owing the company over three million pounds and that would certainly be serious, if not fatal for the company in the short to medium term.

Jason began to withdraw into himself. Much to Zoë's disgust he seemed to lose interest in sex. He found himself laughing at the most unlikely things and getting angry about things that normally wouldn't have mattered. He was, of course, at the early stages of a nervous breakdown brought on by stress, and still the Asian problems continued. The IMF got involved. There were strikes in Korea, hunger riots in Indonesia killing thousands, suicides in Japan and allegations from Malaysia that George Soros (the man who made billions when he helped to ruin Norman Lamont's future by getting Prime Minister Major to take the pound out of the EMU) was personally trying to ruin their country.

All that Jason knew though, was that he was rapidly moving towards the day of judgement when he would either have to buy the currency or find the money for the losses. There was no way he would be able to pay for the losses. The only solution was for the company to buy the currency and somehow hope that it would once again regain its value and solve his problems. He wasn't at all confident about that, but it was the only thing he could do.

With Valentine removed from the company, Jason

began to relax. He started practising to forge the dead chief executive's signature and was sure, when asked, he would be able to produce authorisation for his purchase of four million pounds worth of eastern currencies. The cover story he had concocted was that Richard Valentine was buying a card company based, he'd thought, in Korea. It was a secret deal and all he knew was Richard was convinced it would be a fantastic profit maker. He didn't know where the negotiations stood. All Richard told him was to buy the currency. As it turned out, Richard would have done better to have waited, but all the advice given at the time was to buy ahead due to the strength of the tiger economies. Even our new religious leader, Tony Blair, thought we should try to be more like them. Everybody seemed to expect the pound to fall. As it was, they were all wrong as the pound gained in value spectacularly. Ironically, the Prime Minister doesn't mention the tiger economies anymore, just the Asian crisis.

The more he thought about it, he was more convinced it would work. In fact he decided to go to Silverman himself with his grave concerns about Richard's controversial deal. After all, a one point six million pound loss could not be hidden forever and the chairman should be aware of it at the earliest opportunity. He was so convincing that he almost believed the story that Valentine had authorised it himself. He forged the paperwork and booked an appointment to see Silverman the following morning. He had completely forgotten that Valentine had told him that Silverman knew all about his fraud.

By the time he got home, his mood had noticeably

improved, much to Zoë's relief.

"Well it's nice to see you happy for a change," she said, "I hope it's goodbye for good to that nasty old Mr Grumpy."

"Have I been that bad? I'm sorry Zoë, things have been tough at work what with poor old Richard's murder and I've been depressed, but I'll make it up to you, I promise. Come on, let's go out. We'll go to the Pont de la Tour for dinner. After all, if it's good enough for Tony Blair to take President Clinton and their wives to, it must be good enough for us."

"I thought they got it free in exchange for all the publicity," said Zoë wickedly.

"You're becoming even more of a cynic than me. Just because the owner supported Blair in the election, why shouldn't Tony bring his good friends Bill and Hilary to his restaurant? They would want to thank him for all his help!"

Jason had noticed just how many good friends had been rewarded after the election, titles; changes in planning applications, relaxation of media restrictions; politics in Britain were getting more like the States every election.

It had been a good evening and as Jason drove into work the next morning he found himself singing. Things were certainly looking up. He entered Silverman's lush boardroom feeling confident.

"Sit down, Jason," said Silverman. "Coffee?" indicating the jug and the cups on a tray.

Jason poured himself and Roland a cup and sat down ready to start his performance.

"Roland, how much do you know about the Korean deal?" he asked in a matter-of-fact tone.

"Korean deal? What Korean deal?" asked a puzzled Silverman.

"You don't know about Valentine's proposed acquisition in Korea then? That is strange, I assumed you'd know all about it."

"As far as I'm aware we have no plans to enter the Far East market. To my certain knowledge we never have had. What are you talking about?"

"I apparently know as much as you. Richard asked me to arrange to buy four million pounds worth of eastern currencies to pay for part of the acquisition. I did wonder if it was a bribe or a sweetener but Richard wasn't forthcoming. You know what he's like, or he was like. As instructed I bought the currency, the problem is the tiger economies have turned flat and we've lost one point six million. I presumed you would know all about it. I'm sorry to bring you such bad news."

Roland Silverman looked at him for what seemed like hours.

"This is extremely serious. I'd better have a look at the authorisation paperwork."

Jason handed it over. Silverman looked at it and then his mood changed.

"Do I look simple? Have I got green grass growing instead of hair? You're a bloody crook, Roberts! You've been swindling the company out of tens of thousands of pound using false companies and now you're trying to tell me we've lost one point six million in some bogus currency scam. This bit of paper's a forgery! Both you and I know for this size of deal it needs my signature on it as well."

Jason looked sick. All his confidence evaporated rather quickly.

"What are you going to do?" Jason asked anxiously, hardly expecting another six months' breathing space.

Silverman found this a difficult question to answer. The shares had already dived when Valentine's death was announced. If a financial scandal came out then they would hit the floor. That was the last thing he needed.

"I'm not sure at the moment. I need time to think what's best for the company. In the meantime you're suspended. Go home and talk to nobody. I'll send for you as soon as I've worked out what to do."

Jason did not sing as he drove home. All he could think about were Silverman's words. "You and I both know it needs my signature as well." If Silverman was to meet with a tragic accident then he was off the hook. Yes, if only Silverman could die.

CHAPTER 13

Griggs was looking forward to meeting the famous, or as some of the senior officers in the force might say, infamous, ex-Chief Inspector, Sandy Neil. He might well have retired from the force, but his amazing reputation lingered on. Admittedly, most of the gossip was about the double-page spread he got in News of the World when he won his discrimination case. It couldn't have been very pleasant for him to have his dirty linen washed in public, even if he did win in the end. By all accounts his wife must have been quite a goer, but the Deputy Commander should have known better. Not surprisingly after the headlines, 'Commander has sex with Chief Inspector's wife while assigning him to overnight cases', the Commander had retired early on the grounds of ill-health. Griggs had only ever met the Commander twice, once at a police dance, where he had reluctantly gone with Sharon as he was told it would help his career, and the other was at a lecture given by the Commander about the importance of keeping the family happy to create a contented police force. *He certainly tried hard to ensure that at least one police wife was satisfied,* thought Griggs.

Griggs couldn't say that he was taken by the man.

As far as he was concerned, he was the usual climber, the sort who knew how to use the correct tools at dinner and not disgrace the Chief Constable. There was no chance that Griggs would ever sit at such a table. Nackington Road Comprehensive didn't have the same ring as Harrow and the Dalston College of Further Education hardly matched up to Oxford. No, the only advantage he had over such people was that he could catch villains, while they only seemed good on television. Fascinating as the sex story was, Griggs was more interested in how Neil had arrested Morrison. He had read a paper about it and was very impressed by Neil's lateral thinking which led to the result. The story was that everyone knew Morrison was a wrong-un. He had been investigated by the Inland Revenue, the VAT, Customs and Excise, his local police force, the City of London Fraud Squad and even Scotland Yard. Each investigation was extremely thorough, but always proved to be unsatisfactory. As a last resort it was given to the Serious Fraud Office. Griggs imagined that all the officers were queuing up for such a tantalising case! Chief Inspector Sandy Neil drew the short straw and so had to work out a strategy which was different from everyone else's. He spent the first week or so looking through all the papers from the previous investigations. At the end of that time, he couldn't see any direct area that had not been well covered. He even considered recommending not to bother any further, as in his opinion it would be a waste of the SFO's valuable time. But finally, he thought he could give it one last try. He decided to investigate thoroughly everyone who came into contact with Morrison, the bank clerks, the junior managers, fund managers assistants, all of the small fry. The results were amazing. He found a badly paid bank clerk driving a new Porsche, a telecommunications engineer spending regular holidays in the Caribbean. From these small beginnings, he built up a water-tight case against Morrison, firstly for bribery and corruption then as the contact cracked, he learnt more and more about the major fiddles that gave Morrison his international playboy life-style.

Morrison found out how close Neil was getting and fled to Australia. Neil completed the work, got the charges sorted out and flew to Sydney, where he got Morrison extradited and brought him back home in triumph. His picture was on the front pages of all the serious papers this time, giving him a much fairer press coverage than before. By all accounts Neil was one of the brightest of the bunch in his day and it would be interesting to finally meet him, particularly as Griggs wasn't totally convinced, despite all the evidence, that Mrs Valentine really was a murderer.

Neil arrived on the dot and was shown up to Griggs' personal cupboard, which he shared with a three-drawer filing cabinet, a small desk and two battered old chairs. His first impressions of Neil, as he stood in the doorway, was that he looked far too young to have retired. *In fact*, thought Griggs, *he looks younger than I do. Perhaps Sharon's right, I do need that holiday.*

"Come in, Mr Neil," he said, holding out his hand.

"Thanks, but please, call me Sandy, everybody does."

"Fine, Sandy it is then. Please sit down." He

indicated a battered ladder-back chair that must have come from the original Scotland Yard. "I won't pretend I don't know your reputation, Sandy. Any senior officer that takes the Deputy Commander to an industrial tribunal and wins is never likely to be forgotten. If that wasn't enough, to finally nail Morrison when everybody else had failed. What a way to retire, fly to Sydney, make the arrest, get extradition and return in triumph. To put in a sporting connection, you were a quality player. I have to point out your experience was mainly in fraud, and you have left the force. Which means you are like anybody else, a civilian, your previous service gives you no special rights. When was your last murder case, twenty years ago? The thing about murder, it often tends to be unpremeditated. So it brings out a different set of problems."

Sandy sighed and looked at him with his strong penetrating eyes, willing him to get on with what he had come for – the Valentine case.

"Oh yes, all right – so I'm teaching my grandmother to suck eggs but nevertheless, it was worth saying. You're working for Nicola Valentine and you want my help. That's if I can legally give you any. My best advice then is to give up now, save yourself a lot of time and Mrs Valentine a lot of money. You see it's an open and shut case, I'll give it to you straight as we see it."

Sandy leant back in the uncomfortable chair wondering as it was so old, did Sherlock Holmes use the very same one? He looked across at Griggs. It was important not just to hear what he said about the case but also to be able to judge the man himself. His first impressions were favourable. Griggs was a small dark-haired man with an odd taste in suits. His grey eyes were unusually bright and gave Sandy a distinct impression of a man with a good brain. It would be interesting hearing what he had to say.

"Let's start with the motive, it's normally the key when it comes to murder. Money normally comes into it somewhere. In this case the only one to benefit is your client. We've checked the will, insurance policies and pensions. Everything is left to Mrs Valentine, no other legacies. Fact one – nobody else stood to benefit from his death.

"Valentine was a shit of the first order. This is something everybody agrees on. He was a real ladies' man, a right two-timing bastard. He treated his wife like dirt and he couldn't care less about her feelings. From what I gather he was even at it before the honeymoon was over. Recently he's been so indiscreet with his latest woman, friend Rebecca Fielding, that he would have tried the patience of a saint. I admit by itself it's not a strong motive but it gets worse. She claims her husband wouldn't give her a divorce, however, according to Rebecca Fielding, Valentine had said she was religious and so she didn't believe in divorce. Fielding claims Valentine was going to insist on a divorce on the evening when he was murdered. From what Piers Lamont, her boyfriend, says, she was also going to ask that night for a divorce. Supposing she chose an alternative method of setting herself free?

"All right, I can see from your face you don't buy it, well perhaps I wouldn't if I was in your position.

"There are a lot of other things but let's get on

with the evening of February the fourteenth. You probably don't remember but it was cold enough that night to freeze the balls off a brass monkey. Mrs Valentine claims, after she was dropped off at around eleven thirty she went for a long walk. Said she wanted to get her arguments sorted out. She says she walked for over an hour but she doesn't remember where she walked, nor did she see anybody. Christ Sandy, in over an hour in central London, she saw nobody? Then we're asked to believe she entered the house and saw a mallet lying on the floor. Being a good wife and knowing how important the thing is to her husband she picked it up, grasping it firmly, and put it on the desk. Only then did she apparently see his body. Again, she claims she thought he was drunk and turned him over, getting blood all over her. Now wasn't that convenient?

"Did she then phone for an ambulance? The police? No, did she heck! She sat down and went over her life with Valentine, a sort of golden moments show. I ask you, would you do that? No, of course you wouldn't, nor would any normal person. Valentine died between ten p.m. and two a.m. according to our pathologists. Your client phoned at twelve fifty-two a.m. which means she has one hour twenty-two minutes with no alibi at the time he was killed.

"When you think about it, it's obvious what happened. They had a bloody great row, he probably turned violent and attacked her. She snapped, picked up the nearest object which happened to be the gavel and beat him to death. Self-defence. It happens! The jury will understand. Tell her to go for manslaughter, plead guilty with diminished responsibility. She'll be out in three to four years."

Sandy sat up and looked Griggs in the eye.

"That's excellent advice if she did it, but I don't believe she did, she's far too nice."

"Oh, she's far too nice is it? Are we getting a bit emotionally involved? Oh dear! Mind you, I agree she's a nice attractive lady. We both know that nice people don't kill, do they?" Griggs was warming to his subject now, he smiled at Sandy as he continued.

"Let me tell you a little story. I had a sweet old grey-haired grandmother in here a couple of weeks ago; she reminded me of my own dear departed mother. This nice old lady been living with a man for forty years. It now turns out that she had hated him for most of that time. One day while she was preparing the Sunday roast she decided that enough was enough. She picked up a carving knife and, Bob's your uncle.

"We both know anyone can commit a murder, given the right circumstances, even nice people. I wish you well. She is an attractive lady and if, that's a big if, she is innocent, I honestly hope you prove it. Keep me informed. Now I've got a crime meeting I've got to go to. You don't have to rush off nobody will come in here, so you sit there and finish your coffee. This is the Valentine file. Don't even think about looking at it, as you know that would be improper."

With that, Griggs left with a wink and Sandy immediately delved into the records. It was as he suspected, a fairly thorough look at the other suspects but it was clear that Griggs had been sure it was

Nicola from the start. Sandy couldn't really blame him, in most cases it was the husband or wife or the person who found the body. From Griggs' point of view he apparently had it handed to him on a plate. Sandy didn't learn much new from the files and left, mentally noting that he owed Griggs a favour.

CHAPTER 14

Sandy awoke early the next day with a start. He'd not quite drawn the curtains properly the night before, so the piercing light from the early morning sun beamed directly into his eyes. He came to life immediately; he lay looking at the hideous floral wallpaper which made a perfect combination with the vile colour of the carpet. Sandy reflected that if ever he was going to choose two colours that should never to go together, it would be the colours of that wallpaper and the carpet. He pondered why anybody in their right mind would choose that particular combination. The only sensible answer he could come up with, was that they were not in their right mind. He lay worrying about Nicola's problems and how best to prove her innocence as quickly as possible. He looked across to the empty part of his bed and wished that Nicola was lying there as his wife. Then he knew it was pipe dreams, what on earth would she want with a poor ex-policeman like him, living in this vile furnished flat?

He decided to visit some of the possible suspects. He got dressed as smartly as he could. If he was dealing with smart city types it wouldn't do to turn up as a country bumpkin. He had his usual quick breakfast of toast and thick-cut marmalade specially sent down by an old Scottish aunt, who was convinced he was starving to death after his marriage broke up. He drank his pot of tea then walked round to the garage where parked was his latest pride and joy, the Saab 900 CD turbo convertible that he'd bought second-hand from Mark Cheshire.

The morning was bright and fairly warm for the time of the year so he opened up the hood straight away. As he drove across London to his first appointment at Roland Silverman's house, he reflected that being a private detective certainly had its compensations.

Roland Silverman lived in one of those exclusive squares close enough to Harrods for shopping convenience, yet peaceful enough to imagine you were out in the suburbs. As Sandy arrived at Hereford Square he realised at once he was going to have a problem disposing of the car. In the end he parked in a residents only bay and hoped nobody would notice. The last thing he required that sunny morning was a nasty yellow clamp. The house was a magnificent five-storey building and would be worth millions on the open market. However, Sandy had already learnt that Silverman only rented, for appearance's sake, and from what he gathered he was even finding the rent difficult to pay.

Sandy pushed the heavy brass bell and waited patiently at the top of the immaculate white steps. The heavy blue door was opened by Silverman himself, who wore dark grey trousers with a matching waistcoat, blue striped shirt and the old school tie. At least it looked like an old school tie, but Sandy knew

Silverman went to a state comprehensive and like so many things in his life, it was misleading. There were many things in Silverman's past that he preferred to conveniently forget or gloss over.

"Come in, won't you?" said Silverman. "I was just having my morning cup of tea. Won't you join me?"

He ushered Sandy along a pleasant corridor into a beautiful drawing room filled with expensive-looking antiques. The walls were covered with what looked to Sandy like old masters, not that he knew much about art.

"You have an impressive home," said Sandy, not letting on that he knew it was rented furnished.

"Thank you, I'm rather pleased with it myself. It's my sanctuary. My place to be able to get away from all the commercial pressures. Particularly now that Richard Valentine's dead, I seem to get lumbered with everything. Now if I understand it, you're trying to help Mrs Valentine with her dreadful predicament."

"Yes, that's the position in a nutshell. I'm trying to prove her innocent."

"Oh I've no doubt Nicola is innocent, no doubt at all. I just can't imagine what the police are playing at charging her, it's got to be a dreadful mistake. Probably some drugged-up thieving oaf looking for money for his fix. One reads about it all the time in the papers. I'd be delighted to help in any way possible. Fire away."

Sandy got out his notebook and pencil.

"Can we start with any enemies he might have? Can you think of anyone who might benefit from his death or hate him so much they might murder him?"

"Well let's not beat round the bush. Valentine was not a popular man. Mind you, he didn't care, he did his own thing and ignored the rest of us. He was self-contained."

"How did you get on with him?" asked Sandy.

"Oh, fine. We had a good working relationship. We weren't what you call friends as such but we respected each other's abilities."

"Have you any ideas who might have done it?"

"Only long shots, I'm afraid. As far as I can see it was probably a burglary that went wrong. I doubt if the killer knew him. However, you might talk to Alec Nash."

"What was his relationship to Valentine?"

"Nash sold us his company for twenty million pounds. He was convinced we said there'd be no job losses, he got angry when Valentine sacked most of the staff. Nash even threatened Valentine's life according to Roger Devon, our company lawyer."

"When was this?" asked Sandy.

"Ironically on the morning of his death, the fourteenth of February."

"Yes, that is interesting. Did Valentine say there would be no job losses?"

"Probably, he was a canny negotiator, he didn't care what he said as long as it wasn't written into the contract. He always played a dirty game, he actually enjoyed it."

"Thank you. Can you think of anybody else I

ought to talk to?"

"I don't like to tell tales out of school and all that but Valentine was a great one for the ladies. His latest mistress, Rebecca Fielding, also threatened him. Valentine thought it was rather funny. In fact she threatened him on the fourteenth of February."

"And where can I find this Rebecca?"

"Here," said Silverman, writing on his card. "I've given her address and also Nash's. Wish I could be more help."

The audience was over. Sandy quickly found himself again out in the square. He went back to the car and drove off slowly.

There was something wrong with his interview with Silverman. For a start he found it amazing that Silverman didn't mention Jason Roberts. After all, in anybody's book he must be the favourite. As far as Sandy was concerned the fact that he didn't mention Roberts was significant. He had to have a good reason. Hopefully by the end of the investigation he'd work out what it was.

He didn't take to Silverman, who was a man who'd built up a strong position from nothing. Sandy wondered just how far he'd go to protect it. Murder? Sandy thought it was a distinct possibility.

Next time he saw Mr Silverman, he thought he might possibly mention the row and see how he reacted. In the meantime though, he had an appointment to see Jason Roberts at his country home in Mersham.

He drove back along the embankment, crossing

the Thames at Chelsea Bridge. He then tacked round London until he picked up the A20/M20 and glided off down through the beautiful Kent countryside.

Despite the traffic it only took him an hour and a bit to get down to Roberts' country house. Mersham was an extremely pretty village full of chocolate-box, rose-covered cottages interspersed with the odd mansion with immaculate lawns and shrubberies. After driving round for a while trying to locate the house, he drove up the gravel drive and parked outside at approximately eleven thirty. The door was opened immediately and Roberts came out. Sandy didn't need to be a doctor to realise that Roberts was not a well man. His hair was too long and badly needed cutting. He had either shaved that morning with a blunt blade or he'd done it blindfolded. He'd cut himself in several places and had a large sticking plaster on his chin. His face had a grey, sallow look and his eyes were like two new steaks that needed hanging for a time before they were eaten. Nothing about his outfit went together. The jacket didn't match the trousers and shirt matched neither again. He wasn't wearing a tie and his shoes distinctly needed cleaning. He looked a total wreck.

"Come in," he stuttered, "I've been expecting you. I'm afraid my wife's not here at the moment. She's on a school trip with the PTA but then I suppose you really want to see me. Come in, come in. Would you like a drink?"

Sandy realised that he already had put away a number of drinks that morning. Far more than were good for him, but to be sociable Sandy joined him in a small whisky. That was another good thing about being private, you could at least have the odd drink rather than resort to the old cliché, "Not while I'm on duty."

They sat down together in the sitting room which was pleasantly furnished and decorated. Sandy assumed it was Roberts' wife's touch as it certainly looked a feminine room.

"What can I do for you then?" asked Roberts.

"I'm working for Nicola Valentine, trying to establish her innocence, and I much hope you'll be able to help me."

"Poor old Valentine. He was a nice chap, you know. Gave me my start in the company. Really cut me up, losing him. He was like a father to me, you know. As for Nicola, of course she couldn't have murdered him, it's absolutely silly. So naturally I'll do all I can to help, but I'm afraid it won't be much."

"I understand Valentine was not popular in the business world and he had quite a few enemies."

"Well, that's natural of course. He was a hard man. He did some tough deals. I can't imagine anyone would want to hurt him, though. Leastwise not physically. I know a lot of them would want to hurt him as far as his business was concerned, but then that's what you would expect."

"Wasn't there one particular man that he had a row with?"

"Oh, you mean Alec Nash. Yes, he had a row but I can't imagine Nash doing anything. He did get angry and threaten to kill Richard but it was just words, I can't think for one minute that he meant it."

"Had he got a genuine grievance?"

"Oh yes, oh yes. Richard tricked him. Silly fool didn't get what he wanted into contract. Ought to know better really, a man of his age. He certainly thought we weren't going to shed any jobs but it was always on the cards. What Nash didn't realise was that we had surplus capacity in some of our other more modern factories, all we wanted was the contracts and some of his design."

"Don't they call it asset stripping in the city?" asked Sandy sarcastically.

"Well I suppose it was a form of asset stripping and that's why, of course, Alec Nash was so angry. He could have probably got more money if he'd have broken the company up himself but he felt he owed a duty to the workforce to safeguard their jobs."

"What about women?" continued Sandy. "I gather Valentine was quite a one for the ladies."

"Oh yes, he was. A definite sexual athlete. Never a dull moment. Different one every other day until he met Rebecca."

"Was he serious about this one?"

"Well he might have been, he certainly acted differently about her but he dumped her recently. The one thing Richard would never want is a divorce. It could mean he would lose the one thing he loved."

"Nicola?" asked Sandy.

"No, Redwood. He wouldn't do anything to jeopardise his control of the company."

Oh dear, thought Sandy. *That certainly doesn't help Nicola.*

"How did you get on with Richard Valentine?"

"Oh, wonderfully. We got on like a house on fire. As I said, it was like losing a father. I'm very upset about it."

"Someone at the office mentioned you'd had a bit of a row with him on the afternoon he died. What was that about?"

"Row!" snapped Roberts. "I think that's putting it a bit strong. We did have a few words about the direction the company was going, but then we often had differences of opinion as far as the business was concerned. All directors do, that's why we have a board. I can assure you that it didn't add up to anything."

"Can you think of anyone else I should be talking to?"

"Can't think of anyone I'm afraid. I wish you well, Nicola's a charming lady and she certainly doesn't deserve this. Anything I can do to help, you can count on me."

During the interview Roberts had been pouring into himself regular slugs of whisky and the way he was going he was certainly not going to make old bones, thought Sandy.

As he drove off again back up the A20, Sandy wondered whether Roberts' wife Jane knew how serious their financial affairs were. It couldn't be long before the bubble burst and he lost everything. It would be hard on someone to lose such a beautiful house.

Sandy's last call that day was to a friend from his

days at the Serious Fraud Office. He was hoping that Paul Fisher would be able to shed some light on the financial side of Valentine's company.

Paul's office was situated in a small alley just off Fleet Street. It was conveniently placed between an old inn which Paul frequented regularly and an Italian bistro where he was less of a regular.

Paul Fisher was a small ginger-haired man with boundless energy, he seemed to be always on the move.

"Evening Sandy, too early for a tipple I suppose?"

"Well perhaps a small one," replied Sandy, knowing full well Paul would have one.

Having completed the formalities they sat down in comfortable chairs in the corner of Paul's somewhat chaotic office.

"Well what can I do for the ex-chief brain of the fraud squad?"

"Did you say brain or pain?" asked Sandy. Paul sighed and gave him a quizzical look.

"I'm working to try and prove Nicola Valentine didn't kill her husband. I'd like some help concerning Redwood if you can give me it."

"Anything to help an old chum, besides, you did me a number of favours, I still owe you."

"Right. I want your views on some ideas I've got. Supposing Valentine caught Silverman doing something irregular. Would he report him or would he pretend not to notice?"

"In normal circumstances he'd report it, but with

the Intercard take-over deal on, I'm not sure he'd have done anything. He couldn't really risk the share price going down."

"You mean if the share price dropped it could ruin the deal?" asked Sandy.

"The take-over depended on the value of the share price on the right day. Valentine was paying with paper, if the value of the shares fell then the paper transaction would be less attractive to the seller. If the share price fell below the transaction price then the deal would probably collapse. You know how these things work. Otherwise Valentine would have to pay more in shares. If he issued more shares, though, that would annoy the institutions that have already large holdings in his company so he was balancing on a knife edge. Valentine had also put in a lot of effort and his credibility was riding on the deal. If it had collapsed he'd have lost a lot of face in the city, and as you know they are an unforgiving bunch of bastards. So the answer to your question is that Valentine might have ignored or delayed action. Saying that, there's another problem that you will have to take into consideration."

"Problem aside, you mean in all probability the deal was so important he would not be able to do anything. It's a thief's dream scenario – they win if they get away with it and also if they get caught. What's the other problem?"

"Silverman's been selling his shares in the company. If Valentine knew of any irregularities, and it could be proved he knew, then he'd be aiding and abetting an illegal act. Silverman would be guilty of insider trading with Valentine condoning it. It would

179

ruin them both, I can't see Valentine gambling everything."

"All right. What about Jason Roberts?"

"Well it's the same story except Jason Roberts of course hasn't been selling his shares. He hasn't got any left to sell. I can't imagine that Valentine would jeopardise his big deal unless Roberts had really screwed up," said Paul Fisher. Sandy tipped his chair back against the wall, his face wrinkled in thought.

"Suppose then, Roberts is up to no good and Silverman found out. What would he do?"

"Ironically nothing again, he couldn't afford a scandal because he's been selling his shares and needs to keep selling. From what I've heard on the grapevine he's got a bit of a problem with Lloyds. So he'd probably turn a blind eye too."

"How about this for an idea?" said Sandy. "Supposing Roberts was guilty of, say, a big fraud and Silverman found out about it. If he continued selling his shares he'd be guilty of insider trading."

"Yes, of course. If Silverman knew they were into financial problems any shares he sold after that would be considered insider dealing, in other words using privileged information to make money. If that is the case you've got two good motives for murder. Remember though, we're only guessing. Anyway drink up, we'll pop round the Grapes for a bite to eat and a pint."

"What's the word in the city about the Redwood Group?" asked Sandy.

"Basically, wait and see, wait and see. No quick

judgements but ready to abandon ship if necessary. The shares have fallen quite considerably since Valentine's death and the fund managers would bail out tomorrow if they have more bad news."

With that, they popped next door for a pleasant steak and kidney pie, a pint of Shepherd Neame's best Spitfire ale, and an evening of reminiscences of previous frauds that they had both investigated.

CHAPTER 15

Sandy heard the music long before he got to the house in Oakley Gardens; he didn't know what it was but he recognised it as hauntingly sad music, the sort he knew she played often. Sandy feared the worst as he rang the doorbell. It was a while before she answered it and even though she had tried to conceal the red eyes, it was clear to Sandy she had been crying again. He knew he never saw the real depths of despair she sank into, she was far too proud. He was proud of the way she coped and was glad she did cry privately, otherwise she was likely to suffer a breakdown. He wasn't to know that she had already had one. Nicola needed to get out of that house and so he persuaded her to go out with him for another Chinese meal. He told her it was to get more background information about the case, but he was lying. He found he enjoyed her company so much he wanted nothing better than to be with her all the time.

It was funny how these things of the heart affect you. Just being beautiful was never enough. Love was a mixture of all things – voice, smell, intelligence and mutual respect. Sure, sex fitted into the equation for Sandy, but it was not as important as the modern magazines would have people believe. Sandy liked sex as much as the next man but he wanted far more from any female companion. If he'd have listed the qualities required then Nicola would top his most wanted list, she was perfection. He hoped she felt something for him, but it was early days and the most important thing was to get a not-guilty verdict. After that, who knows? All Sandy could do was hope.

During the evening Nicola told him a bit about her early disasters. How she'd lost her fiancé days before the wedding, how Richard Valentine had rescued her from her trough of despair and how good it had been before they got married. She also told him how quickly Piers backed away once she'd been charged. She laughed and flashed her beautiful blue eyes at him.

"Do you know he was so gutless that he got his mother to phone me to say it was all over? How she enjoyed it too, she never liked me. Don't look so sad, Sandy, it's all right. I know what I'm going to do if you get me off. I'm not destined to have a successful relationship, I'm going to buy a little cottage with wisteria and roses growing round the door. I'll live there in the country with a couple of cats and become a local character."

Sandy didn't say as he would have liked, that he would be quite happy to replace one of the cats. Instead he replied, "I'd better get you home. I've got a busy day tomorrow. I'm driving down to see Alec Nash."

It was still a warm evening as they left the restaurant, so they drove back with the hood down. Sandy deliberately took a longer route so he could have more time with her. When he eventually pulled up outside her house she leant across and kissed him

183

lightly on the cheek, saying, "Thank you Sandy, I've really enjoyed myself."

With that, she slipped out of the car and quickly let herself into the house. She hadn't been in for long before he again heard that sad music.

Sandy sat thinking about the case for a few minutes before he drove off. He was intrigued by the fact that Silverman hadn't mentioned Roberts at all and that Roberts hadn't mentioned Silverman. Could they be in a conspiracy together? Could it be a more complicated fraud than he'd imagined? Did either have a hold on the other? He was sure that between them there was the answer to his problems but he just couldn't put his finger on it at that present moment.

First on the agenda in the morning was the angry ex-company boss, Alec Nash. He lived in a country house in the middle of a golf course. The setting was breathtaking as Sandy drove down the drive. The garden was a blaze of colour – rhododendrons, cistus, roses and ceanothus, were flowing in large banks of brilliant colours, all sorts of reds, white, yellow, mauve and the most incredible blues that Sandy had ever seen. The house itself looked like it needed attention. The rendering was in bad repair and the roof looked in urgent need of replacement. It hadn't been painted in a month of Sundays. Certainly the Nashes cared more about the garden than they did about the house.

The front door was opened by a plump, dark-looking lady wearing a floral dress.

"Mrs Nash?" asked Sandy.

The plump lady giggled.

"No, I'm Mrs Nash's cleaner. I'll fetch Mrs Nash."

With that she went off, muttering to herself, "Me, Mrs Nash," and giggled further at the thought of it.

As a dignified elderly lady came down the corridor Sandy realised how stupid he'd been.

"Good morning," said Mrs Nash. "I assume you're Mr Neil. My husband is expecting you. Do come through."

She led Sandy along corridors and on into an extremely large living room. Everything about it indicated comfort. Most of the furniture was good quality but old. There were ring marks on most of the tables. The Nashes liked to live in a house rather than a museum. Sandy liked that, it made a refreshing change.

Alec Nash was a large grey-haired man who looked like he might have been quite a sportsman in his day. He was comfortably dressed in a pair of old brown corduroy trousers and what had been an expensive sweater. Sandy assumed correctly, as it happened, that when the business was finished he'd be back into his garden. He looked at Sandy for a while, as if summing him up.

"You're a private detective, but you look more like a proper policeman than the other man that came here."

"I was a Chief Inspector before I retired," said Sandy.

"That accounts for it then. How can I help you?"

"As I explained on the phone I'm working for Mrs Valentine. You know she's been charged with the murder of her husband. I don't believe she's guilty and so I'm trying to help her. I understand you saw Valentine on the morning of the fourteenth of February and had a few words."

"Well I wouldn't put it like that," said Nash.

"How would you put it then?"

"We had a bloody great row. I know the man's dead and you shouldn't speak ill of the dead, but he was a shit, a shit of the first order."

Mrs Nash, who was embroidering in the corner, looked agitated.

"I'm sorry Grace, but he was a shit. Anyway I told him so to his face. I half killed him as well. I admit it. I don't have any regret, why should I? I enjoyed it."

"You half killed him?" said Sandy, amazed he was hearing such a confession. "What did you do?"

"Well I was so angry with him and he was so smug I grabbed him over the desk and shook him like a rat. Silly thing to do. Made me feel better, I can tell you. I also told him I'd get even with him. All of this was in front of witnesses which wouldn't be sensible if I was going to kill him that night, would it?"

Sandy had to admit to himself that it wasn't a good build-up for a murder. He also found he liked the old belligerent man.

"I don't suppose you know anything that might be helpful to me about the company or Valentine?" asked Sandy.

"Not really, I'm afraid. In reality I'm one of your best bets, aren't I? You hoped I'd bashed his head in and might like to confess this morning to save you a lot of bother. Sorry to disappoint you, but I didn't.

Mind you, I've got no alibi for the evening. Grace was away staying with her sister. But if you'll take my advice, I'd look elsewhere for someone with a more likely motive for murdering him."

Sandy shut his notebook and changed the subject.

"I must say Mrs Nash, you've got a beautiful garden. It must be wonderful just being able to walk round it."

"It's all Alec's work," said Grace, his wife. "He doesn't have anyone to help him. He works all hours he can on it. He's extremely proud of it."

"Have you enough time for me to walk you round?" asked Nash.

"Yes," said Sandy, "I'd be delighted."

Sandy spent an enjoyable ten minutes walking in that small piece of paradise. He was sad to leave it.

"I think your garden's the most beautiful I've ever been in. Thank you for showing it to me."

As he drove off he could see Alec Nash standing in the doorway. Sandy couldn't imagine Nash going to Valentine's house and bashing his face in. He had to agree that he should look for more fertile ground.

CHAPTER 16

When Nicola suggested going to the opera Sandy's first reaction was sheer panic. He tried to think of a good reason why he couldn't go but he'd already washed his hair and hadn't got any thank you letters to write. Sure, he wanted to go out with Nicola, but he had the horrible feeling he might have more fun filling up his VAT form. He had, in fact, never been to an opera, but instinctively knew he would not like it. Sandy realised that it was important to Nicola so in that case a couple of hours listening to a lot of foreigners warbling shouldn't hurt him. Besides, he could take her out for a meal afterwards and would make even the rack bearable. Nicola had bought two tickets months before all of her present troubles had erupted, to see the Royal Opera Company perform the Egyptian Helen by Strauss at the Royal Festival Hall. She had originally been going to go with Piers, but since his mother had dumped her on his behalf so unceremoniously, she couldn't think of anyone else she would like to ask. The famous opera house in Covent Garden was being redeveloped in a hundred million pound scheme at the taxpayer's expense, so the company was homeless.

"Don't look so worried," said Nicola, when she

invited him, "you'll enjoy it. The music will be fantastic and it'll be worth it just to see the sets and the costumes. They will be spectacular."

Even so, Sandy did worry.

On the evening of the performance he put on his best grey suit, which he had had cleaned especially. His shoes shone so he could see his face in them. He wore his favourite shirt and had tied his tie just right. At least he wouldn't let Nicola down with his appearance.

They took a taxi to the Festival Hall. When they arrived the first thing that hit Sandy was the dress code. He had naively thought that people would dress up for the opera, admittedly some did, but the majority had just not bothered. In fact some looked as if they'd just crawled out of bed.

While he was looking round he noticed the drinks stand. They both wandered over and found that they were being offered smoked salmon sandwiches and champagne for the interval.

"Well, let's do it in style," he said, "would you like to be spoilt in the interval?"

"I think you might need it," she laughed, "better order a bottle."

After arranging this treat Sandy bought them a gin and tonic each and they sat at the corner of the bar watching the world go by. At least Nicola did; Sandy was too busy watching Nicola. Her blue outfit brought out the blue of her eyes, her hair shone under the bright lights and her face radiated a fantastic glow. Just as he was enjoying himself the irritating buzzer started, indicating the performance was about to start.

They had to drink up the gin and tonics quickly and climb the steps and enter the auditorium.

It didn't take Sandy long to realise that there was no curtain, nor set. The orchestra filled the entire stage with a few empty seats, presumably for the singers.

"Ah, perhaps you won't get the lavish sets and the beautiful costumes," said Nicola giggling, "but the music will be good and if you want you can follow it in the programme. There's a complete translation from the German."

Sandy studied the programme and quickly understood the basic story.

"Well I hope Helen of Troy will live up to her reputation," he said to Nicola. "The most beautiful woman in the world, I'll enjoy watching her."

"I think I will prefer Paris. After all, he was supposed to be near perfection."

When the performers arrived they were both in for a big disappointment. The diva playing Helen was rather large; she certainly didn't rank as one of the world's most beautiful women in Sandy's opinion. As for Paris, he was killed off-stage and never appeared. Helen's husband was so odd it was obviously why she'd run off with Paris in the first place.

Sandy found his mind wandering while the performance was on. At first he looked at the audience and was struck with the number of pairs of young men, normally one old and one young. His father warned him about opera and ballet and it appeared to Sandy, he had been correct in his basic assumptions.

He was also fascinated by the conductor, who was the Jonty Rhodes of the music world. He was extremely energetic, jumping up and down like a jack in the box. Occasionally he glanced at Nicola, who was totally absorbed and enjoying it. Sandy resolved for her sake to try to like it, after all, he wanted to take her to the Test Match.

As he sat there he started thinking about the case. Although he was certain that Nicola was innocent, he was still not sure which of all his suspects was guilty. They all had good motives and each of their alibis were not very convincing. He started going over the list in his head.

Roland Silverman, the company chairman. He was clearly in deep financial trouble. Lloyds had all but ruined him and the demands just kept coming in. He had joined three groups and he couldn't have picked a worse three if he'd have tried. He'd borrowed heavily and had sold over seventy-five percent of his shares. It was possible he had done something that Valentine had found out about. If that was so, it would certainly give him a good reason to commit murder. As for his alibi, it was virtually non-existent. According to Silverman he'd gone to meet a Colonel Jones, a fellow Lloyds sufferer who was desperate to talk about his problems. Silverman had gone to the St Ermine's Hotel, near St James and waited in the bar. The Colonel never came; he had decided in the end that he'd had enough and committed suicide, so no alibi for Silverman here. The suicide was genuine enough, but it would have been easy for Silverman to have known about the death and concoct his story. No, as far as Sandy was concerned, Silverman was still his joint favourite.

Mind you, Silverman's financial problems paled into insignificance when compared with Jason Roberts. He was up to his neck in debt and facing total ruin. It always amazed Sandy how men of a certain age suddenly became complete fools. He accepted the girl was attractive but to destroy his life and his wife and children's seemed, to Sandy, completely irresponsible. It was likely that Roberts was on the fiddle, in fact he had to be, just to survive. Again, if Valentine knew or even suspected then he had a powerful motive. His alibi was in many ways worse than Silverman's. He claimed he was so worried about his financial problems that he'd gone out for a long drive in his car, parked by the Thames and just looked at the water. Not only could he not remember exactly where he drove or where he parked but he apparently saw nobody. He did clearly remember, however, looking at the Thames. Valentine's house was close to the Thames so he could easily have been nearby. The other factor that seemed relevant to Sandy was Roberts' appearance. He looked like a man losing his mind and he was therefore unpredictable. He might well have solved his problems by committing murder.

He was just about to review the position of the other suspects when he realised the music was building up to a massive climax. It didn't take his degree in criminal psychology to work out that it was nearly half time. After clapping for what seemed like two or three hours, they eventually pushed their way out towards the stairs and rushed to the champagne bar on level three to grab a table.

"Well? What did you think of it?" asked Nicola.

"It must have been a major triumph judging by the applause. I'm surprised the audience had any hands left. Do they always clap like that?"

"Yes, it's a tradition, it doesn't mean anything, they just like clapping. You seemed absorbed by it. What did you make of it?"

"Interesting," lied Sandy. "I'd need to go more often to understand it properly. The music was good."

It seemed to Sandy that they'd hardly had time to sip the champagne when those nasty warning beepers went again. On their return to their seats Sandy was quickly aware he'd lasted longer than some of the other opera lovers. Quite a number of empty seats were to be seen and to his delight the old couple next to him had left, giving him some extra room for his long legs.

As the opera got going again he drifted back to his suspects. The next one on the list was the angry and disgruntled company director, Alec Nash. Sure, he was annoyed at being made a fool of. He was angry and rightly so. It's always dangerous to sup at the devil's table. However, Sandy couldn't see him killing Valentine because of it. His alibi was certainly weak, staying in all night watching television isn't the perfect cover for murder. He didn't really help his position by admitting he'd slept through most of it so couldn't tell the police about the programmes. Only a fool would organise an alibi like that and Nash did not strike Sandy as stupid. He'd noticed a video and a number of tapes in the sitting room so it would have been easy for him to record the programmes, watch them and then wipe the tapes. No, he didn't murder Valentine, it didn't make any sense. He was a rich man, if he felt that badly he could always give three million or so to his workers. Admittedly they'd only get ten thousand or so each but it would make them realise that he was genuinely duped. This would clearly make him feel better and he'd still have seventeen million left. Even if he'd given them half the money he got from the sale of the company he'd still be left with over ten million pounds. Threats are one thing but carrying out a murder is another. Sandy mentally crossed him off the list.

Next, he came to Rebecca Fielding. Again, she had certainly threatened Valentine, but while she was carrying his child it did seem a bit far-fetched to kill him. The only positive motive was hate and clearly, she loved him. She claimed he was going to ask Nicola for a divorce the night of his death. This was not helpful for Nicola, of course. The fact that Nicola claimed that she'd asked for a divorce and Valentine had refused might not go down well with the jury. Somebody was lying and a pregnant mistress might just get the sympathy vote. She had no financial motive as she had been left out of the will. No, as far as Sandy was concerned she had no real motive to kill him In fact, she was the real loser. He'd have felt sorry for her but for the fact she was sure Nicola did it to spite her. No, he couldn't see any reason to waste any more effort on her. It was Roberts or Silverman. He was not sure which one, however, but his money was on Silverman.

After beating his hands to a pulp for a second time, they left the Concert Hall and walked back to his car. Although he hadn't really enjoyed the opera, just being with Nicola was enough for Sandy. He had parked on Waterloo Bridge. He always tried to park up there because not only was it free, it was also easy to get away from in the after-show traffic. If you used the car parks, it could easily take twenty minutes to get out. It was a surprisingly warm evening and Sandy hoped it would be warm enough to eat outside. He had splashed out and booked a table at the Pont De La Tour, one of the most fashionable and expensive restaurants in London. They parked the Saab in the new Butlers Wharf car park; the original one, right on the Thames, was being redeveloped to provide even more expensive water-view flats.

"Did you know that people queued for thirty-six hours in order to place deposits on these flats? Seems silly really as they won't be able to live in them until the millennium and who knows what property prices will be like then," said Nicola.

"Probably be like those Jaguar super cars, you remember, the price fell so quickly that the deposits were worth more than the cars. You can still buy them new at £125,000 but at the time they were nearly three times as expensive, but who knows? The people who buy these might be lucky. Anyway, here we are at last."

"You can afford to eat here, in Conran's best! Business must be good or have you won the lottery?" joked Nicola.

"Don't worry about the cost, I'm working for a rich widow and we can claim it on expenses. She'll never know," said Sandy in as serious a tone as he could manage under the circumstances. "Young lady, it is not the done thing to kick your host in a world class restaurant, it's not what I would expect from an elderly widow."

Sandy was saved from more serious injury for at that moment they were shown to an outside table under the heater, so as to ensure they didn't freeze. As they sat gazing at the magical picture of an illuminated Tower Bridge and the City lights behind, Sandy was almost carried away with the romance of the moment, but the mood was broken by a dishevelled, drunken man who shambled by carrying a guitar, and glared at them as he went by.

"Wouldn't want to meet him on a dark night," said Nicola, "he looks and unpleasant sort."

They had just been served their starters when the shouting started. The restaurant went quiet as everyone strained to hear what was going on in the reception area. The noise got louder and the man appeared in front of the restaurant, swinging his guitar like a club at the band of five apprehensive-looking waiters who surrounded him and were herding him away from the restaurant. He was shouting something unintelligible as one of the waiters got a little too close and was clumped on the shoulder.

"Come on," said Nicola, "you were in the force, shouldn't you do something?"

"Certainly not!" said Sandy indignantly. "That's uniformed officers' work. Besides that, I'm an old and decrepit retired officer. Give the youngsters a chance, that's my motto!"

It didn't take long for the police to arrive. They appeared from all sides of the restaurant and to

Nicola's delight, a police boat, with its blue light flashing, appeared from the station across the river at Wapping. A second police boat arrived from Tower Bridge.

"It's obviously a quiet night in Southwark," said Sandy, grinning, "I can really imagine they need nine officers to arrest one drunk!"

By now there was quite an international crowd gathered to watch the show. The police handled it very quickly and the man was hurried away in one of the boats.

"I hope the manager of Millwall wasn't around," said Sandy. "He drew a bigger crowd than Millwall usually gets on a Saturday!"

Nicola laughed. The manager, holding his left arm in pain, came round to apologise to the guests, but most people treated him like a hero.

"The man is a madman," he said, "he put one of my waiters in hospital and a chef had to go home."

"There you are," said Sandy, "two shows in one night. I reckon mine was the most entertaining. You should stick with me, I know how to show a girl a good time!"

As the evening went on, Sandy realised that he was falling more and more in love with this beautiful woman. He loved to make her laugh and take the sadness from her, but he knew that there was really no future in it. They came from such different worlds. Still, he was going to enjoy it while it lasted.

CHAPTER 17

They were in the middle of their regular monthly partners' meeting at Pike and Neil. It wasn't a particularly nice day; the unusual warm days had given way to more normal spring weather. Rain was sheeting past the window and almost bouncing high enough off the pavement to reappear again. It was a gloomy grey day and was even more depressing after the recent false summer. The weather was reflected in Cheshire's mood; he didn't seem to be his usual cheerful self. Sandy had briefed them on his progress with the Valentine case and both Pike and Cheshire had listened carefully. The idea of these meetings was that the others could sometimes spot something obvious that the investigator had missed because he was too close to the action. From Sandy's story it was obvious to both of them that he was much more involved in the case than was usual.

"You seem rather close to your client," said Mark Cheshire, the company chairman and the only one with any business experience. "Is this wise? I know we must believe her innocent but the police do have an extremely strong case. You have to face the possibility, however small, that she did in fact murder her husband. It's not professional to get so involved."

"I know she didn't," snapped Sandy, a little too loudly for comfort in the small room. "However, I take your point."

Sandy sat back in his chair glaring across the table at Mark. Peter Pike didn't like it when his two friends were niggling each other. He decided to change the subject and bring a little humour into the meeting.

"Can I tell you about my Post Office job? It's a classic," he said triumphantly.

Both Cheshire and Neil were pleased to get away from the Valentine case and readily agreed.

"If you remember the problem was simple. Regular pilfering of registered parcels from the Borough Road main office. The Post Office investigation boys had been in but had found it difficult as it was so obviously an inside job. This always brings problems from the unions so the management decided to try us before the police. I interviewed all the staff and according to them, there was never a time of day when the registered mail was left alone and the offices weren't manned. They never stopped working throughout the whole day. From their own evidence it was clear that it had to be one of the postmen that was the thief. The office was one of those big old fashioned ones with great big fold-back doors which meant it was possible to get a good view from across the road. I borrowed a heap of a car, a mud-coloured Vauxhall, and sat watching the office. I could hardly believe my luck. At about eleven o'clock, there was a tea break and the entire floor cleared as if by magic. Almost simultaneously a small man wearing a blue anorak with the hood up walked into the office bold as brass and started checking the registered packets. The greedy bastard didn't just take a bundle, he had plenty of time for a good look and to pull out the ones he wanted. He then walked out and a few minutes later the place returned to normal. I followed the thief and noted his address. The next morning I got a member of the local CID to sit with me and we watched an almost identical performance. The man was arrested as he left the premises. When the police searched his flat they found enough evidence to send him away for a decent stretch. The result was the Post Office paid us a large fee and on top of that gave us a bonus as we cleared it up so quickly and they were so pleased it wasn't an inside job. The posties thought I was a super man solving the case, whereas I felt guilty getting so much money for nothing. The funny thing is, how often people forget simple things when questioned."

Sandy listened to the story carefully and found himself wondering if Nicola had forgotten anything. He resolved to interrogate her much more firmly and perhaps walk her round the area. If only he could find a witness who saw her out that night. His thoughts were interrupted when he heard his name being spoken aloud and realised he'd not been listening to what Mark had said.

"Can you do that for me?" asked Cheshire.

Not wanting to admit he wasn't listening, he agreed to whatever Cheshire had asked.

"Yes, I'll help, no problem," he said.

"Good, Mrs Mannering will be here about three o'clock, all I need is you to start the ball rolling and use your own judgement. I've put all we have in the file but it's not much. Incidentally, I'm sorry about Mrs Valentine, but you know I'm right. You should never get emotionally involved, it's a golden rule. Right then, I'm off to the funeral. I'll see you both soon."

As Cheshire left, Sandy realised Mark didn't normally wear a dark suit and black tie. So much for a top detective's observation.

"What funeral's that?" asked Sandy.

"I knew you weren't listening. It's his aunt's funeral. I think he was fairly attached to her. Incidentally, do you know anything about the Mannering case?"

Sandy shook his head.

"You got it bad! Mind you, she is rather special. It's all right for Cheshire, he's got perfection already. I hope it works out for you. Anyway all we know about Mrs Mannering is the fact that she thinks her husband was murdered. She thinks it's all part of a conspiracy, as far as she's concerned, to murder members of the MCC."

"Oh God. Is she sane?"

"Who knows? That's your problem," laughed Peter. "I've got some more financial stuff on Roberts and Silverman for you. The more I get into it the more desperate their positions get. They both have motive enough for fraud and if they were dipping into the treacle and Valentine caught them, it could give you the motive you need. Come on though, I've got twenty minutes. Do you want a pint over the road? I've got to be quick though, I'm replacing Tom on another stakeout job."

On his return from the Slug and Lettuce, Sandy rang Nicola and arranged to go round that afternoon. When he arrived he was determined to try the walk idea before the more aggressive interview. He wondered if it would be better getting Peter Pike to interview her. He wasn't sure he could do it.

The rain had at least temporarily stopped as they came out of the house, both wearing sensible rainwear.

"Now where did you go that night? Think. It is important."

They left the house and turned left onto Oakley Street; at the Thames end they continued along Cheyne Walk past Carlyle's House. Trouble was that Nicola had a mental block. The horror of the night had driven all thoughts of that fateful night from her head. As they headed back along Cheyne Gardens it started to drizzle, making Nicola even more depressed.

"Come on, this isn't working. I can't see going down with flu is the answer, if we cut back down the Row we can get home quickly."

As they were passing a detached house with a wooden fence running round its boundaries, a large black dog suddenly jumped up level with Nicola, snarling and showing its teeth. Nicola jumped back in terror and Sandy quickly grabbed her arm and guided her on past the house.

"A dog! That's what I saw. A dog!" shouted Nicola excitedly.

"Not a great witness, I'm afraid," said Sandy. "Juries don't tend to believe dogs."

"No, silly, not just a dog. A man was walking it. It was a huge dog and I was afraid of it. I've always been slightly afraid of big dogs."

Now this is much better, thought Sandy.

"What sort of dog and what did the man look like?"

"The dog was a great lollopy thing, a kind of overgrown greyhound with a shaggy mane. It seemed to have enormous energy and just bounded along."

"What about the man?"

"That's not easy," said Nicola, "I only saw him for a moment, tallish, well wrapped up. I'd say he was probably much thinner than he looked. Dark hair, I think, but it's all not clear I only saw him for a minute."

"Never mind, it could be gold, if only we can trace him. It shouldn't be that difficult."

They continued with the walk and when they got back to the house, Sandy immediately got her into the car and drove her to the nearest library. They got out some books on dogs and looked through together. After about twenty minutes, Nicola recognised her dog.

"I'm sure this is the one. It's called a lurcher."

"Right, I'll put a few advertisements in the papers, the only thing we now can do is keep our fingers crossed."

When Sandy got back to the office he drafted an advertisement which he hoped might produce results. He realised it was rather a long shot, but then if he could find that man with the dog he was on the way to opening up some sort of defence.

His eventual advertisement read:

"Lurcher owners. Were you walking your dog on the evening of fourteenth of February in the Oakley Street area of London? If so, could you please contact Neil and Pike on a matter of some urgency?"

He put in his phone number and placed it with the Telegraph, Times, Mail, Express and Evening Standard. All he could then do was wait and hope for the best.

Working on the same principle, he thought he'd have another go round the houses. Who knows? He might just pick up something else. He decided to interview everybody who lived in the immediate area of Nicola's house, just on the off chance.

The next morning Sandy set out on his mission. As always, when starting such a surveillance he was hopeful of finding some important new piece of the jigsaw that would mean Nicola would never have to face the ordeal of the court.

At the first front door he was welcomed by an extremely old lady.

"Come in," she said, "you've certainly taken your time."

Sandy was somewhat taken aback; whoever she thought he was, she was in for a disappointment.

"I'm afraid there seems to be some sort of misunderstanding."

"Don't stand there and mumble, young man! Come in, come in, you're wasting time."

The old lady hurried him down the corridor and Sandy had little option but to follow her. She took him into the kitchen where a tap was shooting water like a fountain all over the place.

She was lucky, as one of the few practical things that Sandy was any good at was fixing taps. He looked round and saw what he thought was the stopcock. He turned it off and to his immense satisfaction the fountain ceased.

"Oh well done, young man!" squealed the old lady, almost jumping up and down with joy.

"Have you any washers?" shouted Sandy in order to get his message across.

"There may be some in the cupboard under the sink," she replied, "and there's no need to shout, I'm not deaf."

Sure enough, there were washers in the cupboard under the sink and also a pair of pliers. Sandy stripped down the tap and replaced the washer, he then slowly turned the stopcock back on. To his great relief the washer held and the tap was fixed.

"Even if you do shout, young man, you're certainly a fast worker. How much do I owe you?"

"Nothing," said Sandy, "I'm not a plumber, I've come to ask you some questions. I'm a private detective."

"How exciting. Come in the morning room and I'll make us a nice cup of tea."

She settled him into an enormous armchair and then went back to the kitchen.

"A private detective! Well that's something to tell

them all at the bridge club tomorrow."

A few minutes later she returned with a tray covered with a beautifully embroidered cloth, two dainty cups and saucers and matching tea set, with a small plate of delicious-looking cakes.

"You're spoiling me," said Sandy, tucking into one of the cakes that she offered.

"Not at all. I've never met a real-life detective before. Have you always been a gumshoe?" she asked.

"No," he chuckled, "originally I was a real policeman, a Chief Inspector in the city fraud squad."

"Even better," she said, smiling. "I'll be a real celebrity at the bridge club tomorrow afternoon. Now, what can I do for you?"

Sandy explained about Nicola's plight and how he was trying to help her as he was convinced she was innocent.

"Oh it's all very romantic," said the little old lady, whose name Sandy had now been told, was Mrs Williams.

"What do you mean romantic?" asked Sandy, somewhat dreading the answer.

"Well you are in love with her, aren't you?"

"Is it that obvious?" said Sandy.

"I'm afraid so, young man, you can always tell. So you want to know about Valentine's Day."

"Well, mainly the evening and anything you can tell me that might be helpful."

"I'd like to help but I'm afraid I'm an old crock

these days and retire early. I was in bed by nine thirty, so I couldn't have seen anything. I did however, hear two cars. I don't know if that's any use."

"It could be. Have you any idea of the time you heard them?"

"Well the first one was a powerful car, the engine was large, it was probably a sports model. It arrived about eleven thirty and left almost immediately. It made a deep purring sound as it left."

That would be Piers and his Jaguar, thought Sandy.

"And what about the other one?"

"That was not so close, it left in a hurry though. I'd say about twenty-five minutes later, just about midnight. I can't tell you much about that car other than it must have been an ordinary sort of car. It sounded much like any other."

Sandy was interested in the second car as it could well have been the murderer departing. What was needed was a more extensive check in that neighbourhood. He wondered if he'd get the assistance of the local police. He better have a word with Detective Inspector Griggs.

He thanked Mrs Williams for her help, the cup of tea and the plate of cakes which he'd somehow devoured without even noticing. As he left an obvious plumber arrived wearing the traditional blue boiler suit and wearing a bored expression.

"You're too late," said Mrs Williams aggressively, "for all you cared I could have drowned! The police had to come and fix it for me. Good day."

With that, she firmly slammed the door in his face.

"Bloody old cow!" muttered the workman as he returned to his van.

Sandy laughed as he moved on to the next house. He knocked at the door and when he was just about to give up, a fat, red-faced man opened it. He had a nicotine-coloured bushy moustache and black Grecian 2000 dyed hair. He was certainly not one of the beautiful people.

"What it is you want? I can tell you straight away I don't buy from door-to-door salesmen."

Sandy believed him, but he was sure if it was a door-to-door off-licence, he might have been tempted, he stunk of whisky.

He explained the purpose of his visit and the fat man looked at him intently with his piggy eyes.

"Can't help you old boy, I sleep soundly. Nothing wakes me up. Heard nothing. Saw nothing."

With that, he backed away and firmly shut the door.

The next few houses produced similar stories. It was extremely cold on February the fourteenth and most people would have certainly been in bed if not asleep by eleven thirty.

He almost didn't bother with the final house. It had been a disappointing morning and Sandy was getting peckish. Duty called, however, so he climbed up the final steps, rang the bell and waited. An attractive lady of about fifty opened the door. Once again, Sandy went through his spiel of why he was there. The lady smiled at him.

"I'm terribly sorry, Mr Neil, I would have loved to

help Mrs Valentine but we were skiing in Klosters, as I told the police. The house was completely empty on February the fourteenth."

Sandy was about to go when a voice came from one of the nearby rooms.

"That's not completely true, Mother. I think you should ask the gentleman to come in."

Sandy was shown into a room where an attractive young lady was sitting drinking tea. She was, from her features, the daughter of the owner. Sandy sat down and before he could speak the mother started.

"What do you mean dear? Were you here on the fourteenth of February?"

"Yes, I ought to have told you but I worked on the principle of what you don't know doesn't hurt you."

"I still don't understand. Why didn't you tell me?"

"It's easy, Mum. Charles had asked me to marry him and I just wanted to be sure. A couple of weeks at home seemed to be a good idea of testing our relationship. That's why I didn't tell you. I thought you might be a little old fashioned. Now we are engaged, so the subterfuge was worth it. I should have told you but can't we talk about it later?"

"You're quite right," said her mother, suddenly remembering Sandy was there. "We'll talk about it afterwards. You've got something you feel you should tell Mr Neil."

"Did you see anything on the evening of the fourteenth when you were here, that might be helpful to Mrs Valentine?"

Bella thought for a moment.

"Is Mrs Valentine the rather pretty woman, about thirty-five, who lives almost directly across the road?"

"That would be a fair description of her," said Sandy.

"I think I saw her arrive home that night. A fabulous new green Jaguar XK8 coupé roared up about eleven. I recognised the car because I really fancy owning one, I think they're really cool. The lady got out, and a tall good-looking guy kissed her goodnight; he didn't make much of an effort though. I wouldn't have been satisfied if that's all I got at the end of an evening. He didn't stay long, and after he had kissed her he left. She stood out in the street for quite a while, then all of a sudden she suddenly came back to life and walked off down the road. I didn't see her again."

"You're sure she didn't go into the house, even for a few minutes?" asked Sandy excitedly.

"No, she didn't go into the house then, nor for at least another ten minutes."

Sandy was pleased. That was the first definite confirmation that Nicola did go for her walk. He could now at least be able to prove she was telling the truth about that.

"Did you see anything else that would help?"

"Charles was late. I was getting annoyed so I kept looking out of the window to see if I could see him. I did see a short fat man hanging about. He had an unusual way of walking, he brought his right leg right up to his left leg as he walked. I watched him as at first I thought he might be a burglar. But in the end he must have been just getting some fresh air, because he went back into his house."

"Can you remember which one?" asked Sandy hopefully.

"Well come to think of it, I think it was the same door the lady usually goes into. Have they converted the building into flats or something?"

"What sort of time was this?" asked Sandy. "Was it before, or after the lady arrived by car?"

"Oh, afterwards, but not long afterwards, probably about ten to fifteen minutes later. He might have been there earlier. I have a feeling I saw him but I couldn't swear to it."

"I'd like to get a full statement from you, if that's all right," said Sandy. "It's important we get this on paper and signed. I wonder if you could possibly go down to the offices of Walter Fitzwilliam, the city lawyers. I think what you've told me will be extremely useful and probably important. I'm grateful for your help. I realise it couldn't have been easy for you."

"Yes, I'd be delighted to help. She looks a nice lady. When will I have to go?"

"They'll get in touch with you. They might even be able to do it here to save you the trouble."

As Sandy got up to leave he noticed her mother sitting straight in her seat and he reckoned there would be words spoken after he'd gone. As the door closed he heard the first rumblings of what was to come.

"I think you've been extremely deceitful, dear. I just don't know what's come over you, it's since you've been at that college."

Oh dear, thought Sandy, *I'm not going to be their most popular visitor in that house this year.*

He drove slowly back to his office, parked the car, sat down and put all the relevant facts he had learned down onto paper.

Timetable

February fourteenth, evening. Eleven to eleven thirty, Nicola arrives with Piers and goes for a walk.

Eleven thirty five to eleven forty, unidentified man goes into Valentine's house. NB, **not necessarily Valentine's house, must check.**

Twelve o'clock, car revs up loudly close by and drives off quickly.

Twelve, twenty man with lurcher dog sees Nicola.

Twelve twenty five approximately, Nicola arrives back and finds dead body.

Twelve forty eight, Nicola phones the police.

Death occurred some time between ten and twelve thirty.

Notes.

Front door was unlocked. **Were the police aware of this? Must make sure we tell them.**

Sandy looked at his bit of paper for a while and then picked up the phone and dialled the lawyers' office.

"Can I speak to Fitzwilliam please? Ah, Walter it's Sandy. I've got some useful information about Nicola's alibi. I think we should meet. Can I come down this afternoon? No, shouldn't take long – say twenty minutes. Fine. Four p.m. it is, then."

Sandy suddenly realised he was hungry. When he looked at his watch he was amazed to see it was one forty-five. No wonder Walter was a bit cagey about time. He walked across to the Slug and Lettuce for a pie and a pint. He felt self-satisfied. *A good morning's work,* he thought.

Walter Fitzwilliam was a thin, wiry man in his late thirties. He'd been a key player in a large group practice but decided he wanted the challenge of his own business, so he had taken a large personal gamble on his own abilities and had formed Fitzwilliam and Co. Sandy wasn't quite sure who the 'Co.' was, if it was anybody. He had a feeling Walter felt it sounded much grander than just Fitzwilliam.

He was an able solicitor with excellent contacts in various chambers in the Inns of Court. Sandy had come across him a number of times during his time when he was in the City of London Fraud Squad and also at the Serious Fraud Office. Sandy was impressed with his energy, intellect, and the fact that he wasn't a raging snob like so many in the London solicitors' offices. Roger's office, although in a good area, was not the grandest you'd ever see. The fact he'd bought in his old discarded dining room table and chairs for the reception area didn't help the professional look of the entrance. Sandy didn't care about the superficial look of the place, all he was concerned about was the passion of the man. He knew he would fight with tooth and claw to get Nicola off. That was all that mattered to Sandy.

The main office was small and full of paper,

documents lay everywhere, on the table, the mantelpiece, over the books on the bookcase and also covered much of the floor. Walter was genuinely pleased to see Sandy. He was grateful that in his early days Sandy had recommended clients to him. He knew this present case was important to Sandy and he certainly didn't want to let him down.

Sandy went step by step through the information he'd received on his door-to-door investigation and the details of the lurcher dog story. He was pleased to see a broad smile on Fitzwilliam's face.

"This is good, Sandy, very good indeed. If you can find the dog walker then we can confirm the first part of Nicola's alibi. This will help enormously. No stone must be left unturned as far as this witness is concerned. He must be found. I also like the sound of the mysterious man hanging around. I think he'll go down well with the jury, if nothing else, it will confuse them and cast further doubt on her guilt. Pity the girl didn't see him leave. If we could tie him to the car leaving, then we've got an excellent alternative scenario. Mind you, with what she had in mind for the evening we are lucky to have what we have got. You were lucky she was in when you called and that she was prepared to speak in front of her mother. Not all girls of her age would have the courage. I'll organise someone to get a statement from her. We will make it as easy for her as possible. I also think we want a statement from your old lady, she's useful too. I think I'll send a car for her. From what you have said it will be a treat for her and she could hopefully even remember something else.

"I think we are on the up, Sandy. I've also been

doing some good work. I've been talking to an eminent lady psychiatrist who tells me that Nicola's reactions to the death of her husband are not untypical from the female point of view. It will be important to ensure there's enough women in the jury to understand that, as for most men it seems far-fetched."

"What's next?" asked Sandy.

"Well, I fixed up for Sir Edgar Ramsden to see Nicola on Tuesday. He's good, so she'll have the best defence possible. And as for you, find me that lurcher!"

The advertisement appeared the next day and Sandy desperately hoped for a phone call but none was forthcoming. He had to go to the office to keep his promise to Mark to see the lady about the MCC murders. He wasn't terribly excited about a serial killer knocking off members of the MCC. He knew many people that hated cricket, but murder? He thought not; that was extremely unlikely. He sat going over the bits and pieces of his present case until the appointed time of Mrs Mannering's visit.

He had to admit Mrs Mannering didn't look like a nutter. In fact she looked ordinary. She'd made a great effort with her clothes, which were her good ones. It was apparent that she didn't dress up often as she filled the room with the unmistakable aroma of mothballs. Although she'd made up carefully, her eyes were extremely puffy. It was obvious that she was still distressed about the death of her husband.

"Good morning, Mrs Mannering," said Sandy kindly. "Can I get you a cup of tea or coffee?"

"Might I have a glass of water, please? I don't

drink tea or coffee, it's got too much caffeine in it."

Sandy buzzed out to the secretary and almost immediately a jug of cold water and a glass appeared on the desk.

"Now Mrs Mannering, tell me about your husband's death and why you think he was murdered."

"Before I start, Mr Neil, I think it's important that you understand just how experienced a driver Jack, my late husband, was. He was the chief executive of Glinceo International, the pharmaceutical subsidiary of the American giant Keinzle. As you're probably aware the company has many chemical plants around Britain so Jack was always driving. He was a member of the advanced drivers' guild and regularly took refresher courses at the institute's testing and training headquarters in Saltdean. He normally would drive at least forty thousand miles a year and yet despite this he had never had an accident. You can see he was an able driver. On the day of his death he'd stayed overnight at the Royal Crescent Hotel in Bath. According to the hotel he'd had breakfast early in the restaurant, his car was brought round and he departed about nine o'clock. He never drank while he was on these company trips and this was confirmed by the hotel. At about eleven fifteen he was driving across the Black Mountains when he apparently lost total control of the car and plunged down into the river valley. The car caught fire and exploded. He didn't stand a chance. We'd been married nineteen years and our twentieth wedding anniversary was the day of his funeral."

Telling the story was extremely distressing and Sandy could see tears in her eyes. She sat back and bravely sipped her water. Sandy felt sorry for her, even so, he had to ask the question.

"What did the police say about the accident?"

"They said it was caused by his careless driving, His careless driving!" she screamed. "I ask you. My husband was never careless. As far as they are concerned the case is what you call closed. Mr Neil, I honestly believe my husband was murdered." She glared at Sandy as if to dare him to contradict her.

"I understand that you believed his death is somehow involved with the membership of the MCC. Why do you think that?"

"I bought with me some newspaper cuttings showing details of three separate murders. Each victim you'll see were members of the MCC. What I think is even more interesting there was no apparent motive for any of the murders. The other thing that stands out is they were all very well planned. The only obvious connection I could see is with the MCC."

"So you think it's a cricket-hater? Taking some sort of grizzly revenge?"

"Don't patronise me, Mr Neil, I'm not stupid. No, I think it's some problem with the MCC, I don't profess to know what it is. There has to be a connection otherwise it just doesn't make sense. Four deaths in three months now, I think you would have to agree that's significant."

She seemed far more relaxed after she had finished and sat watching Sandy, waiting to hear his comments.

Sandy looked at her news cuttings briefly and had to admit the deaths were strange.

"You do realise that an investigation of this sort would be expensive. We could easily be talking about tens of thousands of pounds. There's also the problem that we can't give any guarantees that we'll be successful."

"I quite understand that but money is not a problem. My husband was extremely wealthy so he's left me well provided for. I don't care if it costs a hundred thousand pounds. I want my husband's killers brought to justice."

"Good. I'll get the investigation going then and send you a contract to sign. We normally ask for some form of deposit. In this case I think it ought to be something like five thousand pounds. There will, I'm afraid, be VAT to pay on top of that. I'm in the middle of a large case at the moment, so another investigator will be in charge of your case. Our chairman, Mark Cheshire, also wants to be involved as he too is a member of the MCC. He would have been here today but for the unexpected death of his aunt."

"Thank you Mr Neil, I'm delighted that at last something's going to be done."

"Well, I hope we can live up to your expectations."

After Mrs Mannering had gone, Sandy made a few notes for Mark. It was almost certainly a load of old rubbish and he wished Mark the best of luck – he would certainly need it.

Mark would find it easy to work from within the MCC structure, being a member. He took the file through to Mark's office, put it on his desk and then drove back to his flat. He was feeling somewhat depressed as he had hoped for some news from the advertisement but nothing had yet materialised.

It was late in the afternoon. The office was hot and stuffy. Peter was getting a little tired of ploughing through endless records in order to find the evidence needed in a complex fraud case. He'd been at it all day and although he had been used to the painstaking sifting of paper, he'd never much enjoyed it. He realised it was important, but given a straight choice, Peter would always choose surveillance, particularly if it involved a three-strong car chase. But then, what red-blooded ex-spy wouldn't? He was also aware that he needed to know much more about the city and the financial scams that he'd never come across. He was teaching Sandy about his own skills and Sandy was showing him the sort of things he should be aware of when dealing with companies. He wandered down the corridor to Sandy's office for a break and hopefully, for some help.

"Coffee?" he asked as he walked in. Sandy leant back in his chair and stretched.

"Why not? I could do with a break. If you look in that cupboard over there by the window, you'll find a box of Jaffa Cakes. I'm starving."

As soon as the kettle boiled, Peter made two cups of instant coffee, adding milk and sugar to both. He brought them over to the desk and sat down opposite Sandy, who had by this time, already eaten two Jaffa Cakes.

"Any news of your lurcher-walker?" asked Peter.

"No, it looks like a non-starter at the moment. My only hope is that he's been on holiday. I'm going to try repeating the advertisement in a week or so, but I'm not too hopeful. How's your case coming on? Anything come out of those boxes of paper yet?"

"Bits and pieces. Nothing useable yet though. Mark suggested to me there could have been an illegal share-support scheme. I said I'd look into it, but I'd like some quick guidelines. Can you spare me ten minutes?"

"No problem. It's all fairly easy really. In the first place think of company shares as money. The only difference between notes of the realm and shares is that the share price goes up and down. It mainly works on the fear and greed principle. However, there are many reasons why a company might need its share price high."

Sandy held up his hand and ticked off the first finger.

"In the first place, in order to encourage directors to work hard, they normally are given what's called share options. This means they have the right to buy shares at an agreed price sometimes in the future. Normally the price will be well below the market price. The higher the share price, the more profit they will make if they buy and sell straight away. The share price, of course, depends on the company's profit figures, so directors may massage figures in order to keep the share price high."

"You mean over-value the stock or something?"

"Yes, there's a whole range of things they can do like forget liabilities, overestimate work in progress. There's lots of things. You've got to remember that their annual bonuses also depend on the profit figure, which may make them more optimistic about asset values. As a clever man once said, the only thing that doesn't lie in a balance sheet is cash."

He held up the next finger and ticked it off with his right hand.

"Second, companies or directors may have borrowed against the share value. If the price of the shares drop, the bank could ask for more security or call in the loan. This gives another powerful motive to massage the figures.

"Thirdly, and most importantly, companies use their shares to buy other companies. If a price has been agreed when the shares are at, say, five pounds, then it would be disastrous for the shares to fall before the deal is finalised. In the famous Guinness case, many rich friends bought shares to keep the price high. The reason it was illegal was that they were guaranteed a profit and this is what is called an illegal share-support scheme. It's normally very difficult to prove. Of course you do get grey areas. Take an example from the stock market a few days ago. A plc bought a major stamp company for thirteen and a half million pounds. The owner apparently took all his money in shares in the plc. At the time of the purchase, the shares were five pounds fifty. Within a month of the take-over, the plc issued a profit warning that their profits this year would not be as high as expected. The shares quickly dropped to two pounds fifty. The previous owner of the stamp company lost over seven million pounds. I don't thinks there was any question of dishonesty, despite the fact that almost all the main directors sold millions of pounds of their personal share holdings at around five pounds fifty a few weeks before the take-over. It appears that in this particular case, the financial director was totally incompetent. If, however, the directors had known about the problems before or during the take-over, then that would have been illegal."

"You're telling me that most of the directors sold their holdings before the take-over at fife pounds fifty per share?" asked Peter incredulously.

"Yes. But apparently, they were always going to sell. It wasn't something new."

"Well, if it was me, I'd have asked myself why they were selling. The stamp bloke must have been stupid. But then, what do I know? I've been in another sort of world for a long time. I'm a natural cynic."

"However, the point I'm making," continued Sandy, "it's not easy to distinguish between illegal, legal, lucky and unlucky deals. You have to have positive proof and that's not easy. The only way you normally get it is when someone talks. Hopefully that helps you with your case. By the way, what are you going to do about Inge?"

"Good point. Bung us over a Jaffa and I'll tell you."

To Sandy's amazement, there was only one Jaffa Cake left, which he reluctantly passed over to Peter.

"I had some bad news this morning," said Peter, trying to keep his face straight. "Remember that plane crash in India yesterday? Well my old office arranged for Inge to be on the passenger list. That means that I'm officially a widower."

Sandy grinned at him. "I suppose it's about right. As she never existed in the first place it seems appropriate that she should die when she wasn't even there! Talking about Inge, did you two play the part in full?"

"Oh yes. She was an excellent actress and insisted on full reality. Actually I really miss her sometimes. But it will be nice to go out again as a single man. Tell the staff no sympathy. I'll get over my grief quietly. Mind you, if your secretary wants to comfort me, she's very welcome!"

"Forget it! She's engaged and you know we don't like mixing business with pleasure, even if you are officially in mourning."

"In that case, I'll go back to my boxes. Thanks for your help."

Peter sauntered off while Sandy got back to his more serious work, wondering how to get Nicola to feel the same about him as he did about her.

He was looking forward to the evening as he'd arranged to take Nicola to an exhibition of watercolours at the Bankside galleries. He'd been given two complimentary tickets by Mark Cheshire. Art really wasn't his thing, in fact he was the role model for 'I don't know much about art but I know what I like'. He'd arranged to pick her up at about six thirty. They were going to view the exhibition and then eat in a small Greek restaurant.

The exhibition was a great success. Nicola knew quite a bit about the gallery and bought an attractive watercolour by Sir Hugh Casson. When she explained to Sandy that he was the ex-president of the Royal

Academy and was in fact involved in the Festival of Britain in 1951, Sandy began to understand why she was so excited. He was also amazed at how reasonable the price for the painting had been. They spent about an hour or so wandering around the gallery. They then walked back along the Thames walk.

The unseasonable warm weather had now well and truly left England and there was a decided nip in the air. As they hurried along to Coin Street, strong gusts of wind blew them about. On one occasion Nicola was literally blown into his arms. He held her close for a minute. He had a clear chance to kiss her as she looked up into his eyes. But he wouldn't risk it as the last thing he wanted to do was to risk damaging their relationship. They did, however, hold hands after that, which pleased him immensely. He felt like a teenager all over again with the excitement of his first date.

In the restaurant they sat looking over a grey Thames eating their seared tuna steaks served with sundried tomatoes and spinach. They weren't in the mood for wine and so drank still mineral water. Sandy noted the cost was almost the same. Water seemed to get more and more expensive as wine became cheaper.

Nicola asked him how his door-to-door endeavours had gone. He told her the good news. He also confided that they'd had no luck with the advertisement. It was, he told her, early days and hopefully something would turn up within the next two or three days. They strolled slowly back to his car after the meal. Sandy didn't think he'd been so happy in his life. He knew for certain he had to stay with Nicola, if possible for the rest of his life. He just hoped he could persuade her to feel the same about him.

She came in for a cup of coffee and they sat in silence listening to George Shearing while they drank their coffee. Afterwards, he told her about some of his experiences in the Serious Fraud Office.

At about eleven forty-five he drove her back to the house. This time she gave him a proper kiss goodnight. He drove all the way back to his flat singing silly romantic songs. He was not to know at that time just how fortunate it was that he had been with Nicola for the whole evening.

CHAPTER 18

Jason Roberts knew that Roland Silverman's death would have to be well-planned. There must be no suspicion that he was in any way involved. He knew only too well that he would be a principal suspect. After all, it wouldn't take long to find how precarious his financial affairs were. The first problem was how to kill Silverman. The second was where he could possibly do it without being recognised. Finally, as everybody who reads crime fiction knows, he knew he had to have a watertight alibi. The alibi would seem to be the most difficult part of the equation. People tend to be a trifle suspicious when asked to say you were with them when you weren't. They often ask silly questions like, "Why do you want me to lie?" He also came to the conclusion that even the thickest of his friends would connect such a request with the murder of his company chairman. The only sensible answer was Zoë. She would have to be his alibi, after all, he had done everything for her. How could he get her to swear he was with her when in fact he wasn't?

After hours of careful deliberation he worked out what he thought would be the perfect murder, one that even Ruth Rendell would be pleased with. He would steal some sleeping tablets, it shouldn't be a problem, a lot of the office staff use them these days to make long-haul flying easier. They were always careless, with them leaving them in their unlocked desks nobody would be surprised if they lost some, they would assume some insomniac had borrowed them. He would have an early night with Zoë and then feed her the tablets in alcohol. Zoë would be in bed with him when she went to sleep and again when she woke up. Why should she even consider he wasn't there all of the time? The more he thought about it the better it seemed. Now all he needed was a quiet place to murder Silverman close to Zoë's flat at Tower Bridge.

Silverman liked the theatre, he was always boring him about some play or other in the office. Jason found out he was going to the National Theatre on the South Bank to see the London Cuckold, a restoration comedy. Even better, he was to see it on the Bank Holiday Monday. Silverman was a creature of habit, he always parked his silver-grey Mercedes SL380E in the Cork Street car park. He liked to stroll along the Thames before and after the performance as he said it provided him with his daily exercise.

This particular South Bank car park was the most distant from the concert halls. It was always extremely busy during the day, as it served the London Weekend television studio. However, it was quiet in the evening as most visitors to the South Bank Entertainment Complex naturally preferred parking closer to the halls. It was, as far as Jason thought, perfect. With a bit of luck he could leave the flat, drive there, deal with Silverman and be back within the hour.

The first ingredient for his perfect murder was a car that could never be traced back to him. He looked at advertisements in local papers. He was keen to buy from a small garage. As he would be paying with cash it was highly likely that the garage might fiddle the sale to save VAT and tax. That being the case, they might conveniently lose the transaction or not come forward. Jason had always enjoyed acting and had decided to create a part in his murder story for an old man complete with grey hair and beard. He would change his voice, stoop, and perhaps wear glasses. He searched through the car advertisements in the Exchange and Mart; he noticed a hatchback for sale at a small garage in a town called Marston Moretaine. He caught the train from St Pancras to Bedford suitably disguised. While in Bedford he bought a sharp kitchen-devil carving knife. He safely stored it away in a briefcase bought earlier especially for the purpose of carrying the cash. A decrepit local bus ambled its way across the flat Bedfordshire clay lands past endless dusty brickworks to the romantically misnamed Marston Moretaine. The town qualified for full one horse status – it was a total dump. The garage was small, ramshackle, and looking as if it was on its last legs. The vehicle was ideal, a dull red nondescript sort of car, the sort nobody gives a second glance to. It was everything that Jason wanted.

He realised that the garage would expect him to haggle so he decided to enjoy an acting role.

"How much will you give me off the hatchback if I don't part exchange anything and pay you in cash?" asked Jason in a put-on Kentish accent.

"Oh I don't know about that, sir, it's a good little

motor and we will have no trouble selling it. I could I suppose give you say fifty pounds cash discount."

"That's not a discount, that's a bloody insult!" shouted Jason, really getting into the part. "I was thinking more like five hundred pounds, mate. Cash in the hand, with nothing else to sell. I'm the perfect customer paying cash, we both know that. Come on, you can do a lot better than a miserly fifty pounds."

"Five hundred pounds! Christ, I'd lose my job, you're out of your mind, there is never that sort of profit. Look, I'll tell you what I will do, I'll go to one hundred and fifty quid and then I'm virtually giving it away, fair enough."

"No I need much more, I'll have to go back to the other garage. Shame though, I liked your car better." With that, Jason started to leave the showroom.

"Wait, wait! All right, all right, three hundred quid and that's it."

"You got a deal," said Jason smugly, pleased with his negotiating skills. He pulled out a wad of notes that he had obtained using his full range of credit cards from various cash machines. It would be impossible to ever trace them.

"Fair enough but I'll say one thing for you, you're a hard man. I don't know what I'll tell the boss but you certainly have got a bargain."

"Get on with it," said Jason, impatient to be off now he'd had his fun.

"All right. Name?" said the salesman.

"Harold Smith," lied Jason as he filled in all the necessary paperwork. Shortly afterwards he drove his new car back to London. He needed to have it available close by Zoë's flat but in such a way that nobody would take any notice. The ideal place was in Chambers Road which was always busy. He eventually parked it next to a bodywork garage opposite to the London Studios at Chambers Wharf. He reckoned nobody would be interested in a vehicle probably waiting for repair.

Over the Bank Holiday, Jason was on tenterhooks all day. He had told Jane that he had important business to do regarding Redwood. It made a change not having to lie, after all, murdering the company chairman was important and certainly to do with Redwood. He drove up the A20 and met Zoë in Greenwich. They spent the day going round the art and craft market. Greenwich was bubbling with excitement, the sun was out and shoppers of all shapes and sizes, coloured in every hue known to the human race and even a few probably not known, thronged the streets. South East London is amazingly cosmopolitan and the market reflected this wonderful ethnic mix. Zoë had a ball, whereas Jason's mind quite naturally was fixed on his evening's work. So far everything had just been a game, tonight he would have to end another human being's life. He just hoped when the time came he would be up to it. He had left nothing to chance, he'd swotted up on his human anatomy so he knew where to insert the knife to maximum effect. He had misappropriated some sleeping tablets and had ground them up ready for the evening. He had tried to anticipate everything that could go wrong. They bought some sandwiches and mineral water and ate them by the Gypsy Moth 4. It seemed so small to have carried an old Sir Francis

Chichester round the world. Jason could remember being sent an envelope with a special Chichester stamp on it when he was at his primary school. Well, if an old man could sail round the world by himself on that small yacht then surely he could simply stick a knife into Silversmith.

They drove back to Jacob's Island at about six thirty. Zoë tried on her new outfits and gave Jason a private fashion show, twirling provocatively in front of the large glass mirrors. The show gradually became more sexually charged till at last Jason's self-control snapped. Jason was already exhilarated with his plans for the evening and the sight of Zoë playing the stripper was too much. Despite her protests he all but raped her, all but the fact that she found she enjoyed the force and she knew he would never hurt her. They cleaned themselves up again and went out to buy a takeaway pizza from the nearby Cantina. Jason ensured that Zoë drank most of the champagne. True to form, it made her feel sexy and tired. She was delighted to go back to bed to watch television. Jason had never felt so randy; he assumed it was the excitement of the forthcoming kill. They had the television on in the background and this time Jason made it slow and gentle, relaxing her. Jason fed Zoë the tablets, it didn't take long before she was out for the count. Jason then changed into his old man outfit and carefully left the apartment. His luck was in as there was nobody about. He hurried past Springhall Wharf and on into Chambers Road, which was also deserted. He quickly got into the estate and drove carefully to the South Bank.

He'd hoped to park close by Silverman's

Mercedes, he then was going to drive out to block Silverman's exit and ask him a question. As it happened he managed to park next to the Mercedes on the driver's side. He couldn't have wished for it to work out in a better way. He waited patiently, the radio blaring out mindless pop music.

Silverman enjoyed the bawdy romp, he liked Caroline Quentin and was still chuckling to himself as he got back to the park. Next to his car was a dirty estate with pop music blaring out from it rather loudly. A grey-haired was man was fiddling in the boot. He assumed there was something wrong with the man's car, but it still didn't give him an excuse to deafen everyone in the Coin Street area.

Inconsiderate yob, thought Silverman. He walked slowly by to get into his car, carefully avoiding the puddles as he went. He opened the door and was just about to get in when the yob came round, opening the red hatchback's rear door behind him as he came. In doing this he blocked both Silverman and himself from any prying eyes from the few other cars in the park. Silverman at that moment was in that awkward position, half in the car, half outside. The murderer had timed it to perfection.

"Evening squire, sorry about the noise, I'll turn it down. You know how it is, being alone, it helps to have the radio on." The man shouted loudly in a voice that Silverman vaguely recognised.

Silverman took no notice of the man's ramblings until he felt a sudden sharp pain in his back and he felt himself falling into a black void. He tried to call out but his feeble attempt were deafened by the driver now shouting even louder at him.

"I'm really sorry about the noise, Gov, you're right. It is far too loud, I'll turn it down, I'm sorry."

Jason pushed the dead body into the Mercedes' driver's seat, closing the door firmly. He didn't bother to remove the knife; he had worn gloves and he was sure it could never be traced to him. He also realised that it would involve more blood and he already had enough of Silverman's blood on him. He shut all the car doors quietly, switched off the pop music and quickly drove out of the car park. He kept his head turned away from the car park attendant who was far too interested in shutting his hatch to stop the bitter cold air getting in.

It had worked out like clockwork; he had never felt so exhilarated. He stopped the car in a dark patch in Clink Street and removed his overall, gloves and shoes. He put on a new coat, new shoes and gloves which he had bought earlier and stored in the boot, and put the soiled and incriminating garments in a small lead box he had purchased from an office shop under the arches at the back of the War Experience Museum. The old fashioned fireproof box was already heavy but Jason had taken no chances, he had added two large rocks. It was difficult to manoeuvre it to the edge of the Mayflower dock but he was delighted to see the mud bubble and slowly absorb his guilty secret. By the time Jason arrived back at Chandler's Wharf he realised that only fifty minutes had passed. He quickly removed his disguise, put it into his special briefcase and hurried back to the sleeping Zoë. He was delighted to find her dead to the world, though not as dead as Silverman.

Jason removed all his clothes and put them in the

briefcase. He thought you couldn't be too careful, he knew how clever the scientists were these days. He would drop them into a Salvation Army clothes bank in the morning. He had a bath, pouring in some of Zoë's scented oil and washing his hair thoroughly at the same time, using the shower to keep the oil out. He let the water run for a long time as he scrubbed round the bath to leave no traces of his evening's work.

He just couldn't get to sleep that night, he was so exhilarated; he had never felt so good before. He had been dreading that something would have gone wrong but it all went like clockwork. Murder was so exciting and so easy. Jason was also feeling incredible sexy, particularly as Zoë had kicked all the bedclothes off her and her night-dress had ridden up. She was sleeping in a wanton position, her sex fully exposed. Much as he would have liked to take her straight away it was important that he didn't make her suspicious, and waking her out of her drugged sleep at three in the morning would be unusual, he had never done anything like it before. So he waited until around six before he slipped his hand between her legs and started caressing her. He felt her body begin to stir before she even woke up and almost without any real effort from him her body went into a violent spasm.

"Umm, that was nice. What a lovely way to wake up. What's come over you? I thought you be knackered after last night's efforts. You haven't been at the Viagra have you?"

He quickly stopped her laughing by kissing her so hard that he tasted blood. He knew that she sometimes liked rough handling. He wanted her to really remember the morning so he made her come again, playing with her skilfully with his lips and fingers. After a brief rest he managed to make love to her yet again. He was quite sure she would have no doubts that he had been with her all night.

Jason got up while Zoë was in the shower. He put on his disguise – glasses, wig, and false beard. He called goodbye through the door.

"I'm going to Gatwick to meet a client. See you this evening."

"Buy some more Viagra," giggled Zoë, "you'll need it tonight!"

He walked carefully along Bermondsey Wall West past the new building work and then along by the film studios back to the red hatchback. It was important that he got rid of it as soon as possible. He drove down to Brighton, stopping twice, once at a Tesco car park in order to get rid of the clothes in the recycling bank and again to throw the briefcase over a railway bridge into some deep undergrowth. Jason drove carefully, making sure he didn't break any speed limits, for that would be stupid. He had the radio blaring out the latest pop hits and he felt like a teenager all over again.

He parked in a dark corner of a multi-storey car park close to the station. He paid for a day's parking and left the building. He popped into a gents' and removed his wig and beard. He disposed of the glasses easily; he trod on them and then dropped them in a nearby bin. He just managed to catch the ten fifteen London train. He chucked the wig and then the beard out of the train window; he was confident they would never be connected to Coin Street.

By eleven o'clock he was meeting a client at Gatwick Airport. He told him he'd caught the train to save time and as they sped through the Sussex countryside back to London, he reflected on a job well done.

CHAPTER 19

It was approaching midnight and had started to drizzle. The night was black, cold and depressing. Adel Mohammed was looking forward to getting back home where his wife Rita would have a hot cup of tea waiting and a decent stew. After that, his one and only big desire was to get some sleep in his warm bed. He looked round the car park and noticed to his disappointment there was still one car remaining down in the lower level. The car park officially closed at midnight, he was allowed to go home then or when the last car left if that was earlier. He had no obligation to stay behind for even a minute after midnight. All customers were warned with big red notices at what time the gates were locked so it was their own fault if they were locked in for the night. Adel always hung on for at least ten minutes or so if there were cars remaining.

He often found that these latecomers were extremely grateful to find he had waited and as he wasn't well paid, the tips they gave him were important to him.

He looked down at the car and for a moment he thought he could see someone sitting in the driver's seat. He wasn't completely sure, perhaps it had been a trick of the light. He looked again and sure enough there was an outline of a person slumped down in the seat. He wondered if the driver had been taken ill. Although it was cold, wet, and miserable he had no alternative – he knew he had to go and check. He put on his anorak, pulled the hood up and walked slowly down the slope to investigate the one remaining car.

As he got nearer to the Mercedes he could see he was correct in his assumption and there was somebody in the driver's seat. Looking through the window he could see that the man was slumped over the steering wheel, apparently asleep. He banged the window to try to attract his attention. Not being successful, he tried the door, it was unlocked. He opened it and immediately realised something was wrong. As he touched the man's back to try to wake him he found his hand was wet with a warm sticky substance. He then noticed a damp patch in the man's back and realised to his horror that the sticky substance was blood. The man was probably dead. He shut the door of the car and ran quickly back up the slope to the sanctuary of his hut; he locked the door carefully behind him. As soon as he was safe inside he dialled 999 and asked for both an ambulance and the police. Afterwards, he sadly reflected that he would not be home for quite some time.

He rang his wife and excitedly told her his grisly news and that he would be late. He then put on the kettle, switched on his single bar electric fire and waited for the arrival of the police. He didn't have long to wait, however, within a few minutes he heard an insistent *nah-nah* noise coming growing louder and louder followed by the flashing lights.

It didn't take the local police long to establish the identity of the corpse. Roland Silverman had enough gold and platinum credit cards in his wallet to pay off the national debt. He also had in the region of four hundred pounds in notes which quickly took away any idea that it might be a simple robbery. When the information was relayed to the computer at headquarters, it immediately alerted them to the connection between Silverman and Richard Valentine's murder.

It had not been a good day for Detective Inspector Griggs. He had one obvious suspect in his current murder investigation. Everything pointed to a quick and easy solution. He was in the circumstances rather disappointed to find that the main and only suspect was in hospital at the time with two broken legs. He couldn't really imagine him crutching his way across ten miles of London streets without anyone noticing. It was not the best news he could have hoped for. Without an obvious suspect it now looked a complicated and motiveless case. He also had some batty woman who had come to see him and who was convinced the murderer hated cricketers.

Altogether it had been one of those days to forget. He had had a row with Sharon about the holiday, or to be more correct, why they hadn't had one. They had the same row the year before when he was so busy he couldn't find the time to go away. Sharon did have a point, he seemed to remember promising to take them to Florida this year. He always seemed to be breaking promises to her these days.

His three-month-old baby had thrown his breakfast

all over him, causing him to have to go and change and therefore be late into the station that morning. It was the only morning his governor was in early and it was just sod's law that he wanted to see Griggs immediately. He'd gone for a pint at lunch time and some stupid nerd had tripped, throwing his beer over his trousers. Although it had dried, Griggs stank like an old brewery. They say things always go in threes and sure enough, to complete his day he himself knocked over a mug of coffee down his shirt. He was looking forward to getting home to change into some clean clothes but he was stopped by the superintendent, who demanded the paperwork on the Leyton case which he'd been working on. Unfortunately he hadn't got around to doing it and as he had already been in trouble that morning he decided to get it done. That was why he had been in his office late into the night catching up. He wanted to put a complete report on the boss's desk so he'd have it first thing in the morning. It was just after midnight and he was just leaving the station, feeling sorry for himself and realising that Sharon would be cross when the news about Silverman's murder came through.

It was typical of the way his day had gone. He couldn't really imagine that Mrs Valentine had decided to kill all of her husband's board members unless she was a psycho. If that was the case, it was possible that Neil was correct. If so then he'd got it wrong. Mind you, he'd check on her alibi, carefully for this one, just in case. There wasn't a lot he could do at the scene of the crime. The man Mohammed knew nothing useful. There was not a lot for the detectives to do until morning. After the car was examined by the forensic experts, he gave permission for the body to be removed to the pathology laboratory, sealed off the area and went to bed at about three a.m.

Despite his lack of sleep, Griggs was up at seven a.m. He told Sharon that he was sorry about the holiday and told her to get some brochures about Florida then and after an uneventful breakfast he picked up Cook and set off for Chelsea to see Mrs Valentine. In his heart he knew it was going to be a long shot, but he thought he'd get it out of the way quickly.

Nicola was surprised to see the inspector so early in the morning on her doorstep when she opened the door. She assumed it was to do with her husband's death.

"Good morning, Mrs Valentine, I'm sorry to bother you but could we come in? I'd like to ask you some questions. This is Detective Constable Cook, she'll be taking notes."

Nicola took them up the long corridor to the kitchen.

"I've got a pot of fresh coffee brewing. Would you both like a cup?"

They both agreed and shortly they were all sitting round Nicola's expensive antique pine table.

"Mrs Valentine, may I ask you what your movements were last night?" started Griggs.

"I don't understand," said Nicola in a puzzled tone, "why last night?"

"It would be helpful if you could just answer the question please."

241

"If you insist. I was picked up here at about six by a friend. We went to the water-colours exhibition at the Bankside gallery. I bought a Hugh Casson painting. I've got a receipt in my handbag if you want to see it."

Griggs was already interested. The gallery was only five minutes away from the car park where Silverman was murdered. Perhaps it wasn't such a long shot.

"Then what did you do, Mrs Valentine?" he asked, trying not to sound excited.

"We walked along the Thames to a Greek restaurant, I don't remember the name but it's at the Thames end of the Coin Street craft shopping centre."

Better and better, thought Griggs. *She's now only two minutes away.*

"We then walked back to the car which we parked just by the Thames along by the Globe theatre and then drove back to my friend's flat for coffee before he drove me home at about twelve thirty. Now what's all this about?"

"May I have the name of the friend who accompanied you last night please?"

"I think you know him. It was Sandy Neil. I can give you his address and phone number if you like."

"I've already got it on file, thank you," said Griggs, seeing his carefully built murder scenario disappear. However, grabbing at straws he asked, "Were there any times you were not together during the evening?"

"When I made the coffee I was in the kitchen but otherwise we were together all the time. Now I really must insist, what is all this about?"

"Roland Silverman was murdered last night in a Southbank car park adjacent to Coin Street. That's what it's about."

"Roland? Murdered? Oh my god! And you thought I'd become some sort of serial killer I suppose. You thought was working my way through the staff," said Nicola sarcastically.

"No, of course not, but I had to check. You realise we'll have to speak to Sandy to check your story."

As he drove to Sandy's flat he did flirt with the rather improbable theory that Sandy might have killed Silverman in order to put doubt in the minds of the police about Mrs Valentine's guilt. He knew it didn't make any sense. He couldn't possibly believe a copper of Neil's experience being so stupid. No, if Sandy confirmed the story it was the end of that road. He also had the feeling that it opened up the Valentine case yet again.

They arrived at Sandy's flat at about ten thirty. Sandy was still in a good mood. He'd made up his mind to go and see Griggs to see if he'd organise a door-to-door enquiry both for the late car departure and the lurcher dog. He'd been looking at the financial data he'd got on Silverman and was more and more convinced that Silverman was the murderer. In fact he'd put money on it.

He opened the front door and was amazed to see Griggs and Cook outside looking slightly embarrassed.

"Come in," he said, "this is fortuitous, I was about to phone you. Fancy a coffee? It's only instant but you're welcome."

In a repeat performance all three sat round Sandy's

243

cheap second hand B&Q pine-type table drinking the coffee.

"This is official business, Mr Neil. I'd like to ask you a few questions."

"I don't get it," said Sandy, "but fire away."

"Can you tell me your movements last night, sir?"

"Easy, I picked up Nicola Valentine at about six, we went to an art show and then on to a restaurant and finally she came back here for coffee. I took her home about twelve thirty. After that I went to bed, why on earth do you want to know?"

"I suppose you were together all the time? She didn't leave you for say, ten minutes in the restaurant?" asked Griggs hopefully.

"No, not even one minute. She didn't even powder her nose. Now come clean. What's all this about?" demanded Sandy.

"It could be good news in some way for Mrs Valentine. Roland Silverman was murdered last night, close to where you were eating, in the Southbank car park adjacent to Coin Street. You can see why we were so interested in your evening. I have to admit it does make me rather uneasy about the original murder."

"Good, because that's what I want to talk to you about."

Sandy explained about the car engine starting up late at about twelve ten and how Mrs Valentine remembered about the dog-walker with the lurcher and his lack of success with the advertisement. Griggs listened attentively and agreed it was important to check both stories carefully. He said he'd organise a proper door-to-door. Sandy didn't let on that he'd already got a witness to confirm Nicola's departure on the walk.

As Griggs was about to go, Sandy thought he'd be kind.

"I realise you've probably got all the information you want but if I were you I'd look carefully at Jason Roberts."

Griggs grinned at him.

"Once a Chief Inspector, always a Chief Inspector. It's hard to change, isn't it? Mind you, you're right, the answer to both murders has to lie in that company."

When he left Sandy, Griggs went straight round to interview Roberts at the company headquarters. It was obvious from the atmosphere as he entered the building that that news of Silverman's death had reached there. There was an ominous calm throughout the whole building. To have the chief executive and the chairman murdered in a few months was not the usual manner to lose company officials. They had not as yet replaced Valentine, so Jason Roberts was now in charge. Griggs was shown up to his office and Roberts welcomed him at the door.

"Come in, Inspector. I suppose it's about this dreadful business of Silverman's death. How can I help you?"

"As you'll appreciate, sir, we have to eliminate all Silverman's close associates from the enquiry. This is of course very much routine but can you tell me your movements last night please?"

"Does this information have to become public knowledge, Inspector?" asked Roberts.

"Only if it's relevant to the murder enquiry, otherwise of course, if it's not of any interest to us it will remain confidential."

"Fine, because it's a little bit embarrassing. I spent all of last night with a young lady at her flat. We got a takeaway pizza from the Cantina and took it back to her flat, we ate it, had a few glasses of wine, went to bed early, watched television. We have a set in the bedroom, and then went to sleep. We were together all of the evening."

"This young lady, she will of course confirm this story? Can I have her name and address please?" said Cook.

Jason gave Cook all Zoë's details and after they had left he sat back thinking to himself how fortunate he was. With Silverman out of the picture, all the blame for the currency losses could be loaded onto Valentine. If the auditors didn't pick up the bogus companies, which he didn't think they would, then he would be home and dry. He felt sorry for Silverman naturally, but that was as far as it went.

Jacob's Island was one of those new riverside developments so popular nowadays. Griggs could remember Bermondsey Wall West when it was just a derelict street with a few ruined buildings on it. He was amazed at the sudden change. The main development was in the form of a square with water gardens in the centre. A fountain sprung up from the lake and fairy lights lit up all the trees in the grey afternoon light. As usual the British weather confounded everybody. Last week it had been a heatwave and now it was so cold you could imagine snow.

Zoë lived in a separate tower built right over the Thames. Griggs rang the doorbell and after he had told her of who he was, she let him in. He took the lift up to the second floor and was admitted into the flat by an incredibly sexy girl wearing one of those see-through outfits that feature so often in the fashion sections of the tabloid papers. Griggs could easily see what Roberts saw in her. Cook, on the other hand, looked disapproving. *Mind you,* thought Griggs, *even with unlimited money Cook could never look like Zoë.* They walked along a corridor and into the main room. It was enormous, Griggs reckoned he could almost put his whole house into that one room. The views were spectacular. Looking left, it was dominated by Tower Bridge and the Tower of London. If you turned the other way the view went right down to Greenwich and the Millennium Dome with Canary Wharf reaching behind into the dark sky like a space ship. *Must be nice for some,* thought Griggs.

"How can I help you?" asked Zoë.

"It's a routine matter," said Griggs. "We have to eliminate certain people from our enquiries and because of this we need to ask you a few questions. Can you tell me what you did last night?"

"I came home early. I was joined by a friend at about seven thirty. We organised a takeaway meal and ate it with a bottle of wine. We then went to bed early, taking another bottle with us. I think I must have drunk rather too much – I dropped off early."

"What was the name of your friend, Miss?" asked Cook.

"Jason, Jason Roberts."

"With respect, Miss, as you had passed out you couldn't be sure Jason Roberts was with you all the time?" asked Griggs.

"Oh I'm sure he was. I woke up several times in the night and he was always there next to me."

"Do you remember what you were watching when you went to sleep?"

"Yes, I can, ironically it was news at ten. Probably bored to sleep," chuckled Zoë. "I'm afraid I drank far too much champagne which is probably why I passed out. I know one thing, that champagne must have been a cheap one as it sure left an awful taste afterwards. My throat tasted like the bottom of a parrot's cage the next morning.

As Griggs went back to the station he reflected that Roberts could easily have left the flat, killed Silverman and returned to bed again. It wouldn't have taken much to slip the girl something to knock her out for an hour or so. The fact she had such a dreadful taste could easily indicate drugs. He went straight down to see the sergeant in charge of the transport section.

"Bill, I want you to run a few tests for me. Take a car and drive it from Jacob's Island to the Southbank car park at Coin Street. I want the journey time measured for about eleven o'clock to twelve fifteen, there and back. Do it, say, three times in each direction."

If Roberts did do it he needed transport. Griggs had already found out that the parking at Jacob's Island was underground. He sent an officer to requisition all of the relevant video tapes for the evening to see if anything showed up. He was hoping that Roberts used his own car which would then have been recorded.

By early evening his late night was getting to him so he decided, to hell with it, he'd show Sharon a good husband. He was becoming concerned that his son seemed to be unsure who he was. That's the trouble with this job, you never see your family. Perhaps they could book the holiday, they would love Disneyland.

When he got in the next morning the news of the video of Jacob's Island was disappointing if not unexpected. Jason Roberts had parked his car at about seven thirty in the evening and didn't take it out again until eight the next morning. If he did kill Silverman then he had to have another car somewhere in the area. Griggs arranged for an extensive operation to check for such a vehicle.

The videos from the car park were proving quite interesting though, in spite of being of low quality. The cameras revolved round the car park at regular intervals which made it difficult to locate what they wanted. All of the tapes had been sent down to the photographic department and Griggs was hopeful that he'd eventually get some useful pictures. Meanwhile, he hadn't forgotten his promise to Sandy and he set up a blanket door-to-door operation in Chelsea. He also had a team searching Silverman's London house to see if they could turn up anything useful. There was one good thing that had happened about Silverman's death. He managed to dump his other murder enquiry, the one without a motive, onto a lucky colleague – he was welcome to it.

CHAPTER 20

The answer, as both Sandy and Griggs knew, lay in the accounts of the Redwood Group plc. Sandy had already sent for the latest published audited accounts to glance at them, though after so many years in the world of fraud, he realised that the published accounts could often be a work of fiction. The example still in most people's minds was Polly Peck. Here the auditors had given the company a complete clean bill of health only months before its spectacular collapse. As for the Robert Maxwell companies, well, one wonders what the accountants were actually doing. Coming from the Serious Fraud Office, Sandy understood just how creative, creative-accounting could really be.

Looking at most the recent Redwood accounts he saw that Price Waterhouse were the auditors. He was fortunate in that he had a good friend working in their Thames-side Southwark headquarters. He decided now was the time to try to pull in a favour that he was owed. He picked up the phone and arranged to go round to John Holliday's office straight away. It would only take him about twenty minutes to get there.

Sandy had given John some very useful tips both when he was in the City of London Fraud Squad and when he was at the Serious Fraud Office, so John knew that although Sandy was basically a policeman, he did have an excellent nose for financial irregularities. If Sandy thought it was important, then it was worth postponing an internal meeting. As Sandy drove across London Bridge the sun came out briefly and he was almost blinded as it hit the gold on the replica of the Golden Hind and shone directly into his eyes. He turned right in the direction indicated by the parking signs. As he drove past the London Television Centre he realised which car park he was heading for. It was ironic that it was the car park in which Roland Silverman had been murdered so recently. The police roped-off area was still there. Sandy looked at it for a moment thinking how glad that he had been with Nicola at the time. He walked down to the Thames through the bustling Coin Street market. Despite the miserable weather, many people were sitting out enjoying their drinks. As he passed the Greek restaurant he smiled at the memory of their meal. Was it only two nights ago? It seemed like months. The walk along the Thames was pleasant, particularly as he had only just done the same with Nicola a few nights before.

On his arrival at the prestigious headquarters of Price Waterhouse, he had to clear the strict security. This was a necessary arrangement as the public could use their foyer to walk through to the Hays Galleria as they had built over ancient walking rights. Sandy was told by security that he wanted the tenth floor. He took the lift and was met by an attractive young lady who introduced herself as Tig, who, it appeared, was

John's personal assistant. She guided Sandy through the labyrinth of desks to John's private cubicle.

"Nice to see you again, Sandy. I gather you're a private detective nowadays." As John was speaking he poured them both a cup of coffee from a flask that was ever present on his desk and passed an impressive plate of biscuits across to Sandy. "What's it like working for yourself? Must be strange after the Fraud Office."

"The only difference is the backup. I admit I do miss the technical support. Luckily most of it can be bought. On the other hand we are not restricted by rules. The best thing is we can pick our cases. We're being offered far more work than we can cope with. You'd be amazed how much fraud there is today."

Sandy helped himself to yet another chocolate biscuit, wondering at the same time if it was possible to become a chocolate biscuit addict.

"I don't think I would be surprised," laughed John. "In our business we know that only a fraction of fraud is ever reported. Or for that matter ever discovered. When it comes to dishonesty, the computer has a lot to answer for. I assume it is dishonesty that brings you here."

"I'm working on the Valentine case. You could hardly failed to have noticed that Redwood's chairman, Roland Silverman, has also been murdered. It's obvious the answer to both the murders lies deeply hidden in the Redwoods accounts.

"Got anybody in mind?" asked the accountant.

"If I was to bet, I'd put money on the company accountant, Jason Roberts, but that's strictly off the record. You're the auditors, surely with two murders committed already, you could perhaps arrange a spot audit. I could probably get the police to order you to do one but that could take weeks. I'd like something done a little quicker if possible."

Sandy sat back hopefully and found to his amazement he had yet another chocolate biscuit in his hand. It was, to his acute embarrassment, the last one.

John sat fiddling with his braces and looked thoughtful. He suddenly stopped fiddling, smiled triumphantly and said, "What an amazing coincidence Sandy, we received an anonymous letter this morning alleging serious financial impropriety at Redwood. Now it's a rule of the company that we always check such allegations. The accusers normally send the same letter to the press because it would be embarrassing for us if we did nothing about it and it blew up like the Maxwell case. Now if you'd like to write the letter quickly, I'll get things going."

Sandy chuckled as he wrote the poison-pen letter and signed it 'a friend' and passed it over to John.

"What with this letter and your concerns we have every right to make a thorough check. Leave it with me and I'll report back to you as soon as possible."

Feeling pleased with himself, Sandy walked slowly back along the Thames to his car. Just out of curiosity he drove back to Jacob's Island; despite the traffic it took him only seven minutes. That meant if Roberts was the murderer he would only have needed between thirty minutes and an hour to do the deed.

As he arrived back in the office he passed Mark on the way out carrying a suitcase.

"Anywhere exciting?" he asked.

"I'm taking Beth up to Scotland for a short holiday away from the World Cup. Should be fabulous up there this time of the year."

"Wasn't one of the MCC murder victims from Scotland?" asked Sandy.

"All right, it's not just a holiday, but don't tell Beth. I'm checking into the three other murders. I know you think it's all a load of hooey, but I'm not so sure. Maybe it will turn out to be a wild goose chase, but I think it needs to be looked into. Peter's a bit busy at the moment so I'm having a go. If nothing else it's good money and it could help Mrs Mannering come to terms with her husband's death."

"Well I hope you've got your passport, they may declare independence while you are up there. The Scottish Nationalists now have a clear lead in the polls. By the time you get up there Alec Salmon will probably be the King of Scotland."

Sandy wished he was taking Nicola away to Scotland for a few days instead of scratching around trying to prove her innocence. He'd been annoyed that still nobody had come forward concerning the advertisement for the man walking the lurcher dog. He arranged to repeat the advertisements and this time extended it to cover all the national papers. It was that point he realised how silly he'd been. There had to be a lurcher society, club, organisation. He looked up the Kennel Club number in the phone directory and phoned them at once. The Kennel Club were very helpful, providing him with all sorts of addresses. He gave the list to his secretary to work through and hoped she would come up with something useful. There was at least one good piece of news, Griggs had phoned to say they had found a witness that had seen the second car parked in Oakley gardens the night of Valentine's death. Oakley Gardens is one of those snooty ones that don't encourage non-resident parking. The car was a dark blue BMW which was parked in the second part of the road as it doubled back to rejoin Manor Street. The witness, an elderly brigadier, was annoyed as it was in his space and he was forced to park in Phene Street and walk through the cut. Ironically by the time he got back the car had gone so he walked back to Phene Street and drove back to park in his usual spot. He didn't see the driver but at least it backed up Mrs Williams' story, as the old boy could confirm that he was in Oakley Gardens after midnight having returned from an army reunion.

CHAPTER 21

Inspector Griggs sank back into his favourite battered leather armchair. It was early evening which was his favourite time of the day, one he rarely experienced at home. The children were in bed and what was even more unusual, they were both fast asleep. Griggs had arrived home in time to read them a bedtime story, which he always thoroughly enjoyed doing. Sharon had rudely suggested the reason the kids were sleeping soundly was more to do with his boring interpretation of the book than just being tired. She had smugly told him that when she read the story, she always gave the characters different voices, whereas he read as if from a report. It was hardly fair, as she had not only been an infant teacher but was still one of the stars in the local amateur dramatic society.

After finishing his parental duties he had settled down for a pleasant and unusual evening at home. The fire was lit, he was wearing his favourite slippers and he was drinking a glass of Old Speckled Hen. Delicious smells were wafting out of the kitchen where Sharon was preparing his favourite meal, pork and leek sausages with onion mash. He had watched the seven o'clock Channel Four news which was full, as usual, of President Clinton denying that he had had any sexual relations with some junior helper called Monica Lewinski. God, what a fuss the world was making about his sexual lapses. Any half-decent policeman would tell you he was guilty. He was obviously at it all the time. He'd admit it in the end, he always did. It was almost like a game to him. He'd certainly got a different wife to his Sharon. He shuddered to think what she would do if she found he'd been having oral sex with some young probationary policewoman down at the station. The one thing he was sure of was that it wouldn't be enough just to say he was sorry and he wasn't really being unfaithful. It was far more likely that he would get the Bobbit treatment. Even the thought of it brought tears to his eyes. Mind you, you had to admire Clinton's stamina. By the time Griggs normally got home he had just one thought in his head – bed – but in his case it wasn't for sex, he just wanted to sleep. As the news droned on he found himself losing interest and his mind wandered back to his current case.

He was feeling rather self-satisfied. It had been a productive three or four days as far as the Silverman murder was concerned. The video stills had turned up some interesting leads. For a start, there were not many cars left in the car park on the evening of Silverman's death. They'd been able to read the number plates from the enlargements of the pictures and at this moment each car was being checked. He was very interested in the red hatchback car parked next to Silverman's Mercedes. Although they hadn't got any clear pictures of the incident it would appear from the sequence of photographs they had got, that

Silverman was murdered by the man driving the red car. He had cleverly blocked the video camera's vision by leaving his rear door open. Griggs wasn't sure whether this was by accident or with intent. But the result either way was the same, it had proved extremely effective. He'd got the photographic boys to provide a decent enlargement photograph of the vehicle. At this very moment he hoped the local Southwark police were showing it extensively round the area. Shortly he would get the details from Swansea and then he would know who the registered keeper was. It could of course have been the murderer and if so would lead to a quick arrest, however, he wasn't that optimistic. The murderer hadn't made many mistakes and that would be out of character. He had to agree with Neil that the most likely suspect was Roberts and if he was his man, he almost certainly killed Richard Valentine as well, but for the life of him he couldn't see how he did it.

His thoughts were interrupted by Sharon calling him for supper. Afterwards, with his trousers loosened so he could stretch his belly, they sprawled out on the settee. He realised quickly why all the special treatment, he had been buttered up to get him to take a holiday. It wouldn't surprise him if the kids were not really asleep at all, just acting in a large family conspiracy. He didn't really mind and so they spent the rest of the evening looking at holiday brochures of Florida and Disneyland. He'd also agreed that Sharon should book one the next day, after all, he was not indispensable. There were other policemen after all.

When the information did come in from Swansea,

the keeper of the car was found to be a Rob Hunt from 16 Martins Way, Bedford. The local police contacted him quickly and found that he had recently traded the car in part exchange at a garage in Marston Moretaine. The garage confirmed the transaction but had already sold the car on. The new owner had paid cash, which Griggs thought was very significant. They got a good description of the buyer. He was a tall, thin man, with a grey beard and hair. He also wore glasses, but according to the salesman he didn't really need them, as he took them off to check the money and again when he drove off. The salesman assumed they were just worn as a fashion accessory.

By now the photographic unit had managed to isolate a reasonable picture of the estate car driver. The photograph was sent to Bedford and the locals took it round to the Marston Moretaine garage. The salesman was reasonably sure it was the same man who had bought the car, so at least Griggs knew who he was looking for.

The name on all the paperwork for the new owner of the estate was Harold Smith who lived at 16 Martins Way, Bedford. *Mind you, if you believed that,* thought Griggs, *you shouldn't really be in the force.* When the police checked at the address they found it was the home of the local vicar. The Reverend Small not only didn't drive a car but was short, fat, clean-shaven, and didn't bear the slightest resemblance to the man who bought the car. What's more, he said that he had never visited Marston Moretaine, let alone bought a red hatchback, and if you can't believe a vicar, who can you trust? It was exactly what Griggs expected. He knew it wouldn't be that easy. He was looking for a very clever murderer and it just so happened that Roberts had a first class honours degree from Oxford.

Things were now moving very quickly; the next big development came from the Southwark area. There was a garage of sorts on Chambers Street. Both mechanics remembered the red hatchback, as it had been parked next to their store on the far side of the road. The reason they were so sure was because it had been annoying them, it made things difficult to load and unload. They confirmed it had been there since the eleventh of February and had disappeared on the fourteenth, the day of Silverman's death. It wasn't there when they came to work at eight thirty on the fifteenth.

Griggs reflected that Chambers Street was only a minute away from Jacob's Island where Zoë Phillips had her flat and that Roberts was a tall, thin man. Admittedly he didn't have a beard or grey hair or wear glasses, however, all those differences could well be props.

Griggs was more and more convinced that it was Jason Roberts he wanted and started to intensify the efforts in that direction. He arranged for all the security videos in the Jacob's Island, Chambers Street area to be collected and he had a team going through them looking for anything that might be helpful. He also wished he understood accounts more but that sort of thing was never his strength. Luckily though, he knew a man that did, he would go along to the fraud department in the morning.

CHAPTER 22

Berwick Manor Cottage was everything a city dweller would dream of if they ever retired to the country. The cottage itself was covered with wisteria, roses and honeysuckle which disguised most of the black and white beams, but nevertheless it was still a Tudor cottage. The garden was everything a cottage garden should be, filled with Canterbury Bells, Lupins, Bristol Ruby, Hollyhocks and a mass of multi-coloured bedding plants. It had all the appearance of the perfect chocolate-box cottage. To Marjorie it had been home for as long as she cared to remember. She didn't own the cottage, she wished she did, it belonged to the Honourable Lavinia Bentworthy who owned Berwick Manor. Luckily the rent was almost negligible and there had been no increase for many years. Marjorie at one time had been the housekeeper up at the manor and the cottage was partly her reward for being such a loyal and hard-working servant. To Marjorie, everything about the cottage was perfection.

It was right in the centre of the village which boasted a Post Office, an ironmongers, greengrocers, off-licence, delicatessen, butcher, fishmonger and baker. Admittedly they were all in the same shop but

Mr Jones rarely let her down on the things she'd wanted when she went shopping, which was roughly twice a day. Mr Jones' shop was the village club. It was the only place she met other human beings which was why she rarely bought more than one or two things at a time. She always wanted a reason to go back again, so she could join in with the village gossip.

Marjorie was particularly excited, for in the mail had come a letter which told her she had won a major prize, in what she had been told was a national competition. The prize would be delivered to her that evening. Marjorie had never won anything before in her life and she wondered what the prize would be. She could hardly wait for the evening to come so she would find out. The card itself didn't give her any clues to what she'd won, but it did say she had to keep the card safely and produce it when the prize came. Otherwise she would not be able to claim her reward. She had guarded that card as if it was prize certificate, she never let it out of her sight all day, in case for some reason it would get lost and she would lose her one and only prize.

Marjorie lived all alone in the cottage now. Her husband Bill had died of cancer some years previously. Marjorie was poor but her requirements were small and she amused herself by ensuring that the garden was a perfect picture every year. People regularly stopped to admire her work which made her extremely proud.

She was playing patience in the front parlour when she heard the knock on the door. At last, she thought, she would know what her prize was going to be. Marjorie opened the door and the visitor asked to see the card just to verify she was, in fact, the prize winner. He checked it and then put it carefully in his pocket; she noticed he was wearing gloves. She thought how strange that was in the summer but perhaps he had something wrong with his hands. The box that he was holding looked exciting and Marjorie took him through to the kitchen so he could put it on the table. She could hardly bear the excitement. He asked if she had a pair of scissors so he could cut the string.

As she was opening the drawer she felt the first burning stab of pain in her back. She was dead before the carving knife, bought specially for the purpose, had struck its deadly blow a second time. She should have wondered why in summer a man should be wearing gloves but then she was so excited about the prize it never occurred to her. The man removed the box and all traces of his visit, leaving the way he'd come, quietly driving away, another piece of work completed.

Mr Jones was concerned that Marjorie hadn't come into the shop the following day. By late afternoon he thought he ought to go round and find out if there was anything wrong as it was rare that Marjorie didn't turn up at the shop at least once during the day. He hurried down the High and for that matter the only street, to Berwick cottage. He hoped that Marjorie wasn't ill as he was fond of the old girl. He rang the bell and knocked the door. He got no answer; he walked round to the back of the cottage, peering in all of the windows. Looking through the window of the kitchen he could see Marjorie lying on the floor. He ran back to his shop and rang for an ambulance and he also rang the local doctor. He then returned back to the cottage where he had every intention of breaking in, which is what he should have done the first time if he hadn't panicked. He broke the back door window, and carefully put his hand through the hole, avoiding the jagged edges. He managed to turn the key in the lock, allowing him through into the kitchen. When he got there he realised that Marjorie was dead. There was little doubt seeing there was a large carving knife sticking out of her back. It had to be the work of a maniac, he thought, there was no other reason why anyone would wish to kill Marjorie Lowndes.

CHAPTER 23

John Holliday was as good as his word. Within hours of Sandy's visit he'd organised a mid-account surprise audit. The team arrived and John was shown up to Jason Roberts' office.

"Good afternoon, Mr Roberts. I'm sorry to have to tell you but I've been instructed to check your accounts. I'm afraid it's a stock market rule. We have received a letter, suggesting all sorts of financial irregularities. I realise it's probably some sore ex-employee with a grudge, but we do have a duty of care and we have to take it seriously. We'll be as unobtrusive as we can and it shouldn't take more than a few days. Can you let us have an office to work from? Then we'll get set up and get out of your hair as quickly as possible."

Jason felt sick. He knew it wasn't going to be a quick whitewash job, because there was some concern following the deaths of two key executives. It couldn't take long before the currency discrepancy was found. He wondered if he ought to bring it to their attention, before they found it. As for the various bogus companies, it was a matter of how thorough or clever they were. He had a horrible feeling, though, they would be both.

It didn't take long for the first skeleton to pop out of the cupboard. The following morning the head of the investigation team was sitting back in his office, his face wearing a worried frown. He had with him a number of files including the bank statements of Redwood's overseas accounts. Jason knew only too well what was coming next.

"Mr Roberts, we have found a funny discrepancy in your currency accounts. According to the official figures you have four million pounds in Asian currencies. When we checked, we found at today's rates of exchange, there's only two point two million in your bank accounts. Can you explain what happened to the missing one point eight million pounds please?"

If Jason was surprised at the speed they had discovered the first secret, he did not show it.

"I did wonder if I should have told you but I'm glad it's out. The currency was purchased for Richard Valentine. He and Silverman were organising a take-over in Korea, leastwise I think it was Korea. They were secretive about it and didn't include me in their negotiations. All I was asked to do was arrange the four million pounds worth of currency. I did have my suspicions at the time that it was a sweetener, a bribe, you know how some of these deals are arranged. But it was none of my business. It was all above board as far as the company was concerned. I've got full authorisation. The problem, as you found out, is the Asian melt-down. Because of that we're sitting on a large loss. We did hope the currency market would improve and we'd claw back some of the losses but alas, it's not to be. Now you know about it you can advise me how I should account for it. I assume it goes in as an exceptional loss."

John Holliday looked at the chief accountant and smiled reassuringly.

"I can see it must have been awkward for you, Mr Roberts. Surely you were involved in other take-over deals, the Intercard deal for example?"

"I did all the previous due diligence exercises, which is why I was puzzled by this Korean one," answered Jason, cleverly thinking how useful all his drama was proving to be.

"Thank you Mr Roberts, for being so frank. I'll ask how we would like the loss recorded. It is a large amount for this size company though. Remember you're trading on a multiple of twenty-eight times your annual profits. So the amount involved is the equivalent of over fifty million pounds' value on your share price. What makes it even more serious is the fact that at the time Redwood was taking over Intercard plc and using their shares as currency, I'm afraid I shall have to report this to the stock market."

Jason felt sick. Holliday was hinting at criminal activity and that really frightened him.

As Holliday walked slowly back along the corridor to his requisitioned office, he reflected that Sandy had almost certainly got it right yet again.

By the next morning there was no doubt that Sandy had been spot on. His team had uncovered Flat Printing Ltd, a company that had to all intents and purposes totally disappeared. There seemed to be no way they could contact them. The phone was out of action, and the road the factory was located in didn't exist. It had all the hallmarks of a swindle. According to Redwood's records they had bought over three hundred thousand pounds worth of goods from Flat Printing. The records also showed that should have been still in stock but there was no trace either of the goods or the company. Here was the first definite evidence of serious fraud. Later in the day a second bogus company had been discovered and the discrepancies topped five hundred thousand pounds. The company share price now was totally suspect, so as well as the internal fraud, there was almost certainly the question of the illegal purchase of Intercard, for by failing to report these losses and thereby keeping the share price artificially high, the price paid for Intercard was way too little. When this publicity hit the financial press Redwood shares would nosedive. The poor old Intercard shareholders who thought they were getting a good swap, would then find out they had lost over half their money, and that's if they were lucky.

John Holliday walked back to Jason Roberts' office. Jason knew immediately from his face that the game was up.

"Mr Roberts, I'm afraid I have some extremely serious news. Whoever wrote us the letter knew what they were talking about. We've uncovered several serious irregularities. I'm afraid it's my duty to inform you that we've sent for the police. I realise that this is extremely distressing for you after what has happened, but I'm afraid I have no alternative."

Griggs was delighted when he heard the news of the fraud. He himself had not been idle and felt sure it would not be long before he'd have enough evidence to charge Roberts with Silverman's murder.

The car had been found abandoned in a multi-storey car park in Brighton, close to the station, and had been towed back to the forensic lab and was now being examined for any clues that could help.

He'd had a picture of Roberts taken to an artist who'd added beard and glasses. It had been shown to the garage salesman who had no hesitation in identifying him. Even better, a second video from Springhills Wharf, a new development next to Jacob's Island, produced a picture of a similar man leaving Jacob's Island on the evening of the murder and returning later that night. Finally, the forensics experts had turned up some fingerprints and Griggs was hopeful they would prove to be Roberts'. It was time to talk to Mr Roberts yet again, to ask him a few questions about his movements on the day after the murder. He also wanted some fingerprints to compare with the ones from the Brighton car.

Roberts arrived looking extremely apprehensive and sat down opposite Griggs. He just looked down at his feet.

"Would you like a cigarette?" asked Griggs. "Oh, you don't smoke, sorry. Well could you just pass my case over? I've left it on the other side of the desk and I'm dying for one."

Roberts obliged by passing over the case, handling it firmly, and Griggs reflected there should be some quite good prints after he'd left.

Griggs then lit up his cigarette and started the interview.

"Interview with Mr Roberts, started at nine forty-five, present Chief Inspector Griggs and Sergeant Cook. Mr Roberts, as I'm sure you're aware we now have the added complication of the fraud in your company to add to the two murders."

"Two murders?" said Roberts. "I thought Mrs Valentine had been charged with her husband's murder?"

"Charged, yes, but not convicted. The recent events have made us look at that case again."

"I see. So how can I help you?"

"Can you tell me what you did the day after Silverman was murdered?" asked Griggs, in a matter-of-fact voice.

Roberts didn't like the sound of the question. He hoped it was just a fishing expedition.

"Let me see. Ah, yes. I had to meet a South American client at Gatwick. Normally I'd drive of course, but I didn't feel well that morning so I decided to go by the Gatwick Express and left about nine. Caught the train, met my client, then we travelled back together, had lunch in central London and then spent the day together in my offices."

"How did you buy your ticket?" asked Griggs.

Christ, thought Roberts, *I used my bloody credit card.*

"Em, I used cash," lied Roberts. "I was in a hurry and they're always slow at stations with credit cards so I thought it was easier to pay by cash."

There was something about his answer made Griggs doubt him.

"Well, thank you Mr Roberts, but I will need to talk to your client. Is he still in England?"

"As it happens yes, he's here for another week or so. I'll get my secretary to give you his address."

"While I think of it, can you remember what you watched on television the night Silverman died?"

Roberts thought for a minute.

"I can't really remember. I think it was some sort of documentary. It was pretty boring and Zoë had already gone to sleep so I switched it off."

"Well thank you, Mr Roberts."

As soon as Roberts had gone he passed his cigarette case down to the lab. Within twenty minutes confirmation came back that the prints matched.

He allowed Roberts to get back to his office, gave him thirty minutes and then had him publicly arrested on suspicion of the murder of Roland Silverman. Griggs wanted the arrest as embarrassing as possible, for he hoped by getting Roberts angry he just might let something slip. It was obvious that he was a clever customer. Roberts was brought back to the station and put in the cells. Now he was arrested they could talk to the credit card company. It didn't take long to establish that two single tickets to London Victoria were purchased at Gatwick on his credit card. This would tie in well with the abandoned car found at Brighton.

Griggs hurried along to the offices of the Crown Prosecution Service. He went through the case with a lawyer who had no problem with what he proposed.

That evening Roberts was formally charged with the murder of Roland Silverman.

CHAPTER 24

When Sandy heard from Griggs the news about Jason Roberts being charged with murdering Silverman, he was excited yet scared at the same time. He was convinced that Roberts would eventually be charged with both murders and Nicola would then be free. In his heart he wanted nothing else for her but was worried that as soon as the police took that action she would pay his fees and he would have no excuse to visit her. He hoped their relationship was more than just professional but he had little confidence. After all, she was young, rich, and beautiful. Sandy on the other hand was older, poor, and in his opinion definitely not handsome. He'd got one failed marriage behind him. He knew he was dreaming yet he loved her so much it hurt. He couldn't bear the thought of not continuing to see her. Still, it was no use putting it off, he at least could have the pleasure of telling her the good news.

"Nicola, I've got some good news to tell you, I'd like to do it over dinner. Are you free tonight?"

"I'd love to come, I'm not doing anything at all. Where shall we go?"

"What about a film first and then a pizza? I

thought you'd like to see Sliding Doors. It's getting excellent reviews and it's got that superb American actress, Gwyneth Paltrow, playing two English girls. She's supposed to be fantastic."

"It sounds good to me, but rather than a pizza why not come back here to the house? I'll cook you something afterwards."

Sandy got out his favourite grey trousers that he had just had cleaned and to his annoyance, the cleaners had shrunk them, he couldn't do them up. He put them back and selected an older pair, to his horror these were also tight. *Oh my god, it's the chocolate biscuits!* he thought. *I'll have to do some exercise.* That would have to wait. He hurried out and picked Nicola up at six thirty. They went to the early show. The film was brilliant; it was all about how your life could change if you took the right or wrong step at any time. Sandy felt it was very much his position. He didn't want to blow his chances with Nicola, nor did he want to rush things. It was all too important to him.

Sandy hadn't been to the pictures for some time and he was amazed that you actually had allocated seats, just like the theatre. It was also nice to be able to see the film without looking through a haze of smoke. He wondered how many people had caught lung cancer through going to their favourite evening entertainment in the past. He also cynically wondered how long it would be before some bright spark got the idea of suing the Odeon for giving them cancer!

After the film they walked out into the night air, still smiling at the unusual happy ending.

"Now that was the kind of film I like to see," said Nicola. "A good old fashioned romance."

They held hands as they walked back to the car and Sandy felt he was the luckiest man in London.

Once back at the house Nicola set about cooking a porterhouse steak, field mushrooms and a few sauté potatoes. She opened a bottle of Chianti Classico and gave him a large glass to start with.

"Now, I've waited patiently all evening. What is my good news?"

Sandy smiled.

"It is good news too, I promise. Jason Roberts has been charged with the murder of Roland Silverman. I hope it won't be long before he's also charged with the murder of Richard, and then you'll be off the hook."

Nicola could hardly take it all in at first. She hugged Sandy and kissed him.

"Thank you, you've been wonderful."

"I did say hope," said Sandy, "there is still a lot of work to be done but Inspector Griggs is a good copper. I know he'll get it all sorted out."

He noticed then that Nicola was crying. He took her in his arms to comfort her.

"There, there, come on. It's nearly all over, there's no need to cry."

She turned her face to him, looking straight up into his eyes. She moved her lips to his and this time they kissed passionately. Sandy pulled her to him and almost crushed her with his enthusiasm. He felt like crying himself. They broke away eventually and

Nicola looked worriedly at the clock.

"My steak's going to be cremated," she said, "quick, grab some knives and forks from that drawer. I'll bring the supper through."

They ate in a fairly embarrassed silence, neither apparently risking the first conversation opening. Eventually Sandy said, "I'm sorry. I shouldn't have taken advantage while you were so upset."

"Don't apologise. I enjoyed it, but I do think it's a bit soon for me to get involved. You'll have to give me time, Sandy."

"You can have all the time you need," replied Sandy. "You must have realised how I feel about you. You're very special to me."

"You're sweet," said Nicola, walking over and kissing him on the cheek. "I think I need an early night though, let's leave the washing up. I'll do it in the morning."

As Sandy drove slowly back to his flat he was constantly reminded of that beautiful, delicious kiss.

CHAPTER 25

Griggs was getting more and more confident. In his experience, if things went well they tended to continue to go well and onwards to a successful conclusion. His case against Jason Roberts had improved daily. So far he hadn't managed to get Roberts to say much, mainly because he'd been advised by his pompous-looking solicitor to keep quiet and reserve his defence. He felt, though, that this morning's interview should liven things up a bit. He had rather a few unpleasant surprises for Roberts.

"Interview with Jason Roberts, present DI Griggs and DS Cook, and Mr Roberts' solicitor, Mr Montague of Barstock and Montague. Interview started at ten thirty-five a.m.

Mr Roberts, I'd like to take you back to the day after Silverman's death. You said you bought a ticket to Gatwick at Victoria Station and you paid for it cash. That is correct, is it not?"

Roberts looked sullen and nodded.

"Perhaps then you can explain why two single tickets from Gatwick to London were purchased on your credit card at eleven thirty on the same day."

Roberts looked a beaten man. He just sat there staring at Griggs.

"We've also got a picture taken at ten fifteen a.m. of you on Brighton railway station. Can you explain how you were at Brighton Station at the same time you say you were buying your tickets at Victoria?"

Griggs passed the photograph taken from the security video camera across to Roberts and his pin-striped, red-faced lawyer. Roberts still said nothing, he just sat looking as if any minute he might burst into tears.

"It's a good photograph, isn't it?" rubbed in Griggs. "We've got quite a video sequence. Amazing, these security videos. They had one in the multi-storey car park in Brighton, you remember, it was the place you left the car. We've got a good picture of you there."

For the first time Roberts spoke, angrily.

"You can't have!" he shouted.

"Of course you're right, we couldn't have. You were in disguise, weren't you? A grey beard and a wig and some glasses. Look, here's a picture of what our artist thinks you'd look with those on. Here's what the man looked like coming out of the car park in Brighton. Amazing similarity, isn't it?"

"That doesn't prove anything," said the solicitor, "and you know it."

"True, it is, I agree, circumstantial, but it is interesting even so, don't you agree? Particularly when you compare it with these pictures taken by the security camera at Springhalls Wharf on the night of the murder. You do know where Springhalls Wharf is, don't you? It's next door to Jacob's Island. That's where you were supposed to be tucked up in bed with Miss Phillips. This one is on the way out, it's a good picture, isn't it? Here's the same person on the way back. You see that it's clearly the same man who was in the car park in Brighton. Now to complete the set we've also got this one from the car park where Silverman was murdered. If you look again you'll see it's the same man again."

Roberts was sweating and wriggling in his seat. He looked distinctly uncomfortable. Griggs liked the look of him. He knew the shocks were getting to him. He decided to turn the screw a little further.

"Did I tell you that the car was parked in Chambers Road? That's just round the corner from Jacob's Island. Didn't I tell you? Sorry, I should have told you that. Quite a coincidence, wasn't it? So close to your flat, but you had an alibi, didn't you? You were in bed with your girlfriend, that's what you said, isn't it? Pity she was drugged asleep at the time. But then you can't have everything, can you?"

"What's all this to do with my client?" began the solicitor. "He knows nothing about this car."

"Of course, you didn't know. I should have told you, I am being neglectful today. We found his fingerprints on the car."

"As you say, it was so close to Miss Phillips' flat, he might well have walked by and touched it."

"You are right, he could have done, as you said. There is just a small problem about that. You see, these fingerprints of Mr Roberts were inside the car; in several places. That would make it impossible for it to be accidental. Unless of course your client had broken into the car. Let's see, we've got pictures of a man of your build and size leaving Jacob's Island at ten fifteen and again returning at five past eleven. We've got a car used in the murder and your client's fingerprints all over it. We've got pictures of the same man at the scene of the crime. The car was dumped in Brighton, by the station, by the same man at ten a.m. and we've got pictures of your client on Brighton station at ten fifteen. The car was bought in Marston Moretaine and the salesman identified the artist's picture of your client with the beard and glasses. Finally, as I'm sure you're aware, we need a motive and your client will be charged with fraud later today. Part of the charge will relate to forgery of Silverman and Valentine's signatures. Now, have I missed anything? I'm very forgetful today for some reason."

Griggs leant back in his chair feeling pleased with himself. He felt if it were a game of football his team would be leading six-nil. Roberts seemed to be in some sort of pain. His face was contorted, then suddenly the floodgates opened.

"What's the bloody use?" he said. "I might as well get it all over with. I killed Silverman." His voice was flat, his face a mask of despair.

His solicitor looked horrified.

"My client is not well, he's been under a considerable strain and he doesn't know what he's saying."

"Shut up. It's all over, can't you see they know everything? I thought I was so clever. I worked it out to the last detail. I thought it was the perfect murder."

How often, thought Griggs, *had those words been spoken over the years? They always forget something.*

"What about Valentine? Did you murder him as well?" asked Griggs.

"No I did not!" said Roberts indignantly. "That's got nothing to do with me. I admit that from my point of view it was a good thing he did die, but I had no part in his death. I killed Silverman and I'm guilty of fraud, yes, but certainly not Valentine's murder. You can't put that one on me."

CHAPTER 26

Roberts went on to make a full statement. It was fascinating to hear about the lengths he went to ensure he committed the perfect murder. He had certainly read too many detective stories. If Griggs had his way they would ban certain books and stop television providing educational programmes for villains like Wexford. One of his friends from the prison service told him the prisoners' favourite program was the Antiques Roadshow. They watched it in silence, taking notes so they would know what to steal when they got out. The most amazing thing about Roberts was the fact he bought the rail tickets with his company Barclaycard. He was too mean to pay for them himself. All his efforts ruined by one silly slip when he thought it was all over. Eventually Griggs knew he couldn't delay the inevitable, so he went back to his office to make a difficult phone call.

"Sandy, I thought you'd like to know that Roberts has cracked. He's confessed to Silverman's murder and the fraud."

"What about Valentine?" asked Sandy hopefully.

"Er, that's the rub, I'm afraid. He's adamant he had nothing to do with Valentine's murder. I know this is going to be a big disappointment to you but for what it's worth, I believe him. Sorry Sandy, I'm afraid it's back to square one."

Sandy sat back and tried to work out how he was going to tell Nicola. He was so sure it was all going to work out. It didn't make any sense any other way. He still couldn't see Nash as the murderer, nor Rebecca. He knew Nicola didn't do it. So who the hell did? He didn't think he could phone Nicola so he went down to his car to drive over to Chelsea again.

When he got to the house Nicola was in the middle of baking. She had flour all over her face and her hair was a complete mess. Her eyes were red and she was very pale. She looked so vulnerable. Sandy didn't think he'd ever seen her look more desirable.

"I'm making chocolate biscuits. I am treating myself to some serious comfort-eating. I have finished everything chocolate in the house. What brings you here?" she asked, and at the same time she suddenly caught sight of herself in the hall mirror. "God! Look at me, what a sight!" she wailed.

"For what it's worth I think you're a picture of domestic bliss."

"God, Sandy, you're such a romantic." She wiped ineffectually at the flour on her face with the back of her hand and turned back to the mixing bowl. "Come on then, what's the news?"

"It's not good, I'm afraid. There is no easy way for me to tell you. Roberts has confessed to the murder of Silverman and the fraud."

"So we've got to wait to for him to add Richard to his crimes, I suppose," said Nicola.

"No, it's not that simple. I'm afraid he said he had nothing to do with your husband's death."

Nicola started going the colour of the flour all over. She just managed to sit down on one of the kitchen chairs.

"This means I'm still in the same position as before," she said slowly. "I'm still charged with murdering Richard."

"I'm so sorry. I shouldn't have got your hopes up but I was so sure it was Roberts. I'd do anything to go back in time."

"It's all right Sandy, it's not your fault." A small tear started to trickle down her face. She slumped on the kitchen stool, a picture of total dejection.

"Don't worry," said Sandy, putting his arms round her. "I'll make it right, I promise. We've still got the lurcher man, he'll come forward, I know he will."

His sympathy was just too much. Nicola burst into tears and ran off into the bathroom. Sandy sat cursing himself for being so stupid. Why had he let her get her hopes up? He knew these things were always tricky. Eventually Nicola came back minus the flour and with very careful make-up trying unsuccessfully to cover up the worst ravages. She went out into the kitchen and brought out a rather dusty bottle.

"This was Richard's special wine, I thought it might cheer us up."

She poured them both out a large glass and they took them and the bottle through into the living room.

"Are you all right?" asked Sandy.

"Fine. I've got to have faith in justice, haven't I? I know I'm innocent so why should I worry?"

"That's the spirit," said Sandy, thinking of all the mistakes and innocent people sent to prison and just hoping Nicola wasn't going to be one of them.

They spent the rest of the evening finishing that bottle and a second one. Nicola cooked them egg, bacon, and fried potatoes; while they were eating she started to laugh.

"What's so funny?" asked Sandy, pleased to see her more cheerful.

"Richard must be turning in his grave. A 1990 Grand Cru drunk with egg and chips. He'd be horrified."

Sandy helped with the clearing up, stacked the dishwasher and then left Nicola to get some sleep. Although he had been positive with her, he was getting worried. There'd had been no communication concerning the lurcher dog and all his leads with the dog societies had come to nothing. Unless he could come up with something soon, Nicola was going to be tried for the murder of her husband and there was every chance that she could be found guilty. He still had no doubt of her innocence and this was not just based on the fact that he loved her dearly, but he felt instinctively, as an ex-policeman, that she was innocent. He went round to her house the next morning. They sat in her elegant drawing room drinking Earl Grey tea, looking for anything he may have forgotten.

"Come on, Nicola," he said, "there must be something more. We need desperately another suspect. My favourite has been murdered by my second favourite who has confessed to the murder but will not confess to your husband's death, and as for the others, I really cannot see either of them as genuine murder suspects. This means there has to be something else, come on – think! Anybody else your husband's had a row with, anyone he's cheated. There must be something, think!"

"Don't you think I am?" said Nicola. "I've been trying to think for some time. I realise how important it is. I've wracked my brains and I can come up with virtually nothing. There must be jealous husbands but I don't know any. It wouldn't surprise me if he's cheated people – he was a ruthless businessman. I can't imagine anyone murdering him for it, but I suppose it's possible."

"Didn't you say he was annoyed about a letter the morning of his death?" asked Sandy. "What was that all about?"

"Oh he was furious about pensions. He reckoned he'd been robbed and he had put a complaint in to the pension authority, but they turned it down. They said the insurance agent had acted in a responsible and sensible way."

"Had this been going on for long?"

"Oh yes, the trigger point was about eighteen months ago. He was going to put a hundred thousand pounds into a pension fund but he found that the agent, a man called Kon, an appropriate name in the circumstances, was taking nearly fifty thousand pounds in commission. He stopped the payment and tried to get even. He was upset. For once in his life he couldn't manage it, Kon was too clever for him."

"Had he got a file or something on this?" asked Sandy.

"Yes, it's in his desk. I'll get it for you."

She handed over a bulky blue file marked 'pension and insurance', and Sandy glanced through.

"I'll take this away and look at it properly, if you don't mind. Now, anything else?"

"There was a husband, now I come to think of it, that got extremely angry with him. Richard apparently had a steamy affair with one of his secretaries. The husband found out about it and took it badly. He even turned up here once, said he was going to beat the hell out of him. Not that he did, for as usual Richard wasn't here. But he was extremely angry, literally shaking with rage."

"When did this happen?"

"Around two years ago."

"Well, it does seem a long time but people sometimes harbour grudges. I'll see if I can locate this man. Keep thinking though, I need every possible lead you can give me."

Sandy went back to the Redwood headquarters building and talked to some of the girls on reception. It didn't take long for him to find the particular girl that Valentine had been sleeping with. Her name was Sophie Taylor and she lived in Lewisham, close to Goldsmith College. Sandy also got an appointment to see the insurance man Kon, but it wasn't until the next day so he drove out to see Mrs Taylor. She lived in a pleasant flat, in a leafy back street. It wasn't the sort of place Sandy had imagined when he thought of Lewisham.

Mrs Taylor was a reasonably attractive lady, but she had let herself go. The house was a mess. She still hadn't dressed and was in an old towelling dressing gown that had seen better days. She had a small toddler playing in the corner of the room while she had been reading the latest Jilly Cooper bonkbuster.

"Won't you sit down, Mr Neil?" she said. "How can I help you?"

"I'm working on the murder of Richard Valentine and I understand you knew him quite well at one time."

"Oh, it's about that slimy bastard," she said. "Yes, I used to work for him and yes, it's true, we did have an affair. I was stupid. I thought Richard genuinely cared for me. I hadn't been at Redwood long otherwise I would have known about his reputation. My husband and I had been going through a bad patch, mainly about children."

"I gather that your husband was angry about it."

"My husband left me over it. I don't blame him, he had been going for tests, you know, and he found out he couldn't have any children. He was devastated. Well, you can imagine how he felt when I fell pregnant," she said bitterly. "I haven't seen him for nearly two years. I thought I meant something to Richard bloody Valentine, but all he saw in me was a quick screw. I loved my husband and now I'm all alone with Valentine's bastard. I'm glad he's dead."

Oh dear, thought Sandy. Not only was his visit a complete waste of time but he had upset her as well.

"I suppose you thought my ex-husband might have killed him," said Mrs Taylor bitterly. "I can't really imagine him doing anything for me. As for murder, he couldn't even kill a fly. He was as soft as butter."

"I'm terribly sorry for bothering you, Mrs Taylor, but I'm sure you understand I had to at least check. Thank you for seeing me."

As he drove away he wished it was one interview he hadn't gone to.

The next morning he visited the offices of the pension adviser, Mr Kon. He worked from home and the house he lived in was spectacular. There was a Porsche Carrera parked in the driveway. It was obvious there was quite a lot of money to be made out of pensions. Sandy was surprised that Valentine only found out when he was told what the commission was. He'd have thought that by just looking at the car, the house and the lifestyle, he should have realised that anyone who was paying money to this man was paying for it all. Kon was not an impressive man but everything he wore was expensive. There was obviously no love lost between him and Valentine.

"Mr Kon, I'd like to ask you a few questions about Richard Valentine, who I believe you represented for a while."

"I don't represent Mr Valentine anymore," snapped Kon.

"Yes, I understand that, but you did for some time and I just wondered if there's anything in his pensions or insurance business that might give me a lead to what happened to him."

"If what you're trying to say is did I kill him, the answer is no, despite the fact that he caused me considerable trouble. Because of him there was a complete investigation into me by the pensions authority. This was not something I enjoyed. Although I was cleared, it does leave a stain on one's record. However, all of that is hardly enough reason to kill a man."

"I'm sure you didn't kill Mr Valentine, but can you tell me anything about his affairs that might help me?"

"He had a lot of pensions and the money, which will be in excess of half a million pounds, will go to his wife, which won't help you because that's another motive for murder."

"What about life insurances?"

"Well he did have a large endowment policy but he got rid of it."

"You mean he cancelled it?"

"No, I gather he sold it."

"Can you sell endowment policies?" asked Sandy. "I didn't know that."

"Oh yes, there's quite a business in it these days. Look at The Times business section and you'll see quite a number of companies specialising in such activities. Most of the costs of any insurance policy are front ended, in other words all the commission and expenses go at the beginning. Therefore they're much better value if you can buy them later on. People buy them second-hand, keep them going and then get a good cash free lump sum at the end of the endowment period. For forty percent tax payers it can provide an incredibly good return."

"How much was Valentine's endowment worth? What sort of sum are we talking about?"

Kon flipped through some papers and pulled out a blue file.

"Ah yes, here it is, it was originally an endowment for a two hundred and fifty thousand pounds for twenty-five years."

"What happens to it now? Who gets the money?"

"Whoever bought the endowment policy will get the cash payment. It's probably worth over three hundred thousand pounds at the moment so they will be pleased."

I bet they would be, thought Sandy.

"Do you know who has this policy?"

"No, there's no reason why I should. I'm sorry I can't help you."

"Well thank you, Mr Kon, you've been most helpful."

Three hundred thousand pounds! Whoever owned that endowment policy had a good motive for murder.

When he got back to the office he popped into the office of Peter Pike. Peter was playing with all sorts of bank statements, cheque stubs, bills, receipts, and was feeding the information into a computer.

"Come in, Sandy, I could do with a break," said Peter. "This job is driving me up the wall. The answer's here somewhere, unfortunately it's just eluding me at the moment. It would probably do me good to think about something else. What can I do for you?"

"I need to track down someone who's bought a second-hand endowment insurance policy from one of the city brokers."

"Shouldn't be too much problem," said Peter. "Whose insurance policy?"

"Richard Valentine's. It's for a two hundred and fifty thousand pounds and the policy was issued by the Scottish Equitable Assurance company. It was bought by somebody about eighteen months ago. I need to know who bought it and where they live. Whoever bought this policy has benefited by over three hundred thousand pounds. That gives them quite a powerful motive for murder."

"I'll get on to it straightaway, it shouldn't take too long."

Peter was as good as his word, and produced the name and address the following afternoon.

"I've pulled out all the stops for you, I was lucky, it was easy getting to the computer system. One of these days someone is going to devise a secure system and then it will make our lives more difficult."

"All right, cut the commercials. I know you're brilliant, get on with it!"

"The man who bought the policy is one Alan Butler. He lives at The Old Thatched Cottage, Thames Point, near Maidenhead. Judging from the address he would appear to be quite a wealthy man."

Sandy drove down to Maidenhead the next morning. Certainly Peter was correct in his deductions about wealth. Cottage was not the word he'd use for this mansion. He needed a reason to go and see Butler. He went into the village to have a cup of coffee at the Ye Olde Tea Rooms. As he sat drinking the coffee he noticed a petition on the wall. He went across to look at it. It read, "Stop The Bypass". As in most communities, there were plans for a bypass which were violently opposed by a group of local people as well as the professionals that moved in from outside the area. Looking at the protest and the leaflets gave Sandy an idea.

He went back to his car and produced a rather interesting portable printing machine he kept in the boot. He did a bit of work setting up a few lines of text and then printed himself off a few calling cards which read:

DAWSONS
Sandy Neil
Public Relations Executive
Westerham House, Westerham, Kent
01959 564 897

It was a bogus address and telephone number but it looked authentic. Armed with his new identity, he called at Butler's thatched cottage.

A rather odd man opened the door; he was short and tubby with a large fat face, sporting at least six chins which seemed out of proportion with his body.

"Yes?" he asked in a high-pitched voice. "How can

I help you?"

"Good morning, my name's Neil. I'm working for a public relations company that's been employed by Heric Construction to find out the local feeling concerning this bypass. I realise it's quite an imposition to ask you a few questions, sir, but there is a bonus to this. We're going to have a draw for all the people who have helped us. The winner will have an all-expenses paid trip to The Waterside Inn at Bray. The company will provide a chauffeur-driven car to take you there and to bring you back, so who knows? It might pay you to let us find out your views."

"Well I suppose it wouldn't hurt," said Mr Butler in that squeaky voice that Sandy found so annoying. He showed Sandy through into his rather chintzy living room.

Sandy was feeling excited as he followed Butler. Sandy noticed he had a distinctive limp. He had had some problem in the past as his right leg was withered, the effect was as he walked, it moved in an unnatural way against his left leg. Butler fitted perfectly Bella's description of the man hanging about Nicola's Oakley Gardens house on the night of the murder.

"So how do you feel about this bypass?" started Sandy.

"Well, I can tell you we need it desperately. We certainly don't want a few mindless cranks stopping it because they're worried about the red-backed newt."

"Do you think most people in the village want the bypass?"

"Oh yes, I'm sure of it. There are only a few idiots that don't. Most of the people against the bypass are from outside the area. They've arrived to make their protest as they do everywhere else. It's a way of life for them. Everyone will benefit from this bypass except perhaps for the newts, and then they're going to be given a new pond and a special new living area for them. It's being built for them at great expense by the builders. Why on earth should anyone worry?"

While he was talking Sandy had noticed that the oil painting over the blocked-in fireplace seemed to be pointedly outwards, indicating that something was behind the picture, forcing it out. He had his suspicion it might be a safe.

"I suppose I couldn't ask you for a glass of water, could I?" he asked Butler. "I should have taken some tablets earlier and have forgotten. I'm just beginning to suffer."

"Certainly," said Butler, and went out into the kitchen to get him his water.

Sandy quickly moved to the picture and looked behind. As he suspected, there was a safe. He took his aspirin with the glass of water, thanked Butler and left. As he was walking back to his car Butler drove by him in a dark blue BMW.

Sandy couldn't believe that he hadn't at last found the real murderer of Richard Valentine. Butler had a good motive, was identical to the man at the scene of the crime, and he drove a similar car to the one the brigadier had seen in Oakley Gardens. All he needed now was some firm evidence, and that, he was convinced could only be found inside Butler's house.

CHAPTER 27

Alistair had quite fancied Michelle Skinner for some time; lusted would perhaps be a more accurate description. He realised she wasn't exactly the brain of Britain. She ran the office switchboard where he worked with some efficiency. She always was smart in her appearance even if her skirts were rather short and her close-fitting tops were very revealing. She was always giggling round the office. She could see a dirty meaning in almost everything that was said. If double meanings could be a specialist subject on mastermind, she would have a good chance, provided she didn't have to answer questions on general knowledge as well, as she had none. Beautiful as she was, he had to admit that her voice wasn't everything he'd ever wanted. Her constant "All right?" drove him up the wall. Despite all of that, she was an attractive and sexy girl. Alistair hadn't been terribly successful with his romantic conquests lately, in fact the word 'conquest' wasn't quite the way he'd describe what had happened to him in the last few months. He rather fancied his chances now the World Cup had started. All the other men would be obsessed with football and out of the way. Michelle wasn't interested in football and today virtually every man in the office would be off watching the England versus Tunisia match, leaving the field clear for him to take her out.

"Well Michelle," he started in his best chat-up voice, "what are you going to do on your free afternoon? Fancy something to eat?"

"Yea, why not?" she said in that grating voice of hers. "Where shall we go?"

"How about Pizza Express?" asked Alistair, surprised how easy it had been to get her to go out with him.

"Nah. How about my place? It's more comfortable."

He was surprised at her directness, but that was nothing compared to what was to follow. He was used to doing most of the work with the girls and was surprised when she said she'd rather leave the food and get on with the main event.

He'd never come across anyone quite like Michelle before and wasn't sure he ever wanted to come across one again. The only thing he could say was that she certainly enjoyed sex. At last, when even her filthy talk couldn't get him interested, they went out to get some fish and chips. It was then as he was eating his cod, covered with lashings of malt vinegar and salt, he spotted the advertisement.

"Here look," he said to Michelle. "That's me, I was walking a lurcher dog that night. I wonder what it's all about."

"How should I know? You better go round there and find out," she said, "anyway, I've got to go, it was nice though. Perhaps we could do it again sometime. See you around."

Amazing, thought Alistair, *to her it's just simply pure sex; pull a man, go to bed, and look for the next one.*

He noted down the address of Pike and Neil but realised that he wouldn't be able to go to see them the following day as the office had to work longer hours to make up the time lost because of the England football match.

CHAPTER 28

The morning after Sandy's visit to Maidenhead he arranged a meeting with both partners. After the obligatory discussion about the game, Shearer's header and Scholes' wonder goal. He told them about his visit.

"Not only does this man Butler get in excess of three hundred thousand pounds because Valentine is dead, he also looks just like the man seen by Bella Knight whilst she was waiting for her boyfriend the night that Valentine was murdered. I think this man Butler could be the one and if he is, then we should move quickly."

"I know you want a result on this one, Sandy," said Mark, "but you have absolutely no proof of anything against this man."

"I don't know. Butler fits the girl's description and he has a good motive. I know it's not a lot and it wouldn't stand up in court, that's why I need Peter to break in."

"I thought it was going to come to that," said Peter. "I suppose you want a safe cracker as well, do you?"

"Yes, I want the proper job. Is that a problem?"

"Oh no, no problem," said Peter. "It's expensive, in fact it's very expensive. Will your client be able to afford it?"

"Oh I'm sure she'll afford it, besides that I don't think she's got any option. If I'm right then it's worth a lot of money to her to find out."

"The man I'm thinking about did a lot of work for me and some of my friends while I was still working in the service. He's found it's much more lucrative to do this sort of work than actually be a thief. He'll probably charge ten thousand pounds but he will be professional and there will be no slip-ups."

"How do you know there'll be no slip-ups?"

"Well he's been doing it for donkey's years and he's still doing it. That has to be some form of recommendation. All we need is a time when this Butler will not be at home."

"That will be easy," said Sandy. "He's just won a competition, hasn't he?" chuckled Sandy. "I told him somebody would win a prize where they would get a luxury meal at the Waterside Inn at Bray. It couldn't be easier. He wins, we provide the chauffeur car to take him there and to bring him back so we'll know exactly where he is at any time."

"That was good thinking," said Peter, "you're getting better at this sort of thing."

"I just wish you'd thought of a less expensive prize," said Mark, "Couldn't you have given him theatre tickets instead?"

"He might not like the theatre and he might not

want to go out for that. He couldn't resist a chauffeur-driven car and a meal in one of the finest restaurants in England. There is no effort required at all."

Mark sighed. "Right, well, let's get it set up."

Mr Butler was delighted to find he had won his evening at Bray. He had never been to the Inn, so he was looking forward to it. It would be nice to be able to drink a lot and not have to worry about driving home.

The break-in and prize winning dinner was organised for the following Tuesday evening.

Sandy visited the restaurant and explained that the guest was to be treated like royalty, however, he couldn't spend more than two hundred pounds and that included the wine and the tip. That was the budgeted price, but he was sure that they could provide him an excellent meal for far less than two hundred pounds, which would leave them a reasonable tip. Peter's contact was briefed and they arranged to meet on Tuesday afternoon to go through all the final details. Sandy phoned Griggs and told him to be available late on Tuesday evening, as he might have something interesting to tell him. He also warned him he might need a search warrant which would have to be used in conjunction with the Thames Valley local police force, but he'd let him know more about it. Griggs was intrigued but was sensible in not asking any questions as to what they were doing. It might be illegal and if so, he didn't want to know.

The evening was damp and soggy. It had been one of the most disappointing Junes for years, which was surprising as only the year before the country had been warned about drought and how water would never be available again. The general depression hadn't been helped when Beckham had been sent off in the World Cup, making him the most hated man in England. Still, there was always 2002.

They drove in convoy down the M4, turning off and driving round the back of Maidenhead. A message came through on the mobile phone that Butler had already left for his meal and so they were able to go to the house pretty quickly. The safe cracker, who preferred to remain nameless, went straight into action. He climbed up a telegraph pole and clipped a portable phone onto two ends of the main wire and then clipped the wire in the centre. This meant that now, all calls came to his phone.

"We don't want no rozzer calls going through, do we?" he said, laughing in an Irish accent. "They could have one of them automatic phones in the house; well, if they have that takes care of that."

He then climbed up the side of the house to the burglar alarm box and proceeded to spray some form of white foam into it. He came back down again.

"That'll take care of that. Give it a couple of minutes and nothing will ring in that box again."

He then looked round the house carefully and spotted another box and proceeded to repeat the operation.

"Well that's eliminated the alarm system. Now, one of you has got to man the phone, we don't want any helpful callers reporting it down, do we?"

Peter indicated to Sandy that he should do that while he and the safe cracker would go into the house. Sandy watched them deal with the front door, it wasn't long before they disappeared inside. He sat wondering whether they'd find anything, and whether he was right, when suddenly the phone rang. He picked it up.

"Hello, is that Mr Butler?" came a distant voice.

"No mate, no, I'm the engineer. We got a bit of a problem with this phone, see? It'll be all right soon, but at the moment you've got no way of getting through to the house," said Sandy in a put-on accent.

"Well, how long are you likely to be?" came the voice at the end of the phone.

"I should think about twenty minutes. Hey, Burt? How long are we gonna be? Twenty minutes? Yea, Burt thinks twenty minutes too, so I think it'll be twenty minutes."

With that, there was a reassuring click at the end of the line. Sandy was rather pleased at his theatrical efforts. He'd hardly put the phone back when it rang again. He picked it up and this time the voice was more like a robot screaming down the phone,

"Police! Police! Police! Burglary! Burglary! Intrusion into the Thatched House! Police! Police! Police!" it continued to scream, and he was grateful he was receiving the message and not the boys down the local nick. Also, he was quite horrified to realise how easy it was to get round even the most sophisticated security systems.

He sat out there in the damp, drizzling rain waiting for Peter and the safe cracker to come back out again.

Meanwhile, things were going fairly well inside.

Whilst Peter's colleague was working steadily on the safe, Peter was systematically searching the house for anything that might prove to be useful. Eventually, after about an hour and twenty minutes the man opened the safe and Peter started looking through the contents. There were a number of second-hand endowment policies in there as well as the details of those which had already been cashed. Peter wrote down a list of names of those where Butler had benefited from the deaths of the insured people, and all the names of those policies still current that were in the safe. He totalled up quickly the amount of money that Butler had received so far from the endowment policies and it was well in excess of two million pounds. It was an awful lot of money and it seemed too much of a coincidence that so many of the original policy owners had died so soon after selling the policies on. He had a horrible feeling they'd stumbled across a mass murderer, but they'd only know once Griggs had checked the records.

They closed up the safe, made sure everything looked normal, locked the door as they left, the phone wires were re-joined and they hurried away quickly as the chances were that the line would still be active and would phone through to the police indicating a break-in. They phoned the names through to Griggs and asked him to check them as quickly as possible to see if there was anything known about any of them.

Sandy had a feeling he should know something about one of them. The name Gregory rang a bell. He knew he had read it somewhere recently. Then it struck him, the man had been murdered. It was the totally motiveless killing he read in the paper. That meant that at least two policy-holders had been murdered and Sandy didn't believe in coincidences. He phoned Griggs and told him to check the Gregory file straight away. Sandy thought that Newbury was the town but he could be wrong. It wasn't long before Griggs came back to say that Gregory was indeed murdered in Newbury. There was one other name that came up quickly from the list, a Mrs Lowndes, who was also a murder victim in Essex. He was going to organise with the local police force to get a search warrant to get into Butler's house as soon as possible. Peter's colleague didn't feel inclined to hang around.

"I'll be off then, I'll just take my ten thousand notes if you don't mind and then I'll be on my way."

Peter handed him a bulky envelope which he opened, looked briefly into it, and smiled a big toothless grin. "Well thanks mate, I'll be off then. Remember, any time you want any assistance in matters that I have skills, you know what I mean, you only have to ask. It's nice putting them to use where they're doing good."

With that, he drove off.

Sandy reflected how easy it would have been if he could have used such methods in the force, but of course they were illegal. He felt absolutely elated for at last he knew he'd cleared Nicola's name for good. His instincts had been a hundred percent correct. She'd done nothing and was just a victim with a lot of circumstantial evidence against her.

They stopped for an egg and chips at a Happy Eater on the way back to London. Although it was late, Sandy was sure that Nicola would appreciate a phone call. He used the pay phone in the cramped lobby of the café. He would have preferred to be with her at the time so he could see her face as the news sunk in, then the excitement and joy following. The news, he thought, was too good to leave her to have even one more troubled night. The phone rang and rang she was obviously in bed, perhaps he should have waited after all. At last a sleepy voice answered, giving him butterflies in his stomach. He loved the sound of her voice.

"563 7746, Nicola Valentine speaking."

"Do you want the good news or the bad news?" he asked cruelly.

"Oh God I don't know. Yes I do, give me the bad news first, Sandy."

"I spent ten thousand pounds of your money tonight!"

"What on earth did you spend that sort of money on?" asked Nicola, suddenly completely awake.

"A safe cracker!"

"A what?" screeched Nicola. "And did you say ten thousand pounds!"

"Yes I did, on a safe cracker! That's also the good news, as he found the evidence to get the real murderer charged with Richard's death. It's all over Nicola, thank God. I've done it! You're free at last. This time it won't go wrong, I promise. Come and see me in the office tomorrow and I'll tell you all about it."

CHAPTER 29

Mark shook Sandy's hand. He was grinning like a Cheshire cat.

"You see!" said Sandy smugly. "I was right all along about Nicola."

"You've done a fantastic job, well done! I've got one big worry though," said Mark.

"What's that?" asked Sandy, worried that he might have overlooked something.

"You're not going to have to fall in love with all your female clients, are you? If that's the case I'll have to allocate them all to Peter."

"Get on with you, I want to marry Nicola, that is if she'll have me. I've loved her since the beginning. I don't fall for just anyone."

He went back to his office to patiently wait for Nicola. After about forty minutes the internal phone rang.

"Mr Neil," said Sandy's secretary, "there are two people outside to see you. There's Mrs Valentine and a young man called McKenzie who says it's urgent."

Sandy walked out into the lobby. There was Nicola

and a young man of about twenty-six, maybe slightly older, sitting looking at Nicola with great interest.

"Can I help you?" said Sandy.

"Well I hope I can help you," said the young man. "My name's Alistair McKenzie, I've come about your advertisement."

"My advertisement?" said Sandy.

"Yes, about a lurcher dog. You were advertising for someone to come forward who'd been walking a dog on the fourteenth of February. Well I was walking a lurcher dog on that night. In fact I saw this lady while I was out, I recognised her as soon as she arrived."

Sandy laughed. "Why didn't you come forward sooner? It came out three weeks ago."

"Well I never saw the advertisement until the night before last. I was eating my fish and chips and there it was, so I thought I'd better come in and see what it was all about."

Both Sandy and Nicola were killing themselves laughing.

"I don't see what's so funny," said Alistair indignantly. "I've come here in good faith, and all you do is laugh at me."

"I'm sorry, we are not laughing at you," said Sandy, "if you'd have come in a couple of days ago you'd have been a hero. Mrs Valentine was charged with a murder that she didn't commit. One of the problems was that she was out walking at the time the murder took place, but nobody could give her an alibi. You would have been perfect. However, in the last couple of days the real murderer has now been caught and so it's not quite so important. We're grateful to you that you have turned up. As you see, your evidence could have been crucial, it could have prevented a dreadful miscarriage of justice. It's just that the morning after the arrest doesn't quite have the same impact as it would have done a few days ago."

"There is still the question of the reward, isn't there?" said Nicola, winking at Sandy. "After all Mr McKenzie has come a long way, and as you say, it could have been so important to me and I am very grateful."

"Oh yes, of course, the reward. In all of the excitement I almost forgot the reward. If you'd like to come into my office I'll write you a cheque. How much was it, can you remember Nicola?" Sandy asked pointedly.

"I think it was five hundred pounds, wasn't it?" said Nicola.

"Yes, of course it was." Sandy smiled and disappeared into his office to get the cheque.

Alistair was, to put it mildly, rather pleased with his reward. By the time he was sitting in Sandy's office he had already spent it in his mind on a holiday to Greece. He could see it clearly – golden sand, turquoise water and romance. He was rudely shaken out of his idyllic daydream.

"Name and address?" asked Sandy. "I'd better have it for the records."

Just as Alistair was leaving, Inspector Griggs arrived looking pleased with himself, which was not surprising as he had just spent an enjoyable twenty minutes with the Assistant Commander and his Superintendent while they congratulated him on his excellent work. He could see promotion, close by, which would mean he could move house, something that would please the missus greatly.

"Good morning, Inspector? Can you believe it? This is Alistair McKenzie. He was the man walking the lurcher dog, he's just seen the advertisement and come forward," said Sandy.

"We won't need him now," said Griggs, "you'll be glad to know that all charges have been dropped against Mrs Valentine. I'm sorry that I doubted you for a minute, but as I said to Sandy at the beginning, I would be delighted if he proved you innocent. So I am. You did a good job, Sandy. Well done. I just thought I'd like to tell you how pleased we are with you all down at the station. There's a few people probably owe their lives to you. You uncovered one of the nastiest murderers I've ever come across. We know already of three of his victims, but I have a horrible feeling by the time we've finished we're going to be talking about a lot more. Ironically, you caught him with virtually the same trick as he often used to murder his victims."

"How do you know all of this? Has Butler confessed already?" asked Sandy.

"No, course not, he's as innocent as the driven snow. Or should it be pure? But you know what I mean. His solicitor is threatening us with God knows what. To hear him you would have thought he'd been charged with fouling the footpath when he hadn't even got a dog. All of the three murders we've looked at so far, Lowndes, Hill, and Gregory all have one thing in common – they all were excited about winning a competition. We checked on all of the other policies Butler had bought and got lucky with one, a Mrs Coleman. She had been informed by letter that she had won a large prize, that's how he did it. He wrote to them and told them they'd won a prize which he would deliver to them personally. They had to produce the card to prove they were the actual prize winner. That was so that he was sure he got the right person and it meant they'd let him into the house without him having any problems. He always removed the prize card after he'd murdered them. In Mrs Coleman's case, of course, he never got round to it. She would have been his next victim. We've fingerprinted her letter card and envelope and bingo, Butler's prints are all over them. We've already got, as you know, a lot of other evidence, but once we look carefully we'll soon find stacks more. His car has been taken away; it looks clean enough but I guarantee it will still give us plenty, the same goes for his clothes. No, Mr Butler can shout and rave all he likes, he's going down for a long time. I doubt if any judge would recommend any early release. In my opinion, he should get the rope; he has forfeited the right to live. We estimate he's netted over two million pounds from these horrific crimes already. There was evidence in the safe to indicate he had another six or seven victims lined up. It was almost the perfect crime. There was no obvious motive for any of the killings, nobody ever thought of an old insurance policy. Now it's out in the open it's certainly something that the police will be looking for if similar cases should arise in the future. I've also been asked to thank you by three other officers whose cases you've solved for them. I can see why you were known as one of the top men in the police force in your time. You've certainly lost none of your skills going out into the private sector. Well, Sandy, I wish you luck in the future. Perhaps one of these days our paths will cross again. Remember, I owe you a favour and a big one at that. I can't stop, I've got lumbered with a motiveless murder again. I thought I'd got rid of it but my colleague's got himself transferred and I've been given it back again."

Sandy started to chuckle.

"What do you think so funny?" said Griggs.

"It's just occurred to me, it's the old cliché, isn't it?"

"What do you mean the old cliché?"

"Well, in all of the old films and plays we used to watch as kids, the butler always did it!"

THE END

Postscript

Sandy asked Nicola to go away for a holiday to try to forget the dreadful experience she'd had. Much to Sandy's amazement, she agreed. They planned to drive slowly through the Burgundy wine region of France.

Inspector Griggs was reassigned to the murder case, the one he had been grateful to get away from. By a strange coincidence the victim was a member of the MCC.

Zoë Walker's flat was repossessed by Redwood plc as it was bought fraudulently. Zoë, however, fell on her feet and is now the mistress of a city stockbroker, living, ironically, in the penthouse in the same building.

The Wenchester Building Society were trying to evict Jane Roberts and her family from the house in Mersham. However, she was putting up a considerable fight. It was highly likely she might be able to stay the owner of the property as she never gave her permission for it to be remortgaged by her husband, Jason.

Mark Cheshire was trying to make some sense out of the MCC murders but was thoroughly enjoying his new role as amateur detective.

Bella married Charles and now lived on the Isle of Lewis, much to her mother's disgust as she hardly ever sees her.

Alistair McKenzie is still looking for love.

16322986R00178

Printed in Great Britain
by Amazon